What reviewers are saying about
Vital Signs, Book Three in the Baxter Series:

"Kathy Herman keeps the pace moving in *Vital Signs.* The book shows how God provides exactly what we need—even in the hardest of times."

NANCY MOSER, AUTHOR OF *THE SEAT BESIDE ME*

"A multifaceted and fast-paced tale where tragedy meets hope and "losers" are given second chances. *Vital Signs* is a reminder to appreciate life and the possibility of redemption in the worst of circumstances. Good job, Kathy!"

MELODY CARLSON, AUTHOR OF THE
DIARY OF A TEENAGE GIRL SERIES

"If you're looking for a gripping story that will keep you turning the pages, *Vital Signs* is for you. Kathy Herman knows how to raise the stakes with every scene, and how to reassure us that no matter how hopeless things seem, God really *is* there for us all."

NANCY RUE, AUTHOR OF *PASCAL'S WAGER*

Vital
Signs

THE BAXTER SERIES BOOK THREE

KATHY HERMAN

Multnomah®Publishers *Sisters, Oregon*

VITAL SIGNS
published by Multnomah Publishers, Inc.

© 2002 by Kathy Herman

International Standard Book Number: 1-59052-040-8

Cover design by Chris Gilbert/UDG DesignWorks
Cover image by John Rizzo/Photonica
Background cover image by David Bailey Photography

Unless otherwise indicated, Scripture quotations are from:
The Holy Bible, New International Version ©1973, 1984 by International Bible Society, used by permission of Zondervan Publishing House

Multnomah is a trademark of Multnomah Publishers, Inc.,
and is registered in the U.S. Patent and Trademark Office.
The colophon is a trademark of Multnomah Publishers, Inc.

Printed in the United States of America

For information:
MULTNOMAH PUBLISHERS, INC.
POST OFFICE BOX 1720
SISTERS, OREGON 97759

Herman, Kathy.
    Vital signs / Kathy Herman.
        p. cm. -- (The Baxter series ; bk. 3)
    ISBN 1-59052-040-8 (trade pbk.)
    1. Illegitimate children--Fiction. 2. Missionaries--Fiction. 3. Birthfathers--Fiction.
4. Quarantine--Fiction. 5. Viruses--Fiction. 6. Twins--Fiction. I. Title.
    PS3608.E59 V58 2002
    813'.6--dc21   2002008541

02 03 04 05 06 07 08—10 9 8 7 6 5 4 3 2 1 0

To Him who is both the Giver and the Gift.

Acknowledgments

I owe a special word of thanks to Carrie Gill, whose excitement about the way God's sovereignty was presented in this story persuaded her to discuss it at Bible Study Fellowship even before the manuscript had found its way to Multnomah Publishers.

To Jim Smithies, Pastor of Lay Ministries at Bethel Bible Church, whose unabashed outpouring of support has watered the very roots of my creativity.

To Brenda Elrod, Environmental Health Director of Smith County, Texas; and Dan Hart, Sanitarian, Smith County Health Department, for helping me to understand professional response tactics for epidemics, quarantines and public safety; and to the Centers for Disease Control for detailed on-site and on-line information regarding viral hemorrhagic fevers and epidemic control techniques.

To Dr. Dick Hurst, retired family physician, for his valuable input on medical issues and for sharing a past experience from his family practice that influenced a key event in the story.

To Will Ray, Professional Investigator, State of Oregon, for his assistance in constructing a realistic profile of the CWD and for valuable input regarding interactions of different agencies of law enforcement.

To my sister and tenacious prayer warrior, Pat Phillips, thanks for standing firm, especially during the times when the enemy sought to sabotage the writing of this story.

To Susie Killough, Judi Wieghat, Barbara Jones, and the ladies in my Bible study groups at Bethel Bible Church as well as my dear friends at LifeWay Christian Store in Tyler, Texas—thanks for your faithful prayer support.

To Doris Warren, super saleslady of the known world, thanks

for putting more of my books in the hands of customers than anyone else in the country. It's a blessing to watch you in action!

To June Lininger, Rosy Halley, and Sue McKay, for your wholehearted and shameless promotion of the Baxter Series. Oh, that I could bottle your enthusiasm!

To my family and friends, who still get excited every time I do—thanks for sharing the adventure day by day.

To my readers who have encouraged me, either in person or by e-mail or snail mail—thanks! It means so much that my books are making a difference. Your words have blessed me more than you know.

To the retailers who sell my books and support this series— thanks for your partnership. What a wonderful industry we serve.

To my editor, Rod Morris, thanks for your gentle but firm direction. I have such respect for your ability to fine-tune my work.

To the staff at Multnomah, thanks for exemplifying God-honoring business practices and cutting-edge professionalism! I'm privileged to be part of the family.

And to my husband, Paul, whose light shines brightly where mine was never meant to reach—thanks for thinking out of the box, for unlocking doors I would never have chosen, and for giving me a gentle push through each new threshold of opportunity. Can there be any doubt we were meant to be partners?

And to our Father in heaven, without whose blessing none of this would matter, I offer these words from cover to cover and ask that those who read them will come to embrace Your wondrous sovereignty.

PROLOGUE

The hall clock chimed three times. Blake Thomas lay in the dark, fever scalding his face, sweat soaking the sheets. He felt worse by the minute and dreaded the thought of spending even one day of his furlough laid up with the flu. In spite of feeling exhausted, he had held up well during last night's "welcome home" reception at the church.

Blake had so looked forward to returning to the love and fellowship he remembered as the preacher's kid at Cornerstone Bible Church. He and Melissa had spent the past two years on the mission field in a remote area of the Amazon basin, and had rarely made contact with the outside world.

But they were expecting their first child in a month; and as much as they embraced the formidable challenge of sharing the Good News in one of the most isolated places on earth, they had no desire to entrust the birth of their child to the uncertain skills of the village women.

Blake stared out the window at the moon beyond and realized his eyes were not focusing. He tried to ignore his aching muscles and turned his attention to the sound of Melissa's deep sleep. The trip home had been wearing for her, especially the arduous river journey back to civilization. He knew that after their baby was born, sleep could not be scheduled. Right now, he was glad she could rest, and was becoming increasingly concerned that he couldn't.

Blake kicked off the top sheet, and felt the air conditioning sweep over him. Yearning for cool weather, they had planned their trip home in the fall. But after Melissa became pregnant, not even the sticky Baxter summer could dissuade them from returning to share their baby's birth with the church family that had so generously supported them.

Pain shot through Blake's head, causing him to wince, sweat rolling into his eyes and ears. He decided to wake Melissa, who kept a stash of natural remedies and always had a better sense of what to do. He turned on his side and gently shook his wife. "Melissa?… Honey?…" He pressed his hand to her cheek. She was burning up!

Blake fumbled until he found the lamp switch. He turned on the light and noticed red spots on his pillow. He wiped the perspiration from his face and saw blood on his fingers! He tried to stand up, but his legs gave way and he fell against the dresser, then onto the hardwood floor. The fever's heat turned to chills and his body shook.

The room felt as though it were spinning. Blake dug his fingers into the floor and retched until he vomited blood. He tried calling out to Melissa but the words were caught in his throat the way they were in his nightmares. *Lord, take care of her…*

Suddenly, it seemed as if one side of the floor had been raised at an angle, and he was slowly sliding off, everything turning to gray fuzz—and then nothing.

ONE

J ed Wilson sat in the waiting room of Baxter Memorial Hospital, his fingers tapping the arms of a chair that had ceased to be comfortable hours ago. He heard the sound of a baby crying. His daughter Jennifer was the only one in delivery tonight, and he wondered why no one came to get him.

He picked up the remote and started to channel surf, then turned off the TV and began thumbing through stacks of magazines he'd already looked at.

He counted baby carriages on the wallpaper, teddy bears on the carpet, and tiles on the ceiling. His eyes glanced at the waste can overflowing with an empty pizza box, two candy bar wrappers, two Coke cans, and a crumpled package of Chee-tos. He popped two Rolaids into his mouth and started pacing.

How was Rhonda doing as Jennifer's labor coach? Though he had no desire to be in the delivery room, after hearing a baby cry, he was flooded with excitement. How long before his wife came rushing through the double doors, announcing the birth of their first grandchild? Jed looked at his watch, feeling a twinge of regret that pacing had also been the full extent of his participation the night Jennifer was born.

Jed heard a baby cry again. Why didn't someone tell him what was going on? He sat down and heaved a heavy sigh. What did he expect at four-thirty in the morning? The place was practically deserted.

But he noticed a flurry of activity at the other end of the hall, and flashing lights of an ambulance outside the emergency room door. He got up and peeked through the glass on the swinging doors that led to the delivery room. No sign of Rhonda or Jennifer. He decided to walk down to the emergency room and investigate.

Two people, blood-soaked gauze wrapped around their heads, were being removed from the ambulance. The EMTs seemed to be in a big hurry. They pushed the gurneys through the emergency entrance then disappeared through another door. He wondered why they were wearing surgical masks.

The other set of double doors burst open, and a familiar voice called from down the corridor. "Jed! Come see," Rhonda Wilson said. "Hurry!"

Jed rushed toward her. "Well, what is it?"

Rhonda smiled, then turned and began walking briskly the other direction.

"Come on, babe, at least give me a hint." He moved faster, until he caught up to his wife.

She took his hand and pulled him quickly down the hall.

"Can't you just tell me? What's the big mystery?"

"Oh, Jed, they are so cute!"

They? he thought before saying it. "They?"

"Look!" She prodded him into Jennifer's room.

After exchanging glances with his daughter, his eyes zeroed in on two blue caps.

"Surprise! You have twin grandsons. Identical!" Jennifer said.

"Two?"

Jennifer smiled. Rhonda shrugged.

"Why didn't Alex tell us?" Jed asked.

"Well, Dad, my insurance wouldn't pay for those tests that tell you everything. Do you want me to give one back?"

Jed was vaguely aware of something said over the speaker system and hospital staff scurrying outside. "What are you going to name them?"

"I don't know. I was so sure it was a girl."

"Jen, may *we* hold them?" Rhonda said, sounding almost giddy.

"Sure. Here..."

Rhonda took one of the babies and put him in Jed's arms. "There you go, *Grandpa.*"

"Uh, remind me what to do." He laughed nervously. "I haven't done this in a long time. As I recall, I wasn't very good at it back then."

"Well, it's a whole new day," Rhonda said.

Jed studied the child he was holding and shook his head. "Jen, he's perfect. I can't get over it—twins?"

"Yeah, Dr. Harmon gave me such a hard time about my weight, I think he felt bad."

Jed lifted his eyebrows. "Isn't batting a thousand, is he? Maybe that's why he's hiding from us."

Dr. Harmon breezed through the door. "Now, Jed, who says I'm hiding? The way I see it, I delivered twice the goods. Pretty exciting, I'd say. Though the credit goes to Jennifer."

"I'm still in a state of shock," Jennifer said.

"I think you were supposed to be surprised." Dr. Harmon avoided eye contact. "Here, let me snap a few pictures for you." He picked up the camera on Jennifer's nightstand.

"I got several of Jennifer and the babies earlier," Rhonda said. "How about getting a shot of all five of us?"

Jed got up with one baby and sat next to Rhonda on the side of Jennifer's bed.

"Hold it right there...smile..." Dr. Harmon snapped the picture.

"One more…perfect." He handed the camera to Jennifer. "That's the second time they've paged me. I'd better go see what's up. Congratulations, Jennifer. You did well. Your coach didn't do too bad either." He smiled at Rhonda.

"Alex, can I see you outside for a minute?" Jed said.

The two men left the room and stood facing each other in the hall.

"How long have you known?" Jed asked.

"About a month. I heard two heartbeats."

Jed threw his hands in the air. "Then why didn't you tell her? Jen's been struggling with whether or not to raise one baby as a single mom. How's she going to deal with two?"

"Did Jennifer seem upset to you?" Alex asked.

"Well, no. Not really, but—"

"Listen, Jed. I've been your family physician for twenty years. This was a tough call…"

"Meaning what?"

"I prayed about this long and hard before I decided not to tell her."

"That's a cop-out."

"Jed, all of us at church had been praying for Jennifer to decide what the *Lord* wanted her to do. Had she known she was carrying two babies, she might've closed her mind, so I kept quiet and decided to let God handle it. I think it was the right call."

Jed sighed. "Alex, if I didn't know you as well as I do, I'd probably punch you in the nose."

"And I'd probably understand."

Jed raked his hands through his hair. "We're not set up for twins."

"I know. No doubt the church will throw another baby shower and make sure Jennifer has everything she needs. Listen, Jed, I really need to answer that page. If you want to talk some more, call me tonight at home."

Jed looked at the door to Jennifer's room, and then at Alex. "They *are* cute. It's not like you withheld news of some terminal disease or something…"

"They're fine, healthy boys, Jed. A double blessing."

"Yeah, you're right." Jed extended his hand and shook Alex's and then embraced him. "Let's pray Jennifer sees it that way."

Dr. Sarah Rice backed her Cadillac DeVille out of the driveway and drove toward Baxter. She turned on her cell phone, looked up the home number for county health director, Dr. Ivan Roesch, and pressed the button.

"Hello," said a sleepy male voice.

"Ivan? It's Sarah Rice. Did I wake you?"

"I'm not sure yet."

"Well, here's a wake-up call for you: Two patients were admitted through emergency forty-five minutes ago with symptoms of hemorrhagic fever."

"Hemorrhagic fever? *Who?*"

"That missionary couple. You know, the pastor's son and daughter-in-law from the Bible church—the one Ellen Jones did the feature story on?"

"The ones who just came home from the Amazon?"

"Yes," she said. "They're starting to hemorrhage. Burning up with fever."

"Who treated them?"

"Two EMTs, two ER doctors and a few nurses. The EMTs weren't immediately sure what they were dealing with. They answered a 911 call from Pastor Thomas's home. Apparently, the couple is staying there. The pastor said he heard a loud thud and ran upstairs to see what happened. His son had fallen. Vomited blood. He thought the bleeding was from the fall."

"What about his daughter-in-law?"

"Semiconscious. Same symptoms. It's not good, Ivan. I'm on my way to the hospital. Meet me in my office as soon as you can."

Jed studied Jennifer's face as she held one of the twins. She looked tired, but the glow was undeniable.

"I had blond hair when I was born." Jennifer brushed her fingers gently through the baby's hair.

"Not this much," Rhonda said. "Yours was like peach fuzz."

"Hey, Pastor Thomas just went by," Jennifer said. "I'll bet he's looking for us."

Jed poked his head into the hallway. "Bart? Hey, Bart…we're down here…" Jed turned around and stared at Rhonda. "He rushed through the double doors. Guess he didn't hear me. I can't imagine he'd start his hospital visits this early after being up late at the reception. I'm sure he was there long after the three of us left."

"I didn't know anyone else from church was in the hospital right now," Rhonda said.

Jed shrugged. "I saw two people being admitted through emergency. Looked like a car wreck."

"I hope it wasn't someone we know." Rhonda turned to Jennifer. "Honey, you look tired. Why don't you take a nap? I'll get the nurses to take the twins to the nursery for a while. Your dad and I can come back later."

"Thanks, Mom. I really am tired."

"Besides, I'm sure your dad can't wait to tell that macho crowd at the highway department you had twin boys. The testosterone level should be off the charts." Rhonda carefully put the babies in Jed's arms and then hit the call button.

Jed looked at one twin and then the other. "Okay, guys, what are we going to call you?"

"Later, Dad. We'll name them later…please…just let me crash."

"Go ahead. I'll just play with Bert and Ernie here." He expected to evoke a round of protest, but Jennifer was already out. "Poor kid. She *is* exhausted."

The nurse walked through the doorway and over to Jed.

"One nice thing about bein' here is the mothers can decide when they wanna rest. It doesn't work that way when they go home." The nurse took the newborns from Jed with skilled ease. "Come on, baby boys, let's give your mama a break. She's not gonna get many of those for a while."

Dr. Sarah Rice arrived at the hospital just after 6:00 A.M. and found a bearded man dressed in surgical scrubs, gloves, mask, and goggles, pacing in her office.

"For not being a morning person, Ivan, you certainly rose to the occasion."

"For your information, I've already initiated barrier nursing procedures and called state epidemiology. You'll notice the protective clothing on your desk."

"I'm impressed," Sarah said. She put on the gown over her clothes, then the mask, goggles, and gloves. "All right. Let's go see what we're up against."

They walked to C Corridor and stopped outside a glass room where a handwritten quarantine notice was posted on the door. Two young patients lay on the other side, hooked up to IVs. A small staff of medical personnel, wearing protective gear, worked to stabilize them.

A gray-haired man leaned against the glass, looking dazed. Sarah recognized him from the newspaper story.

"Pastor Thomas? I'm Dr. Sarah Rice, the hospital's chief of staff. And this is Dr. Ivan Roesch, Director of the County Health Department."

"How could this happen so quickly?" Pastor Thomas said softly, his eyes fixed on the two patients.

"We're doing everything we can to make them comfortable," she said. "It's important we find out what we're dealing with."

Pastor Thomas turned to Sarah, his eyes vacant. "Melissa's pregnant. Our first grandchild."

She touched his shoulder. "I know."

"Pastor, we need to find out who they've been in contact with," Ivan said. "Especially from the time they became symptomatic."

"We never noticed any symptoms until we found them half-delirious."

"Didn't they mention feeling achy? Hot? Tired?"

"Those kids never complain about anything. They did seem washed out, but we thought it was from the long trip home."

"Did you say there was a reception?" Ivan asked.

"Yes, all evening. Over two hundred people."

"Was there a reception line?"

Pastor Thomas nodded, then sighed and leaned on the glass. "Our church family is close, and many have known Blake since he was a little boy. There was a lot of hugging and kissing and tears of joy. If only we'd waited a few days…"

Sarah felt a cold chill. She looked squarely at Ivan and didn't say a word.

TWO

By 7:45 A.M., Baxter Memorial Hospital was abuzz with concern. Hospital personnel was divided into three groups so Dr. Sarah Rice could meet with one group at a time while the other two handled patient care and administrative duties.

As she prepared to address the last group, she took a sip of water and spotted Ivan Roesch's white beard at the end of the second row. She nodded slightly in acknowledgment of his presence.

"The purpose of this meeting is to give you *details,* not speculation, about a medical emergency we're facing. At approximately 4:35 this morning, Dr. Melvin Helmsley and Dr. Allen Gingrich treated two Emergency Room patients, one male and one pregnant female, who had been transported by ambulance from a rural residence in Norris County. The attending EMTs charted symptoms of high fever, vomiting, diarrhea, and pharyngitis—and for those of you here who are not medical personnel, that means throat inflammation. Also noted was conjunctivitis, or inflammation of mucus membranes in the eyes. Both patients are exhibiting peculiar skin eruptions, which appear as white rings about the size of a quarter. Also some hemorrhaging from nose and ears. The male patient had vomited blood. Drs. Helmsley and Gingrich have given an initial diagnosis of viral hemorrhagic fever, or VHF, of unknown origin. State epidemiology has authorized our sending blood serum, urine, and stool samples to the Centers for Disease Control to see if we can get an antibody match."

The group began talking among themselves, and Sarah could see the alarm on their faces.

"What this means, ladies and gentlemen," she said, raising her voice, "is we have work to do. Since we haven't determined the baseline contact, and since the two patients have recently returned from a remote area of the Amazon basin, Dr. Ivan Roesch from our country health department has initiated a lockup quarantine until we receive further direction from the state."

Sarah glanced at Ivan and read the slight shaking of his head as a signal for her to proceed without involving him.

"State epidemiologists are already on the way, and I'm told that state health officials have contacted the Centers for Disease Control. For now, *C* Corridor of the hospital is officially under quarantine. Medical personnel and family members who've had direct contact with the infected patients have been isolated in *C* Corridor until they receive further direction or are cleared by state health officials.

"In addition, barrier nursing procedures requiring the use of gowns, masks, gloves, and goggles are mandatory for those having contact with the infected patients.

"Supportive care is currently being administered to these patients. Again, for those of you not on the medical staff, that means keeping fluids balanced, providing oxygen and blood trans-fusions—doing everything possible to prevent them from going into shock. Realistically, there's little chance the unborn child will survive.

"Every precaution is being taken to insure the safety of hospital personnel. I cannot emphasize too strongly the need to stay calm and use sound judgment. The public will take their cues from us. And in order to insure the accuracy of information, only official hospital spokespersons will be allowed to talk to the media. I expect each of you to support this effort by not fostering gossip or speculation.

"A request will be issued for volunteer medical teams from nearby communities to be ready to offer their assistance should this situation escalate. But right now, we're doing everything we can to contain this virus. I'm counting on each of you to conduct yourselves as professionals.

"For those of you not working in C Corridor, you are free to move about. I do ask that you use scrupulous hygiene practices, not only here, but also at home. With everyone's full cooperation, perhaps we can keep this virus from spreading.

"I'll get back to you after I've consulted with health officials, and will answer questions at that time. Now, if you'll excuse me, I need to prepare for their arrival."

Sarah turned and left the room by the side door.

Dr. Roesch met her in the hallway, and they walked toward her office.

"I'm worried about public reaction, Ivan. People will be frightened no matter how we present this."

"Sarah, *I'm* frightened. Why are the patients hemorrhaging at the onset of symptoms? I wouldn't have expected to see this manifestation for several days. It's not consistent with my understanding of viral hemorrhagic fevers."

They walked in silence down the long corridor, the heels of their shoes clicking on the shiny tile floor.

When they reached Sarah's office door, Ivan turned to her, his fingers stroking his white beard. "It might be prudent to be unavailable for comment."

Sarah sighed. "Right. And just how long do you think we can pull that off?"

❧

Sarah sat at her computer, accessing everything she could find on VHF, when her phone rang. She glanced up and saw the intercom button lit.

"Yes?…"

"Dr. Rice, health officials are here."

"All right. Show them in." She looked at her watch and then turned to Ivan, who was sitting at the conference table in an adjoining room. "Did you hear?"

"How'd they get here so fast?" He gathered the papers spread in front of him and began putting them in his briefcase.

Sarah walked to the door, surprised to see three men walking in her direction. She'd been told to expect two health officials.

"Good morning. I'm Dr. Sarah Rice, chief of staff," she said, extending her hand. "And this is Dr. Ivan Roesch, director of the Norris County Health Department."

"I'm Dr. Spencer McFarland from state epidemiology; this is my colleague, Dr. Yo Wong."

Sarah was struck by the physical contrast in the pair. Dr. McFarland stood tall and lanky, with wavy red hair and mustache. Dr. Wong was at least a foot shorter, with a thick mound of black hair cut in a straight line above his round spectacles.

Sarah's attention was drawn to the third visitor, a distinguished, silver-haired gentleman whose demeanor instantly commanded respect.

"And this is Dr. Lionel Montgomery from the Centers for Disease Control," Dr. McFarland said. "I thought it wise to involve the CDC as soon as possible."

Dr. Montgomery smiled. "If the truth be known, I think Spencer wanted a test flight in my new plane."

"You flew in?" Ivan asked.

Dr. Montgomery nodded. "Drs. McFarland and Wong happened to be in Atlanta for a health symposium. We felt it wise to address this matter expeditiously."

"Gentlemen, please have a seat." Sarah closed the door and then took a seat next to Ivan. "Dr. Roesch and I are anxious to hear what you have to say."

"Thank you." Dr. Montgomery folded his hands. "Permit me to get right to the point. On the way here, we reviewed what we know of this situation. And before I proceed, I want you to respond to one word: *Ebola.*

"Just hearing the word evokes an emotional response, doesn't it?" He looked at Sarah and then at Ivan.

"Following each new outbreak, the media flooded the networks with graphic images of victims dying a slow, agonizing death. Add that to the fact that there exists no vaccine or therapeutic treatment, and imagine how an 'informed public' would react if they thought there was an outbreak here."

Sarah glanced at Ivan and noticed he was shaking his head.

"Back up a minute," Ivan said. "Unless I'm missing something, what we have here is an *unidentified* VHF. Neither the early bleeding nor the ring-shaped skin eruptions are consistent with Ebola. And active cases have never been reported outside of Africa."

Dr. Montgomery nodded. "Precisely! *We* know that. But the public will jump to its own conclusions no matter how emphatically we deny it. If you want to create a panic, start describing the hemorrhaging associated with this virus to John Q. Public. I guarantee you'll need the National Guard to contain the chaos."

"So what's your suggestion?" Ivan asked.

"My suggestion is we adhere to our oath: First do no harm. And that would seem to include *not* telling people more than they're prepared to handle. There's no harm in our not revealing everything until we have the facts."

Ivan stroked his white beard. "Dr. Montgomery, what do you think we've got here?"

An eerie silence settled around the table. Ivan had beaten Sarah to the question, and her pulse raced as Dr. Montgomery moved his eyes from doctor to doctor. "I think what we've got is a very short time to contain a very big threat. And if we don't?... God help us."

THREE

D ennis Lawton turned in his room key at the Ellison Suites and walked toward the dinky rental car parked outside. The first-class flight from Denver to Atlanta had been easy enough to book at the last minute. But the only rental car available was a compact. When he drove out of Atlanta, he had lasted only a couple of hours before his legs begged to stretch out and he was forced to find a motel.

Dennis opened the driver's door, then turned around and lowered himself onto the front seat, careful not to bang his head. He slowly pulled his right leg into the car, then brought in the left, his thighs wedged against the steering wheel. He shifted his weight until he could bend his legs and his head wasn't touching the headliner.

He studied the map for a moment, then started the car and pulled onto the highway. Comfort wasn't foremost on his mind.

About a year ago, he'd started seeing Jennifer Wilson. A mutual friend had introduced them at a party, and Dennis was instantly drawn to the pretty young woman from Baxter. He found her refreshing, especially after all the shallow women he'd been with.

They were together for a few months, but nothing serious ever developed—at least, nothing they planned…

Dennis had awoken to the phone ringing and groped for the receiver. "Hello."

"Dennis, it's Jennifer."

"Wilson?"

"Uh-huh. Can you talk? Or have you got *company?*"

"No, it's okay. How've you been? I haven't seen you around."

"I left Denver and am living with my parents. I've been dealing with something the past few months, and it didn't seem right not to tell you."

"Tell me what?"

"I'm pregnant."

"You're what?" Dennis started to grin. "Wait a minute, it's April Fools' Day. You almost had me."

"This is no April Fools' joke, Dennis. The baby's due in July."

"Are you nuts? Why didn't you get an abortion—save yourself the hassle?"

She sighed. "I knew you'd say that."

"So, who's the father?"

"Oh, pleeease! You're the only man I've ever been with, and you know it."

Dennis paused, his mind racing through the past. "What do you want, Jen?"

"I don't want anything."

"Yeah, right."

"I doubt you'll understand this, but I've asked Jesus Christ into my life. I'm a Christian now. Things are different."

"Are you giving up the kid?"

"Actually…I'm trying to decide whether or not to raise the baby as a single mom."

"Have you gone off the deep end?"

"No, but thanks for your vote of confidence."

"Jen, why would you even consider raising a kid alone?"

"I'm not alone. I've got my parents and my church family behind whatever choice I make."

"Well, what about me? Why should I be stuck with *your* choice?"

"I'm not sticking you with anything, Dennis. I don't want a penny from you. I just thought you deserved to know…"

Her words still ticked him off. Dennis cracked the car window and let the fresh air flood his face. Deserved to know? He didn't *want* to know! How dare she put him through this? It wasn't fair—not to him or the kid. He had hated growing up without a dad. Now, thanks to Jennifer's *choice,* another kid would know how awful it felt.

To top it off, his Grandfather Bailey was on his case to get this matter settled. And it was he who signed Dennis's paychecks. Patrick Bailey was a powerful man with deep pockets, and Dennis knew he wasn't about to let his grandson's indiscretion end up costing him.

Dennis caught his reflection in the rearview mirror, and he searched the blue eyes staring back at him, feeling a twinge of shame. He had used his good looks to seduce more women than he could keep track of. Jennifer had been especially challenging; but he manipulated her insecurity, and winning her over didn't take long. It also didn't last long. She's the only woman who ever broke up with him.

As he drove up and down the green hills toward Baxter, he wrestled with what to say to Jennifer. She was due in three days, and he didn't plan to hang around.

Dennis entered the Baxter city limits and double-checked the directions he had gotten off the Internet. He continued on the main highway until he spotted Chelsea, then turned right, drove two blocks, and pulled up in front of a stone house nestled in a stand of pine trees. He read the name on the mailbox. *Wilson.* He spotted a yard sign and pulled forward so he could get a better look. On the plastic sign was a stork holding two bundles, announcing this morning's birth of twin boys. He sat dumbfounded. *Twins?* How could she do this to him?

He saw a Mustang and a Silverado parked in the driveway and suddenly felt conspicuous sitting out front.

Dennis pulled away from the curb with his Grandfather Bailey's words echoing in his head. *Don't come crying to me, boy. You're thirty years old. You know better than to let this happen! No gold digger is going to get her hands on my hard-earned fortune because you didn't protect yourself. Find a way to make this go away—or I will!*

Dennis decided to find out where the hospital was. There was no point in leaving until he said what he had come to say.

FOUR

D ennis pulled into a parking space at Baxter Memorial Hospital and turned off the motor. He sat for a few minutes, rehearsing again everything he planned to say to Jennifer, then pulled himself out of the car and walked toward the main entrance.

He went to the information desk and inquired where he might find Jennifer Wilson, and was told Room 121, *A* Corridor. He thanked the lady and walked briskly down the hall marked *A* Corridor.

When he got to Room 121, he found a sign on the door: *No Visitors. Mother Sleeping.*

Dennis turned around and leaned against the door, his arms folded, and heaved a sigh of disgust.

"I see you've encountered a dead end," said a female voice.

Dennis was startled to see a nurse standing there. "Uh, yeah, looks that way. Do you have any idea when she'll be up?"

The nurse shook her head. "Would you like to see the twins?"

"No, that's okay. I came to see their mother."

"Well, since she's asleep, let's go sneak a peek."

"It's really not necessary."

"Of course, it is," she said. "You have bragging rights, after all."

"You think I'm the father?"

She looked at him and smiled, her eyes twinkling.

Dennis looked away. "All right. A quick peek."

The nurse led him to the nursery and they stood in the hallway, looking through the glass.

"Aren't they handsome?" she said.

There were a number of empty bassinets, but only two babies in the nursery: Wilson boy #1 and Wilson boy #2. Dennis stared at them in their little blue caps, wondering if his own father had ever laid eyes on him.

"They look like you," the nurse said.

Dennis felt the heat color his ears.

"Follow me. I'll show you something." The nurse unlocked a side door and then led him to a room behind the nursery. "Have a seat."

"Where are you going?" Dennis asked, feeling surprisingly at ease with her.

"Stay put. I'll be right back."

Dennis sat down and closed his eyes, trying to relax. Seeing the babies hadn't been so bad. But how would he handle seeing Jennifer? What if her big hazel eyes filled with tears? He never could stand to see her cry.

He wondered if her hair was still down to the middle of her back. Jennifer had a natural beauty that couldn't be manufactured in any beauty salon. He liked everything about the way she looked, and still had a whole drawer full of sketches he couldn't bring himself to trash.

"Here you go," the nurse said.

Dennis's eyes flew open, and she placed a baby in each of his arms before he had wits enough to protest.

"Here, let me show you how to support their heads...that's it.

Good. You've got it. Now go ahead and spend a few minutes with them."

"But I've never done this—"

"Don't worry. You're doing fine. Just remember to support their heads." She patted his shoulder and quickly left the room.

"Hey, wait—" How did he get railroaded into this?

The baby in his left arm was staring at him with dark, questioning eyes.

"Stop looking at me like that. You think this was *my* idea?" He wanted out of there, but what was he supposed to do with a kid in each arm?

All of a sudden, a different nurse charged through the door, wagging her finger at him. "What are you doing? This area is restricted to authorized hospital personnel only!" She plucked one of the infants from Dennis's arms and placed the child in a glass bassinette. "How did you get in here?"

"Some lady in a pink uniform let me in."

"Good try, but our staff wears *blue*." She snatched the second child from him. "That door is always locked. We can't let just anybody handle these babies. I don't know what you're trying to pull, but you're in big trouble, buster." The fierce look in her eyes left no mistake who was in charge.

She picked up the phone. "This is Martha Sullivan in the OB wing. Give me security!"

Jennifer Wilson was awakened by health officials and told she would need to be quarantined, as would all those who attended the church reception.

Jennifer dabbed her eyes. "It's a little overwhelming."

"I know," Dr. Lionel Montgomery said. "But since you gave birth just hours after being exposed, we don't believe the babies are at risk for developing the virus. However, you and your parents need to be isolated at home for the ten-day incubation period. It's critical that you not leave your home or come in physical contact with anyone, other than authorized health professionals, during that time."

"You're not infectious now," Dr. Alex Harmon added. "But you're at high risk for developing this virus. Should you become infectious, you could pass this virus on to your babies."

"But ten days seems like forever!" Jennifer said. "I've hardly had a chance to hold them, and now I won't even be able to see them." She wiped her tears with a Kleenex and blew her nose.

"I know this is difficult," Dr. Montgomery said. "But a ten-day quarantine may well prevent a health crisis. We feel this is a necessary step to protect you, your newborns, and the rest of the community. We need your full cooperation."

"If I don't develop the symptoms in ten days," Jennifer said, "can I bring the babies home?"

Dr. Montgomery nodded. "But we might recommend the quarantine be extended if things go a direction we aren't expecting."

"I don't have anyone to take care of my babies if my parents are being quarantined, too. My insurance won't cover it."

"Dr. Harmon has an idea," Dr. Montgomery said. "I'll let him tell you about it."

Dr. Harmon leaned forward. "Jennifer, several retired nurses have volunteered to take shifts and care for the twins free of charge, so you don't have to worry about insurance issues. There's a clinic across the street where the hospital maintains a nice apartment for visiting physicians. It lends itself perfectly to round-the-clock care for the babies."

There were voices in the hallway and then a knock at the door.

"Excuse me, doctors," said a man with a badge. "We have a security issue that can't wait."

"Miss Wilson," Nurse Sullivan said, "I found this young man in the back room of the newborn nursery. I have no idea how he got in, but he was holding your twins. Unless you can give me some reason not to, I'm going to turn him over to hospital security."

"Dennis?" she said in disbelief.

"You know this man?" Nurse Sullivan said. "He *claims* he's the father."

"Uh, yes," Jennifer said.

"Yes, you know him?" said the man with the badge. "Or, yes, he's the father?"

"Well, yes—I mean, of course I know him because he *is* the father."

Nurse Sullivan's eyebrows gathered. She turned and faced Dennis, her arms folded, her weight resting on one hip. "Then why'd you sneak in there? I would've brought those babies to you."

"Look, I didn't even want to see them. Some lady in a pink uniform took me down to the nursery because Jen was asleep, then unlocked the door and stuck me with both kids before I realized what was going on. She's around here someplace."

"Uh, if you'll excuse us," Dr. Montgomery said, rising to his feet, "we need to be going. Miss Wilson, as soon as you're released, someone from the health department will escort you home."

"Jennifer, everything's going to work out," Dr. Harmon said. "I'll be back to talk to you about the clinic when the arrangements have been made for the twins."

The doctors filed out of the room followed by the security guard.

Dennis looked at the nurse, then at Jennifer. "What's going on? What quarantine?"

"Two missionaries from our church were admitted with some awful virus," Jennifer said. "They're being isolated in C Corridor. But a bunch of us were exposed at a reception last night, and they've asked us to stay quarantined at home."

"The babies, too?"

Jennifer's chin quivered. "No, they're keeping me away from

them for ten days since I could develop the virus."

Dennis took a subtle step backwards.

"She's not infectious," Nurse Sullivan said. "But she's been exposed."

"I can't have any contact with them until the quarantine's over…" Jennifer's voice cracked. "Volunteers are going to care for them in a clinic across the street."

"I need to get back to the nursery." Nurse Sullivan looked at Dennis. "I have my eye on you." She brushed past him on her way out the door.

There were a few awkward moments of silence.

"Dennis, why are you here?" Jennifer said.

"To make sure we're clear about some things."

"What things? You're off the hook."

"Yeah, that's what you *said.*"

"And you don't believe me?"

"Jen, how are you going to raise two kids by yourself?"

"The same way I'd raise one: with the help of my parents and church family. And with a lot of prayer."

"Have you even thought about letting someone adopt them?"

"I decided against it."

"*You* decided? Well, *excuse* me. I almost forgot: You're the only one with a choice in the matter."

"I'm keeping the boys, Dennis. Now, if you'll excuse me, I'm exhausted. I was in labor all night."

"Well, for your information, this is a big pain for me, too. How come you waited to tell me until it was too late for an abortion?"

"I never considered an abortion."

"Is that so? Well, you'd better rethink adoption, Jen, because your little scheme won't work."

"What are you talking about?"

"Go ahead, tell me it never occurred to you that my grandfather's got big bucks."

"Get out! I don't have to listen to this. I made the choice to keep the boys because I *want* them."

Dennis stood staring at her, his arms folded, his jaw set.

"I don't believe this," she said. "You honestly think I'm after money?"

"Grandpa thinks you—"

"I don't care what *Grandpa* thinks. Speak for yourself!"

"Okay…if I had anything to say about it, I would've paid for an abortion. But I'm not going to pay for the next twenty-one years for a choice I had no part of. Grandpa agrees with me."

"Is that supposed to be a threat?"

"Want to take him on?"

"You're pathetic. If I decided to sue you for child support, I'd win in a heartbeat. Your grandfather's influence doesn't reach that far."

"He always gets what he wants."

"Save your breath, Dennis. I'm not after money. I absolved you from all responsibility for the upbringing of these two little boys. Now, get back to your life and stay out of mine."

Dennis stared at the floor, his hands in his pockets. "So…I guess this is good-bye."

"I can only hope."

"Come on, Jen. I'm just protecting myself. No hard feelings."

"Try *no* feelings."

Dennis walked to the door and turned around. "I hope you'll be happy. I'm just not cut out to be a dad. I wish I were different."

"That's two of us."

"Good-bye, Jen."

Jennifer waited until she heard his footsteps turn the corner, then buried her face in her pillow and sobbed.

Dennis turned the corner and nearly ran into Nurse Sullivan.

"Leaving so soon?" she said.

"I'm outta here."

"So I *heard*."

"Look, I don't want any trouble."

"Is that so? Then think about this: You might be able to wipe those little boys out of *your* mind, but they can't wipe you out of *theirs*. Oh, I know your type—more than willing to place the order, but suddenly AWOL when the freight arrives. Well, let me tell you something, buster. This freight is fragile, and if you walk away, some part of those little boys will stay broken on the inside, and you're going to have to answer for it someday."

"With all due respect, Ms. Sullivan, it's none of your business." Dennis took a step forward and she blocked his way.

"Every child born here is my business, *Dennis*. I can't make you do the right thing, but I'm not letting you leave without a guilty conscience."

"Nice try. It didn't work."

She moved aside, a smirk on her face. "Give it time."

FIVE

O n Monday evening, Jennifer Wilson sat with her parents in the living room of their Baxter home, awaiting the six o'clock news. She dabbed a tear from the corner of her eye, suddenly aware that her father was looking at her.

Jed pushed the mute button on the TV. "What are you thinking about, Jen?"

"Oh…that Dennis's behavior shouldn't surprise me." Jennifer pulled her feet up on the ottoman. "But how could he think I was after his money? That's not what I want from him."

"I know," Jed said. "But if he doesn't want to be part of your lives, you sure don't want him around. Look what a lousy father I was."

"But you didn't abandon me, Dad. That would've been harder to deal with."

"At least you know where he stands," Rhonda said.

"Yeah, no mystery there," Jennifer said. "Six-feet-three. Hollow. No heart."

"Hey, the news is coming on." Jed turned up the volume.

"Good evening, ladies and gentlemen; I'm Jonathan Smith."

"And I'm Monica McRae. Welcome to the KJNX evening news. Shortly before four o'clock this morning, an ambulance was dispatched to the home of Pastor Bart Thomas and his wife, Penny, who reside on County Road 256 just north of Baxter. Pastor Thomas called 9ll after discovering his thirty-year-old son, Blake, bleeding and unconscious on the floor in an upstairs bedroom, and Blake's pregnant wife, Melissa, unconscious on the bed. The couple was transported by ambulance to Baxter Memorial Hospital where they were treated by two Emergency Room physicians, who were unavailable for comment. But hospital chief of staff, Dr. Sarah Rice, told KJNX earlier today that Drs. Helmsley and Gingrich recognized severe flu-like symptoms and took immediate action to isolate the patients. She indicated that blood, urine, and stool samples have been sent to the Centers for Disease Control to see if the virus can be identified and if a vaccine is available.

"Dr. Rice also told KJNX that an official lockup quarantine is now in effect in C Corridor of Baxter Memorial Hospital. Marcus Payne is standing by live. Marcus…"

"Monica, I'm at Baxter Memorial Hospital with chief of staff, Dr. Sarah Rice. Dr. Rice, what's the status of the situation tonight?"

"We feel the situation is under control. I met early this morning with hospital personnel. Those who were off today were called in for a special briefing. C Corridor of the hospital is completely quarantined—off-limits to everyone other than authorized medical personnel.

"Barrier nursing procedures are now being implemented, which involves the use of protective gear, such as gowns, masks, gloves, and goggles for authorized persons entering the quarantined area. We're optimistic that we can contain this virus without it becoming a nuisance to public health…"

Nuisance? Jennifer thought. This was more than a nuisance. Her life had been turned upside down…

Jennifer had stood on one side of the glass at the hospital nursery while Nurse Sullivan stood on the other, holding up one of the babies. Jennifer studied his face and wondered if he'd look the same ten days from now. Would she even recognize him?

By the time Nurse Sullivan brought the other boy, Jennifer's eyes were clouded with tears and she could hardly see him. She put her hand on the glass as if to somehow touch her son. When the man from the health department wheeled her away from the nursery and out the front door to begin her ten days of isolation, she had never felt emptier...

"Dr. Rice, do you expect the young couple to recover?"

"I'd rather not speculate. But they're otherwise healthy young people."

Jennifer sat up straight and looked at her parents. "What does *that* mean?"

She had hugged Blake and Melissa at the reception, then sat talking with Melissa, looking through photographs. How sick were they?

"Baxter is quiet tonight and health officials are optimistic that they have this virus isolated. Public safety remains their primary concern, but health officials stress that there is no cause for alarm. KJNX will keep you informed of breaking news as it happens."

Jed put the TV on mute. "Odd they didn't mention the home quarantines."

"I get the feeling they're not telling us everything," Jennifer said.

Rhonda shrugged. "They probably don't know everything yet."

"They knew enough to keep my babies from me..." Jennifer's voice cracked.

Jed got up and put his arms around her. "It's going to be all right, honey. A good night's sleep, then some quiet time to pray and think things through, and things will look a lot better."

"Will they?" Jennifer nestled in her father's arms, wondering if Dennis had given their two sons a second thought.

∽◦∾

Dennis Lawton sat in a motel near the Atlanta airport, eating gourmet pizza while he watched the evening news.

Health officials from the Centers for Disease Control gave every indication that things in Baxter were under control. He could hardly wait to catch his 7:30 A.M. flight to Denver.

Ellen Jones opened the front door and was met with the aroma of the pot roast she had put in the oven on her lunch hour. She walked to the kitchen and saw a stack of mail on the countertop.

"Guy, where are you?"

"Right here." His arms slipped around her from behind. "How'd it go?"

Ellen closed her eyes and leaned against his chest. "Suffice it to say I'm one beat-up newspaper editor."

"What happened?"

"Health officials aren't talking."

"Why not?"

Ellen turned around and faced him. "That's what I want to know. They dodged my reporters and my phone calls."

"Not very professional."

"That's what I thought." Ellen picked up an oven mitt. She opened the oven door and started poking the pot roast with a fork. "Did you catch the evening news?"

"Uh-huh."

"Sum it up for me."

"Okay…the Thomas couple was admitted to the hospital early this morning with severe viral symptoms. *C* Corridor is quarantined. The CDC has been called in. Health officials are waiting for the virus to be identified. Dr. Rice says things are under control at the hospital. Personnel working in the quarantine area are being required to wear gowns, masks, and goggles. That's the gist of it."

"Was there any mention made of home quarantines?"

"Home quarantines? No. Just C Corridor at the hospital… Honey, did I say something wrong?"

Ellen took off the oven mitt and dropped it on the counter. She shut the oven door and looked at Guy. "They're holding back. My source at the hospital told me this virus is causing hemorrhaging."

"That's unsettling. How reliable is your source?"

"Infallible."

Guy's eyebrows gathered. "What do you know about the home quarantines?"

"Over two hundred people were exposed at a church reception last night. We think they're all being quarantined at home."

"And health officials aren't *talking?*" Guy said.

"Won't even return my calls. I'm not about to beg until they decide to throw me a crumb. I'm running the story. After they read tomorrow's headlines, they just might change their minds about talking to me."

SIX

Assistant Manager Mark Steele turned on the Open sign at Monty's Diner, and a few seconds later the front door opened.

Mort Clary came in, put a quarter in the jar, and picked up a newspaper. "Mornin', Rosie," he said as he sat at the counter. "Got my caffeine?"

"Here you go." She set his cup on the counter.

The door opened again and in walked George and Hattie Gentry, Liv Spooner and Reggie Mason on their heels.

"Good, the paper's here," George said. "Wanna see what Ellen's got to say about this virus situation over at the hospital."

"Mmm...I do love the smell of bacon frying," Hattie said.

"Want your usual?" Rosie held her green pad and took the pencil from behind her ear. "Leo's got the grill fired up."

Mark glanced out the east windows of Monty's Diner. The morning sun looked like a red ball stuck to the horizon. He leaned against the wall and began to read Tuesday's issue of the *Baxter Daily News*.

Virus Warrants Quarantine
Health Officials Remain Hushed

A young couple was admitted to Baxter Memorial Hospital early Monday morning, exhibiting symptoms of an unidentified virus. Details of the illness are not being discussed, though health officials say that due to its potentially infectious nature and unknown origin, a lockup quarantine is now in effect in *C* Corridor of the hospital.

Blake Thomas, 30, son of Pastor and Mrs. Bart Thomas of Baxter, and his pregnant wife Melissa, 28, were admitted to emergency just after 4:30 yesterday morning, after being discovered unconscious at the home of Blake's parents. According to a reliable hospital source, the young couple's symptoms include high fever and hemorrhaging.

The pair returned Friday after two years on the mission field in the Amazon basin of South America. On Sunday night, they were honored at a welcome reception at Cornerstone Bible Church and hours later became symptomatic, which raises concerns about the potential level of exposure.

Dr. Sarah Rice, chief of staff at Baxter Memorial, made this public statement: "Barrier nursing procedures have been implemented, which involves the use of protective gear, such as gowns, masks, gloves, and goggles for authorized persons entering the quarantined area. We're optimistic that we can contain this virus without it becoming a nuisance to public health."

However, when questioned by a reporter from this newspaper, Dr. Rice excused herself and did not comment on the detailed nature of the severe symptoms, or reports of an estimated 230 other people, involving as many as 70 local families, health officials have isolated in home quarantines throughout the city.

As of Monday evening, reporters from this newspaper had spoken with persons in 47 households who have been officially placed under quarantine by the Centers for Disease Control, a detail not openly discussed by health officials who remain strangely unavailable for comment.

Mark heard Mort Clary's voice and looked up at the counter. He tucked the paper under his arm and moved closer to the conversation.

"I got my ideas about all this," Mort said. "Them bioterrorists can spread all kinda diseases before anybody realizes they done it."

"This couple just got back from the Amazon," George said. "That's probably where they picked it up. Will you stop with the bioterrorist thing?"

"Do ya really think them health higher-ups are gonna spit out what they know, Georgie?"

"Knock it off, Mort. The newspaper didn't even imply bioterrorism."

Rosie Harris finished reading over George's shoulder, then side-stepped along the counter, pouring coffee refills. "I *would* like to know what this home quarantine thing's about. It's odd that KJNX didn't mention anything about it on the news."

Reggie Mason held up his cup. "What's the deal with this hemorrhagin' stuff?"

"Remember them Africans," Mort said. "Bleedin' ta death, droppin' like flies? Ecoli—or somethin' like that? Could be right here and we'd never know till we all up and die."

"Mort, you're paranoid." George dismissed him with a wave of his hand. "Health officials know what they're doing. That's what the quarantine's all about."

Jim Hawkins laid his newspaper on the counter. "Has anyone here talked to someone who's quarantined?"

"I have," Liv Spooner said. "My next-door neighbors, the Wilsons."

"What are they being told?" Jim asked.

"Same thing we are. But I can tell you this: Their daughter had twins yesterday morning at the hospital and officials won't let her touch them. They've got Jed, Rhonda, and Jennifer quarantined at home. But those babies have been placed somewhere else."

Rosie stopped pouring. "That doesn't sound good."

"Told ya. Could be the end of the world as we know it," Mort said.

Mark Steele rolled his eyes. "Do you lay awake at night, thinking up this stuff?"

"Scoff at me all ya want, Mr. High and Mighty Assistant Manager. But you ain't gonna change my mind."

"Maybe not. But I *am* going to change the subject."

Ellen Jones walked down the hall and stood outside Mayor Charlie Kirby's office. It was only 8:25. She didn't want to appear too eager for this meeting. She heard voices at the other end of the hall, then saw Sheriff Hal Barker and Police Chief Aaron Cameron round the corner.

"Hi, Ellen," Aaron said. "Good story. Raised some fair questions."

Hal lifted an eyebrow. "Probably someone's blood pressure, too."

"I'm glad Charlie called this meeting," Ellen said. "Now maybe Ivan will tell us what's going on."

Aaron looked at his watch. "Well, it's almost eight-thirty. Shall we?" He held the door.

Ellen walked inside and saw Mayor Kirby and Dr. Ivan Roesch standing in the reception area.

"Welcome," Charlie said, giving Ellen a hug. "I've missed seeing you at church."

"I feel guilty leaving Guy on Sunday mornings," she said.

Charlie shook hands with the others and then led the group down the hall to a conference room where they were seated around a table and offered beverages. He was his usual jovial self, but Ellen detected some tension in his voice.

Charlie took a sip of water. "Each of you is an influencer who understands the dynamics of this community. We know how to work together. But we need to be on the same page if we're to be a positive influence out there. Ivan has agreed to address all of our concerns. So without further delay, I'll pose the first question. Ivan, *is* the medical community reluctant to talk openly about the virus?"

Ivan Roesch cleared his throat. "The CDC doesn't think it's wise to release details that will create more unanswered questions, causing even further speculation."

"Is that a *yes?*" Ellen asked.

"I suppose it is."

"What can you tell us about the home quarantines?" Aaron said.

"Home quarantines have been mapped off into ten districts of seven households each. One safety monitor has been appointed for each district and will check every day with each of the seven households to watch for viral symptoms, address any health concerns, and insure the conditions of the quarantine are being met.

"Each safety monitor will also assign and coordinate the use of other volunteers to insure that those being quarantined have groceries, medicines, or whatever else they need. As of this hour, at least one volunteer has been assigned to each of the seventy quarantined households. Both safety monitors and volunteers will observe barrier nursing procedures."

"It sounds like you expect everything to go like clockwork," Hal said. "But what if there's a snafu? What if those being quarantined decide they aren't going to comply?"

"Sheriff, the people involved are all from the same church. They're cooperative and concerned. I don't expect trouble."

"But what if you get it?" Aaron said. "I don't have enough officers to tackle anything that big."

"I suppose that's true. But again, we don't expect trouble."

Ellen twirled her pencil over and over like a baton.

"Do you have questions, Ellen?"

"Indeed I do, Ivan. Why were none of the facts you just mentioned released to the media so people in this community would've known what's going on?"

"Our energies were focused on getting the quarantines organized. I'm sorry if we neglected to provide information on your newspaper's timetable."

Ellen didn't say what she was thinking. "May I consider this *official* confirmation that there are seventy households under quarantine?"

Ivan nodded. "Yes. And the official number of persons quarantined, counting those in *C* Corridor, is 238."

"Do you know where the Thomases contracted the virus?" she asked.

"Not yet. But the CDC has already teamed up with the World Health Organization and is working hand in hand with them to retrace the patients' travel route from South America. We hope to know the source of the virus within a few days."

Ellen leaned forward on her elbows, her eyes searching Ivan's. "I have an unconfirmed report that these patients are hemorrhaging. Is that true?"

Ivan sighed and began to stroke his beard. "Look, Ellen, this is an area where we need to enlist your professional discretion. We don't want to inhibit your access to information, but we also feel a responsibility not to give the community information that will only raise unsettling questions we can't answer. Surely you can understand our desire to prevent widespread, shall we say, 'jumping to conclusions'?"

"That's precisely why I'm here," Ellen said. "And you still haven't answered my question."

"It's not a good idea to tell the community everything we know until we can tell them exactly what it means."

Ellen mused for a moment. "You know, it was never my intention to get ahead of health officials. But I asked these questions yesterday and didn't receive the courtesy of so much as a returned phone call. KJNX made no reference to home quarantines on their broadcast, so I know they weren't informed. Be glad I did my homework. You're really playing with fire when it comes to KJNX—you're lucky they didn't make up something."

"They're aware this is sensitive."

"Oh, come on, Ivan. They can hardly be trusted with the truth. Give them half-truths, and you're courting disaster. Frankly, I'm amazed they didn't blow this story up to epidemic proportions."

"Well, we're a far cry from an epidemic."

Ellen lifted an eyebrow. "But 238 people quarantined in a town the size of Baxter warrants considerable attention. *Not* telling people can evoke more panic than explaining the truth. Can't we work together to keep the community informed in a reasonable manner?"

"Our number one concern is public safety. The number one concern of the local newspaper seems to be telling the truth, the whole truth, and nothing but the truth. Too much information in this situation could actually be harmful, if you get my point."

"Maybe you could elaborate a bit more on your point?" *Just say it, Ivan. Stop beating around the bush.*

"My point is: The public knows just enough about viral hemorrhagic fevers to be dangerous."

"Like Ebola?" She waited for a reaction, but he didn't flinch.

"Ebola is one such VHF. But there has never been an active case outside of Africa. However, in the public's eyes, 'if it looks like a duck, walks like a duck, sounds like a duck…'"

"Then it must be a duck," Ellen said. "So, tell us, Ivan. *Is* it a duck?"

There was a long pause.

"More like a *strange* duck, Ellen. The CDC hasn't yet identified it. And if the dreaded *E* word is said out loud, we could have a real panic on our hands. People tend to freak out, if you'll pardon a nonmedical expression. Am I making myself clear?"

"Yes. Quite. So at what point do the people need to know? After someone dies? When there's an outbreak? Ivan, if you aren't forthcoming with people all along, at what point can you really expect them to trust you for the truth?"

"Everything that's being said is true. We just haven't elaborated. Our oath is 'first do no harm.' Can you imagine how harmful panic would be?"

Ellen leaned back in her chair. "Underestimating the community's ability to handle this seems more harmful to me. The *Daily News* has always, and I mean *always,* been a reliable source of information. Since we plan to be here long after this virus is gone, I'm hard pressed to see how withholding important information will do anything to foster the trust between the paper and the people who live here.

"And in my opinion, presenting the true story is more important than thinking for people. There's an expression, 'The truth will set you free, but at first it might make you miserable.' So be it. Give them the truth and let them decide what to do with it. I don't mean to be arbitrary, but we find ourselves at an impasse."

There was a long pause.

"May I make a suggestion?" Charlie said. "What if each of us focuses on what he or she does best? Ellen, you can't solve any of the health issues, but you can report them. Ivan, you aren't responsible for what people think or how they'll react, but you can work diligently to contain the virus. Hal and Aaron, you can work to keep the peace. I can encourage and bring people together. By focusing our efforts on what we do best, we can set the tone for the rest of the community."

"Seems reasonable," Ivan said.

Ellen nodded. "I respect what epidemiologists and the CDC are doing, and I plan to keep a levelheaded approach in reporting this story. As long as health officials don't attempt to regulate the truth, there's no reason this has to be combative."

"I'll talk to them," Ivan said. "Their intentions are good."

"Well then, it seems we're in agreement." Charlie looked at his watch. "Are there any other questions?..." He pushed back his chair and stood up. "Okay, then, let's focus."

SEVEN

Dennis Lawton sat in the airport coffee shop trying not to scowl. His flight had been canceled due to high winds, and the announcement he just heard didn't leave much hope of getting to Denver anytime soon. More severe thunderstorms were moving into the area, and if the winds didn't delay everything, the lightning probably would. He sighed. At the moment, he was surrounded by a whole coffee shop full of disgusted travelers who were mirroring his frustration. The last thing he expected in July was a weather delay.

"Would you like more coffee?" the waitress asked.

"Sure, why not? Who knows when I'll get a flight to Denver?"

"Everyone's complaining. Sorry for the hassle. At least it's good for business."

"Yours maybe, not mine. My grandfather's expecting me back at work before noon. And he doesn't like being disappointed."

"Well, he can't expect you to control the weather."

Dennis looked at her and rolled his eyes. "You don't know my grandfather."

"You may not get out today even if the weather clears.

Forecasters say high wind warnings will be in effect."

"I hope they're wrong. I need to get home."

"I can think of worse places to get stuck than Atlanta. You can stay entertained right here in the airport. Wander around. It beats sitting."

Dennis looked outside. "Think I'll stick close to the gate, just in case."

"Good luck."

Dennis took a sip of coffee and watched the endless flow of stranded travelers in the concourse. No one was smiling. He saw a flash, then heard a loud clap of thunder that shook the building. The lights in the coffee shop flickered for several seconds. He downed his coffee, picked up his check, and headed for the register.

Jennifer finally awoke around noon, her fears overriding her faith. Was she equipped for the next twenty-one years of motherhood? She hadn't been a happy child herself and still had hang-ups about men. Was she even capable of instilling a good self-image in her boys? She hadn't planned on raising two. Could she make enough to support them?

"Oh, you're awake." Rhonda was standing in the doorway.

"Come in, Mom. I'm just lying here, going nuts."

"What's wrong?"

"Why can't I have simple faith like everyone else?"

"Like everyone *else*? Don't kid yourself, Jen. Simple faith is what we start with and, hopefully, what we end with as mature Christians. But during the time in between, we tend to complicate it."

"But you and Dad have simple faith."

"Not all the time. It's a constant choice to trust God to do what He says He'll do, especially when so much depends on it."

"Like what?"

"Well, like trusting Him to cover the finances while your dad isn't working. He doesn't have any vacation or sick time left. The bills don't stop coming because we're quarantined."

"How can you *not* worry, Mom?"

"It takes practice. Today I'm fine with it, but I'm not sure how I'll be doing ten days from now. Our church family usually pitches in when someone needs help, but this time, most of us are quarantined and have the same needs. We *can't* help each other. We have to trust the Lord."

"Mom…if I'm scared…does that mean I don't have faith?"

Rhonda stroked Jennifer's long hair. "No. But it's a good indication you're not exercising the faith you have."

"I want to. But suddenly I'm responsible for *two* babies. What if I didn't hear God? Maybe I should've considered adoption more carefully."

"Jennifer, you did consider it. You looked at every aspect of it for a long time. Your dad and I and a whole lot of people from church sensed the same answer as you did to all those prayers. This feels right even if doesn't make a lot of sense. You're not willing to part with them, are you?"

"No. I'm just overwhelmed. Was I wrong not to want child support?"

"I don't know, honey." Rhonda took a Kleenex and handed it to Jennifer. "You've always been independent. Your experience practically guarantees you'll get the management position when the Vitamin Hut opens in September. And you won't have to worry about paying child care."

"Mom, you offered to take care of the baby—not babies. It'll be too much for you."

"Don't get ahead of the Lord, Jen. It'll all fall into place. If living by faith seems difficult to you, then you're no different from the rest of us. Simple, unquestioning faith comes easy to us as children. But when we're old enough to want control, it's harder to trust His sovereignty."

"So you don't think I'm awful because I'm scared?"

"Of course not. As you see His hand in your life, you'll learn to trust Him." Rhonda put her arms around Jennifer and held her close.

"I really love you, Mom. Thanks."

"Honey, you feel warm. Why don't you get out of that long gown and into something comfortable?"

Jennifer wrinkled her nose. "I can hardly wait till I'm out of maternity clothes."

"After you eat, I thought we could call the clinic and check on the babies. Have you thought any more about names?"

"I can't decide."

"It's risky to keep your father waiting. If he keeps calling them Bert and Ernie, it's liable to stick."

Dennis awoke with a start. For a moment, he forgot he was lying on the floor in the waiting area of Gate 17. He looked around sheepishly, hoping he hadn't been snoring. At least the lights were still on. His watch told him that almost an hour had passed. But flight 1692 to Denver was still posted at the gate as "delayed." He stayed stretched out on the floor, wishing this miserable day would end and he could get back to his life and put this all behind him.

Dennis knew he should call and let his grandfather know what was going on. Instead, he reached under a seat and grabbed a copy of *USA Today*, laid it across his face, and went back to sleep.

Jennifer sat with the air conditioning blowing on her, trying to cool off. She felt exhausted and depressed. Was she experiencing the postpartum blues Dr. Harmon had told her about?

"Jen?" Rhonda said softly. "I made lemonade. Would you like some?"

"Thanks, Mom. Got anything for the blues?"

"Just happy thoughts of two little boys coming home soon."

"At least we know who's taking care of them at the clinic," Jennifer said. "Flo sounded nice."

"But?…"

"But I hate having to ask questions about my own children." A clap of thunder made the windows rattle. "Are these storms ever going to clear?"

"They say it's going to last all day and maybe even tonight. Your brother said they closed the airport in Atlanta. He's stuck."

"Mark called?"

"While you were asleep. He asked about you."

"Hmm…overjoyed I had twins, I'm sure."

"Mark loves you, Jen. He'll learn to love the boys, too. He has to get used to the idea of your being a mother."

"Yeah, me, too."

"Your dad and I are going stir-crazy. Want to play cards or something?"

"Maybe later. I'm wiped out."

"Okay, honey. Why don't you take a nap?"

The doorbell rang at the Wilsons'. Jed looked through the peep-hole and saw a man covered in a white gown, mask, goggles, and gloves, holding an umbrella.

"Who is it?" Rhonda asked.

"Must be the safety monitor." Jed opened the door and felt a surge of steamy heat.

"Mr. Wilson? I'm Vince Mulloy, the safety monitor for district two of the quarantine."

"Come in." Jed held open the screen door. "Bet you're miserable under all that. Is it really necessary?"

"Yes, sir. Just a precaution."

Introductions were made, and then Vince sat down with them and went through his checklist. Jed and Rhonda supplied the answers and then asked some questions of their own. In fifteen minutes, they were finished.

"I need to record your vital signs before I leave," Vince said. "Your daughter's, too."

Rhonda stood up. "I'll go wake Jennifer."

Jed studied Vince as he opened his bag and laid out what he would need. What did this guy look like? He sounded young.

"Does the protective clothing make you uncomfortable, Mr. Wilson?"

"I feel like a leper. I suppose I'll have to show myself to the priest when the quarantine's over?"

"Nah. We just throw you to the lions."

Jed smiled. "A man after my own heart. Feels good to joke about it. Cuts the tension, you know?"

"I sure do."

"Have people been cooperative?" Jed asked.

"Oh yes, sir. Everyone's been great. I understand you all go to the same church."

"Yeah, we go to Cornerstone Bi—"

"Jed! Jed, come in here—*hurry!*"

Jed rushed down the hall to Jennifer's room. Rhonda met him at the door.

"What's wrong, babe? What is it?"

Rhonda clutched his arm, her eyes full of panic. "Jennifer's burning up!"

EIGHT

D r. Sarah Rice walked down *C* Corridor and found Pastor
Thomas and his wife looking through the glass wall of
the isolation room. She stood next to them, her eyes
fixed on the green curtain around Melissa's bed.

It was several minutes before Pastor Thomas broke the awkward silence. "Are you a believer, Dr. Rice?"

"Yes, I am. Since I was thirty-five."

"Blake accepted Christ when he was six, Melissa when she was
eleven. These kids are completely sold-out to the Lord. As soon as
they got married, they were off to some remote rain forest to bring
the Good News to the lost. Never once heard them complain."

"You must be very proud," Sarah said.

"I am. Penny and I love them so much. We could hardly wait to be
grandparents." The pastor's chin quivered, and he wiped a tear from
his cheek. "They would've gladly served the Lord even if He never gave
them a child. Why—" His voice cracked. "Why did He bless them
with a child, let them come home to share their joy, and then?…"

Dr. Rice swallowed the emotion. "It's beyond our ability to
grasp."

Pastor Thomas held his wife's hand to his cheek. "With all our heart, we trust in His sovereignty and His goodness…but it's so hard to let go."

From behind the green curtain, a nurse emerged carrying an infant's body, which had been sealed in an airtight bag and covered with a towel.

Dr. Rice blinked the moisture from her eyes and focused on the clock above Blake's bed. *Time of death: 4:52 P.M.*

Dennis looked up when he heard rain pelting the windows at Gate 17. Trees were swaying. Limbs were down. Thunder rumbled in the distance. He might as well call his grandfather and get it over with. He wasn't going anywhere, and it was already after four o'clock in Denver.

Dennis got in line, lamenting that he had forgotten to bring his cell phone on this trip. He waited and listened while each person in front of him explained his or her circumstances. He shifted his weight from one foot to the other and suddenly wished he had a cigarette, even though he'd kicked the habit five years ago. When the chatty woman in front of him finally hung up, he picked up the receiver and dialed. He heard the phone ringing.

"Hello, Patrick Bailey Insurance Agency, how may I direct your call?"

"Hi, Sheila, it's me."

"Ah, Dennis. Mr. Bailey's been using your name in vain most of the afternoon. Shall I transfer you?"

"Yeah, thanks."

"Good luck."

While Dennis was on hold, his attention was drawn to the voice of a man nearby talking on the phone.

"What do health officials think?… That can't be good. What about the brats? Okay—the *twins?*… Dad, this is lousy news. How long before you know something about Jen?... Is she at Baxter Memorial?..."

Dennis's eavesdropping was suddenly interrupted by his grandfather's voice.

"Dennis? Where in tarnation have you been? I've been pacing the floor most of the day. I expected you in the office by noon!"

"Sorry, Grandpa. I'm stuck in Atlanta. The weather's horrible and planes have been grounded all day. I kept thinking I'd get out, but it's not going to happen." Dennis strained to hear the other voice but found it impossible to concentrate.

"Do you hear me, boy?"

"Uh, I'm sorry, Grandpa, it's noisy here. I didn't catch what you said."

"I *said*—did you see that girl?"

"Yeah, I saw her."

"And?..."

"She's not going to be a problem."

"Good."

"Listen, Grandpa, I'm calling from a pay phone. It's too noisy for me to talk. I can barely hear you. I have no idea when I'll get a flight out, but I'll call you as soon as I know something. I didn't want you to worry."

"All right, Dennis. Get here when you can. I held up my end of the bargain. I haven't said a word to your mother."

"Thanks, Grandpa. It's best left between you and me. See you soon. Good-bye."

Dennis kept the receiver to his ear and resumed his eavesdropping.

"I'm stuck. My connecting flight to Denver was canceled. I'll never make the meeting...Yeah, Dad, I'm sure God can take care of it—whatever. I'll check back later to see how Jen's doing. Try not to worry...yeah, okay."

Dennis heard the young man hang up. He waited a few seconds, and then hung up the receiver and followed the guy. The man appeared to be in his early twenties, dressed business casual, carrying a laptop. He had light brown hair, was about five-foot-ten, give or take. Slim build. Cocky attitude. He followed him into a food bar.

"Excuse me." Dennis tapped him on the shoulder. "Are you Mark Wilson, Jennifer's younger brother?" When the man turned around, Dennis instantly saw the family resemblance.

"Yeah. Do I know you?"

"Not exactly. I'm Dennis Lawton, Jen's ex-boyfriend. I overheard your conversation on the phone a few minutes ago, and it sounds like the situation in Baxter is getting worse."

"So *you're* the bad boy?" Mark's piercing brown eyes seemed to size him up. "I use you for target practice in my sleep."

"Look, I was in Baxter yesterday and know all about the quarantine. Have things begun to escalate?"

"Now you care?"

"Well, of course, I care," Dennis said, realizing how ridiculous that must sound under the circumstances.

"You've got a weird way of showing it."

"I don't blame you for hating me, but—"

"Just stay away from my sister."

"I heard you say she's in the hospital."

"You heard wrong."

"Well, are the boys all right?"

"What boys? Go back to Denver. *Denver?*" He grimaced. "They better not put me on the same flight with you. I don't wanna breathe the same air."

"Look, Mark. Let's don't make a scene. I just want to know—"

"I don't care *what* you wanna know, Lawton. I'm not telling you anything. And stay away from my sister. I mean it." Mark turned on his heel and began to walk down the concourse.

Dennis felt his face get hot. People were staring. He left the food bar and went looking for an airport TV.

NINE

D ennis sat in an airport lounge listening to CNN, and looked up when he heard Baxter's name mentioned. He recognized the main entrance to Baxter Memorial Hospital and realized this must be a clip of an earlier broadcast. Dr. Sarah Rice stepped forward to make a statement. A number of news crews and reporters were present. A hush fell over the gathering as she began to speak.

"After the sudden onset of labor, which lasted only three hours, the infant daughter of Blake and Melissa Thomas was stillborn at 4:52 P.M. eastern daylight time. An autopsy will be performed to determine the cause of death. Melissa Thomas remains in serious but stable condition."

"Dr. Rice, did the baby have the virus?" a reporter shouted.

"I don't want to speculate. Let's wait for the autopsy report."

"Was Melissa aware that the baby was stillborn?"

"I'm not going to comment on that."

"Dr. Rice, in light of this new development, what are the chances the parents will survive?"

"As I said last evening, these two young people are otherwise in good health. With the level of supportive care we're providing, we remain optimistic."

"Dr. Rice, KJNX-TV reported that a young female patient who had been exposed to the virus was admitted this afternoon with a high fever. Can you confirm that?"

"Yes. But the young woman's exposure to the affected patients occurred less than twenty-four hours prior to her developing a fever. That's an inordinately short incubation period. Let's not jump to conclusions."

"Can you give us her name?"

"Jennifer Wilson. That's all the questions I have time for. If you'll excuse me, I must get back to work."

As a policeman escorted Dr. Rice back inside the building, reporters continued to fire questions.

"Dr. Rice, there are unconfirmed reports that the patients are hemorrhaging. Did the Thomas baby bleed to death?"

"Is Jennifer Wilson hemorrhaging?"

"Shouldn't people be worried? Why aren't health officials giving us more information?"

Dennis sat frozen, his pulse racing. He tried to recall everything he had overheard of Mark's phone conversation. The words made frightening sense as they came echoing back to him.

Hemorrhaging? No one mentioned that before. And why did the doctors tell Jennifer she wasn't infectious? Was he at risk? Were her babies?

Dennis's mind retraced his every step at the hospital. He was sure he hadn't had close contact with Jennifer. If only that nurse hadn't conned him into holding the babies.

Dennis got up and wandered down the concourse. After a while, he stopped and leaned against the wall outside a gift shop and watched the steady flow of stranded travelers rushing to go nowhere. He'd never thought seriously about dying. He didn't even have his life figured out yet...

"Mom, who is this in the picture?" Dennis had asked.

"Where'd you find that?" She plucked it out of his hand.

"In the attic. You said I could look through the cedar chest... It's my father, isn't it?"

"I thought I tore up all those pictures."

"Can I see it?"

"He's a louse, Dennis. No point in giving him a second thought."

"I just wanna look...please?"

His mother sighed and turned loose of the photograph.

Dennis studied the stranger whose blue eyes looked just like his. "What if he's changed, Mom? Maybe he'd be happy to see me."

"He doesn't know how to be happy." His mother snatched the picture from his hand and tore it to pieces...

Dennis never told her that he didn't know how to be happy either.

He kept filling the emptiness with things, but the aching never went away for long. When he was old enough to use his good looks, he became involved with one woman after another. But when his bed was empty, so was his heart. What was wrong with him? His life had been a total waste. *Here lies Dennis Lawton: A pathetically unhappy and self-serving nobody.*

Dennis blinked several times to clear his eyes. He put his hands in his pockets and started walking briskly down the concourse in the other direction.

Jennifer had drifted in and out of a fretful sleep, aware that she was in the hospital. *Lord, please take care of the babies. They're so little.*

She saw someone standing at her bedside, covered in protective clothing.

"You're awake," the woman said. "How are you feeling?"

"Run over."

"Let's see if your fever's gone down."

Jennifer opened her mouth and received the thermometer under her tongue. She nodded off until the woman's voice startled her.

"Hmm…your fever's down to 102. By the way, I'm Helen. I'll be your nurse tonight. If you need anything, just press the button on the side of your bed."

"Do I have the virus?" Jennifer asked.

"We're waiting for the lab results. You just rest, darlin'. I'll be back to check on you periodically."

When the nurse left the room, Jennifer closed her eyes and drifted back to sleep.

Dennis had waited in line for thirty minutes, hoping to rent a car.

"Next."

Dennis stepped up to the counter. "Have you got a midsize?"

"I'm sorry. All we have left is a limited number of subcompacts."

"They're like sardine cans. Don't you have *anything* else?"

"Not tonight. We've been swamped with people tired of waiting out this storm. I expect to be out of options within the hour."

"All right, I'll take it. I'll just have to stop every half hour and make sure the blood's still circulating." Dennis smiled wryly. "The worst that can happen is I'll lose my legs."

"He can have mine," said a gray-haired man approaching the counter.

"Your legs?"

"No, my car. I changed my mind. I'm not driving in this mess."

"Well, looks like this is your lucky night," the agent said to Dennis. "If you'll be patient for just a little longer, I'll get the paperwork switched out."

"That'd be great." Dennis turned to the gray-haired man.

"Thanks, mister. Can I give you a lift?"

"No, I'll take the hotel shuttle."

When the paperwork was completed, the agent directed Dennis to a bus that would take him to his car.

Dennis picked up his bag and walked to the door, where he was met with a blast of muggy air and the sound of thunder. He got on the bus and a few minutes later arrived at the rent-a-car lot.

He stepped down into a puddle up to his ankles, then hurried inside the office and got the keys. With a magazine shielding his face from a blowing sheet of rain, he went out the door and ran to space number seven.

A few minutes later, he was driving a red Ford Taurus out of Atlanta.

TEN

On Tuesday evening, the skies over Baxter started to clear as the wind blew out of the west, bringing the humidity level down to bearable.

Ellen Jones strolled arm in arm with Guy around the town square. "Feels good to unwind," she said. "Thanks for getting me out of the house."

"There's a respectable showing tonight," he said. "I guess everybody's glad to be outdoors after all the rain."

"There's more to it than that, Guy. After Dr. Rice made her statement about the Thomas baby being stillborn, I can almost feel the unsettledness banging like a loose shutter. The winds of apprehension are definitely picking up."

"You promised not to get intense until we walked around the square at least once."

Ellen smiled and squeezed his arm. As they walked, her eyes sought out a huge magnolia tree that had been there ever since she could remember. Steam rose from the sidewalk, much to the delight of two small children who squealed and tried to catch it.

In the center of the square stood the Norris County Court-house, its reddish stone walls and rounded white pillars a contrast to the green lawn and towering shade trees. Ellen glanced up at the clock tower just as it chimed eight o'clock. The sun still felt hot as it dropped lower in the western sky.

"The breeze feels good," Guy said. "Watch out for the puddle." He pulled her to the other side of the sidewalk. "All right, Ellen. You made it all the way around the square without commentary. I know you're dying to say something."

"Guy, did you notice what's missing?"

He looked around. "I give up."

"Tourists."

"Hmm…I guess all the bad press scared them off."

"Very funny," she said.

"Ellen, as your attorney, I'm advising you to lighten up. It's such a nice evening. Let's take another stroll around the square, and scratch day two of the quarantine off the calendar."

"I can't exactly put the situation on the back burner, Counselor."

"All work and no play makes Ellen a dull girl."

"Honestly, you and your clichés."

"If you can't say somethin' nice, don't say nothin' at all."

"Guy, this is scary."

"The only thing we have to fear is fear itself."

Ellen laughed. "Okay. Okay. I get the point. How's this for light-hearted: Last one to the park bench at Holmes is a rotten egg?" Ellen took off running with Guy on her heels.

By the time Dennis got to Ellison, he could see stars overhead and noticed a drier feel to the air. He pulled the car to the side of the road and got out to stretch his legs.

He breathed in the rich, unmistakable scent of earth after a rain. He spotted a restaurant that appeared to be open. A full meal sounded good after a day of fast food in the airport. He got back in the car and drove a block, then pulled into the parking lot of Mrs. Wright's Kitchen.

Dennis went inside and ordered from the all-you-can-eat menu. He savored a home-style dinner of baked ham, scalloped potatoes, green beans and corn bread, and then asked for a second helping.

He lingered over his food, trying not to talk himself out of what he was about to do. What did he have to lose?

"Can I get you anything else?" the waitress asked.

Her voice startled him. "Look what time it is. You should've pushed me out of here fifteen minutes ago. Sorry."

"I hated to bother you. You seemed deep in thought. Are you all right?"

"Yeah. Can't quite shake the situation in Baxter. Did you hear that couple's baby was born dead?"

"Just about every customer I had tonight mentioned it. Know anyone over there?"

Dennis nodded. "An old girlfriend and her two kids."

"My sister lives there. I'd be afraid to go near the place right now. I told her to come stay with me."

Dennis looked at the bill and gave her twenty dollars. "Keep the change."

"Sir, your bill was only—"

"Yeah, I know."

"Thanks. That's very generous. Be sure and come back."

Dennis stood up and walked out of the restaurant, wondering what the odds were that he would be coming back—ever.

Billy Joe Sawyer had spent the evening at Ernie's Tavern, hanging out with the guys in his militia group. He emptied the glass pitcher and downed another beer, listening for the umpteenth time to all the penny-ante opinions about the Thomas baby's death. All they ever did was *talk!* Sawyer shoved back his chair and stood up, twelve pairs of eyes fixed on him.

"We all know what killed that baby!" Sawyer said. "You think they're gonna tell us the truth?"

"Buncha liars!" someone shouted.

"They tell us what we wanna hear!" shouted someone else.

Sawyer nodded, his eyebrows raised. "They told my mom she was cured of cancer. Six months later I buried her. Who knows how many are in that hospital bleedin' to death while their germs are spreadin' over here?" Sawyer moved his eyes from face to face. "Are we just gonna sit by and do nothin'?"

"What do you expect us to do?" Bo Ritter said.

"We're the Citizens' Watch Dogs!" Sawyer raised his right arm, his fist clenched. "What do you think we've been trainin' for?"

"To protect our God-given rights," Bo said. "But that ain't what this is about."

Sawyer bent down, his face in front of Bo's. "Should we just roll over and play dead till we *are* dead? If this isn't protecting our rights, I don't what is!" Sawyer stood up straight. "Who's man enough to stand with me?"

Sawyer stood alone in the silence that followed, his heart racing, his fists clenched.

"I am!" shouted one man, rising to his feet.

"Me, too!" cried a second.

"Count me in," said a third.

One by one, eleven men rose to their feet. Finally, Bo stood up.

Sawyer felt a surge of adrenaline. How long had he waited for this chance? "It's high time everyone knows who we are and what we stand for! Let's go show 'em!"

Sawyer led the way outside where they piled into three pickups and headed for the ammo shed.

∽०∽

Sawyer drove his pickup ten miles to the Baxter city limits, Bo riding in the passenger seat and two men riding in the truck bed. He glanced in the rearview mirror and saw two sets of headlights. "Are those Watch Dogs?"

Bo turned and looked out the back window. "Yeah."

Sawyer slowed at First Street and made the final turn. As he approached the town square, he rolled down his window, pushed on the accelerator, and began firing his pistol into the air.

Hooting and hollering, Sawyer drove the lead pickup once around the town square. When he slowed, the two men jumped out of the back and ran to the center of City Park where they drove a tall stake, carved with the initials CWD, into the ground directly in front of the courthouse. Cheers resounded from those in the trucks as the pair lit the kerosene-soaked tip.

Seconds later, the two zealots hopped back in, and Sawyer sped away, leading the convoy to the assault target.

Jennifer Wilson woke to the sound of screeching tires, then gunfire and breaking glass. She heard voices shouting and tried to remember where she was.

Someone burst into the room. "Hit the floor!"

Jennifer felt herself being pulled down beside the bed as bullets ricocheted off the walls. Something crashed through the window, spilling flaming liquid across the room and igniting blankets folded on a chair.

"We have to get out of here," Jennifer said. She turned and saw Helen lying in a pool of blood. Jennifer shook her. "Helen! Helen!"

She grabbed the nurse by the wrists and dragged her body out into the hallway. Jennifer gasped for air and went into a coughing spasm.

The sound of the fire alarm blared over the pandemonium. People were running up and down C Corridor. Some had fire extinguishers.

Jennifer felt dizzy. She backed up until she could feel the wall, then slid down to a sitting position, her arms hugging her knees. She felt a deep, burning sensation and noticed blood seeping through the front of her gown.

Someone came rushing toward her, the voice far away and indistinguishable. The sounds of chaos became muffled and surreal...and then silent.

"Gimme that phone." Sawyer grabbed the cell phone from Bo and entered the numbers he had written on his wrist.

"Hello, this is Margie."

"Is this the *Daily News?*"

"Yes, it is. But the only people here this late are—"

"Listen carefully, lady." He spoke in a deep, raspy voice. "I'm only gonna say this once. We're the Citizens' Watch Dogs—the CWD—and we've spoken. They can't keep the truth from the people—"

"Excuse me, who did you say—"

"Shut up! Tell those liars at the hospital that the *people* have spoken. We won't sit back and let that virus take us out. What we did tonight? There's more where that came from. This is war." *Click.* Sawyer grinned and tossed the phone back to Bo. "Any questions?"

Bo said nothing. He popped the top off a beer and handed it to Sawyer.

Sawyer tilted his head back and took a big gulp, feeling invincible on the throne of his shiny black pickup. He laughed and jabbed Bo with his elbow. "Power to the people!"

༄

Dennis's eyes were heavy, and he tried to stay focused on the road. Three sets of headlights zoomed past him in rapid succession, shaking his car. He sat up straight and rubbed his eyes. He could have kicked himself for not staying in Ellison for the night.

A few minutes later, he entered the Baxter city limits and noticed the air seemed smoky. Up ahead he saw a fire truck and a sheriff's squad car pull onto the highway and speed toward downtown. Suddenly wide-awake, Dennis decided to see what was going on.

ELEVEN

Dennis followed the flashing lights to the town square and saw people running from all directions toward City Park. A sizable crowd had already gathered and was watching something burning in front of the courthouse. Police officers held back onlookers.

Dennis pulled up to a parking meter and stepped out of the car. "Anybody know what happened?"

A young man turned toward him. "Lots of shooting—somebody whoopin' it up. Might've been one of those drive-bys like they've had over in Ellison."

"What's burning over there?" Dennis asked.

"Can't tell. The cops won't let us get close. But most of the smoke's coming from the hospital. Someone said there was a fire."

"Fire? Are you sure?" Dennis said.

"That's what I heard."

Dennis backed the car onto Baxter Avenue, then pulled forward to the intersection and made a right on First Street. Before he reached the hospital, he noticed the road up ahead was barricaded. He turned down a side street, parallel parked, and walked back to First.

He stood with a group of onlookers and tried to size up the situation. A string of vehicles with flashing lights was parked between the barricade and the hospital. On the circle drive outside the main entrance, firemen corralled medical staff and patients and took them back inside.

"What happened?" Dennis asked.

"A fire of some kind," said a man in a terry cloth bathrobe. "Looks like it's out now. I'm going back to bed."

"Do you know of a clinic across from the hospital?" Dennis asked.

"Yeah, there's one on the street behind it. It's not open at night, though."

"Thanks." Dennis took off running down First. When he reached the barricade, he cut through yards, angling his way to the street behind the hospital. He ran along a row of quaint houses-turned-businesses and finally spotted a sign: Hunter Clinic. He bounded up the steps to the front door, glad to see lights on and the place undamaged.

He rang the bell and looked through the beveled glass on the door. Through the sheers, he could see a large entry hall papered in red and tan striped wallpaper and, at the far end, a wooden staircase. A door on the left of the entry hall was closed. But on the right, he saw French doors covered in lacy panels. The lights were on.

Dennis banged on the door. "Hello. Is anybody in there?" He rang the bell again.

Finally, the French doors opened, and an elderly woman came out into the entry hall. She saw him standing on the front porch and walked to the door and opened it.

"Young man, another fright like that and they'll be puttin' me six feet under. It's the middle o' the night, for land's sake. What took you so long to git here?"

"Well, I—"

"Don't matter no how. I'm just glad to have help." She opened the door and let Dennis inside. "Had a scare a while ago. Still don't know what happened. I heard poppin' o' some kind, and then smoke was pourin' outta the hospital. Mercy me! If them flames woulda spread, I'd've had a time gittin' them babies out by myself. You are from that volunteer agency, ain't you?"

"Actually, I'm—"

"They been tryin' to git me help. But after the babies' mama took sick, them other volunteers backed out. I was beginnin' to think nobody'd come. You ain't afraid?"

"I held the babies at the hospital," Dennis said. "I've already been exposed."

"Nah. Them boys was born just hours after their mama was exposed. That ain't long enough to git it *or* give it."

Dennis wasn't so sure.

"But people's afraid," she said. "And newborns need holdin'. Sometimes they flat *demand* it. Ain't no room here for nobody whose scared a gittin' sick."

"I'm here to help," Dennis said. "But you'll have to train me."

"How much do you know about carin' for infants?"

"I—uh—well, nothing. But I'm willing to learn. And I can stay around the clock. I don't have to be anywhere else."

"Praise God, you're an answer to prayer, boy. And just in time to get showed around before their two o'clock feedin'. You ain't been through nothin' 'til you try feedin' and changin' two hollerin' babies by yourself. Makes you wish you'd growed a few more arms. What did you say your name was?"

"My name? Uh, Ben…Ben Stoller."

"I'm Florence Hamlin. Call me Flo."

Dennis looked into her gentle brown eyes. "Okay, Flo. Teach me how to do this. Even if I'm all thumbs, ten thumbs are better than none."

౦౦

At 2:00 A.M. Dr. Sarah Rice sat at the table in her conference room with Drs. Roesch, McFarland, and Wong, Police Chief Aaron Cameron, Sheriff Hal Barker, Mayor Charlie Kirby, and Ellen Jones.

"This won't take long," Dr. Rice said. "But since we're all here at the hospital, let me update you on tonight's situation.

"Suffice it say, *C* Corridor is out of commission. Fortunately, the fire was put out quickly, and damage was confined to that wing. And, thanks to state-of-the-art fire protection and damage control planning, the smell of smoke in the other two corridors is hardly noticeable.

"Patients not requiring isolation have been moved to *A* Corridor. Those quarantined have been moved to *B* Corridor, where barrier nursing continues.

"Chief Cameron and Sheriff Barker have teamed up and provided officers to patrol the exterior of the premises until we get direction from the FBI."

Dr. Rice paused, aware that her hands were shaking. "Tonight's bloodbath posed a serious risk of spreading the virus. We owe a great deal to the medical staff for their quick and courageous response.

"However, we did incur casualties—five people suffered gunshot wounds…two have died. Four nurses are being treated for smoke inhalation. Of course, exposure to blood during the attack has increased the number of people now being quarantined. And after I found out what precipitated tonight's attack, I don't mind telling you I'm one *very* distraught Chief of Staff…" Her voice failed. She motioned for Aaron Cameron to speak.

"Dr. Rice is referring to a phone call made to the *Baxter Daily News* following the attack," Chief Cameron said. "Ellen, why don't you fill them in?"

Ellen pulled a three-by-five card out of her briefcase. "Minutes after the attack, a man called the newspaper and talked to my assistant. This is verbatim what he told her: 'Tell those liars at the hospital that the *people* have spoken. We won't sit back and let that virus take us out. What we did tonight? There's more where that came from. This is war.'" Ellen looked at Ivan Roesch. "The statement speaks for itself."

"They've declared war on this hospital," Dr. Rice said. "If the community wasn't paranoid before, they certainly are now. We need to change how we're perceived in the media."

Dr. Montgomery nodded. "Though it was never our intention to be untruthful, we can no longer afford to be protective. These radicals have already claimed two lives. And right now, the community has more to fear from them than from the virus. We've had no experience in managing VHF quarantine in the U.S. population. But it appears we would do better to address the unsettling questions than face the attacks of any more frightened citizens."

"Frightened citizens?" Sheriff Barker said. "My bet is this CWD has been looking for an excuse to explode their toys. I've studied groups like this. If not the virus, they'd find something else."

"Chief, what do you know about this group?" Mayor Kirby asked.

"This is the first I've heard of them. The torch they left burning on the square had the initials CWD carved on the base. That, and what Ellen shared of the phone call, is all I know about the Citizens' Watch Dogs."

"The FBI probably has a file on them," Sheriff Barker said. "I'll bet Jordan Ellis will give us an earful."

"Excuse me," Dr. Rice said. "Could we get something settled here? When the sun comes up, the media is going to be camped on *my* doorstep. And I'm not willing to jeopardize my patients and staff to run interference on this anymore."

"I agree," Dr. Montgomery said. "From this point, let's be completely direct."

◦◦◦

Ellen went in the front door and was surprised to see Guy sitting on the couch reading a novel.

"It's almost time for you to get up," she said. "Have you even been to bed?"

"No. I've been waiting for you."

Ellen sat next to him. Guy put his arm around her and pulled her close.

"This is exactly what I warned them about," she said. "Only worse."

"Come on, Ellen. Even you didn't figure on some radical militants attacking the hospital."

Ellen fought back the tears, her chin quivering. "Jennifer Wilson was shot. They're not sure she's going to make it."

"I'll bet Jed and Rhonda are beside themselves."

"Those poor little twins," Ellen said. "What a way to come into the world."

"I wonder what the people from your church are thinking now?" Guy said. "Unfortunately, when you use religion for a crutch, it's bound to give way at some point."

"The ones I've talked to seem to be holding up. Pastor Thomas is a rock. And Charlie did a great job at the meeting this morning. I'm sure Jed and Rhonda will find the strength to handle it."

"Yes, I'm sure they'll all find a way to make God the fairy godmother in this. They have to. Otherwise, their belief system would topple."

Ellen moved his arm and got up. "I'm too exhausted for this. Why can't you just accept the fact that there might actually be Someone greater?"

"I just don't. And I'm concerned you're beginning to believe it."

Ellen started up the stairs and then turned around. "If you're so concerned, why won't you read *Evidence that Demands a Verdict?*

Try to shoot holes in it. I'm more than willing to discuss it with you."

"I haven't had time."

"No one *has* time, Counselor. You make time."

Dennis was feeding one of the twins his two o'clock bottle and noticed it was almost empty. "Didn't take *him* long."

"You're doin' just fine, Ben. You got the hang of it real good. He's a cute one, you know."

"Flo, they look exactly alike."

"Well, there you go. I can say it no matter which one you got. What're we gonna call these babies? We can't keep callin' 'em Number One and Number Two—like some diaper disaster." She chuckled.

"Hasn't the mother named them yet?"

"Don't think so. Poor thing. I wonder how she's gittin' along? Guess we'll just have to keep prayin' she gits well since their daddy took off and don't care nothin' about 'em."

TWELVE

Wednesday morning's sun invaded the east windows of Monty's diner and patrons began pulling the café curtains. Assistant Manager Mark Steele lowered the thermostat while Rosie Harris turned on the ceiling fans.

"I wonder what's holding up the *Daily News?*" Mark said.

Rosie fanned herself with her order pad. "If we don't get facts pretty soon, Mort's liable to start writing a made-for-TV movie script to go with his bioterrorism paranoia."

"I heard that." Mort Clary whirled around on the stool. "You won't be laughin' fer long."

"Want more coffee?" Rosie said. "*To go?*"

"I ain't leavin' till I know what the paper has ta say."

Minutes later, the door to the diner opened and a man walked in with a bundle of newspapers. "Sorry it's so late. We had to wait on a special insert about last night's attack."

"Everybody stay put," Mark said. "I'll pass out the papers. You can drop your quarter in the jar on the way out."

"Order up!" Leo shouted.

"You're on your own, boss," Rosie said. "Duty calls."

Mark picked up a stack of papers and handed them out, then took one for himself and pulled out the insert.

Five Shot in Hospital Attack—Two Dead
Citizens' Watch Dogs Threaten More Violence

Mark shook his head in disbelief as he read the details, then went back and read them a second time. A few minutes later he moved closer to the counter, where the conversation was heating up.

"This is an outrage!" Hattie Gentry said. "How can this group possibly justify gunning down helpless people?"

"I knew it'd come ta this," Mort said.

George Gentry shot him a look. "The Citizens' Watch Dogs aren't bioterrorists, Mort. Not even close."

"Okay, Georgie, all powerful and all knowin', why do ya suppose them watch dogs went ta firebombin' the hospital?"

"Because they're paranoid," George said. "And stupid. Their shooting up the hospital could've turned this into an epidemic."

Mort's eyebrows gathered, his eyes squinting. "But supposin' this CWD was really intendin' to *spread* the virus, not wipe it out? The attack woulda been the perfect smokescreen."

George rolled his eyes. "I give up."

"Well, I sure don't wanna get the virus," Reggie Mason said.

Hattie nodded. "We're all scared. But the violence those half-wits brought to this community should scare us more than the virus. *They* need to be quarantined permanently—behind bars."

Rosie poured Hattie a refill. "The whole thing's frightening. Suppose they're just waiting to find out the body count before they hit again?"

Reggie cupped his hands around his mouth. "The score after the first round of play: The Citizens' Watch Dogs 2, the virus 1."

Rosie thumped Reggie on the shoulder. "How *dare* you make a game out of this? People are dead!"

"Sorry, I just wanted to lighten things up. This stuff's heavy."

"It's going to get heavier when they release the names of the ones who died." Liv Spooner started to cry. "Those two victims are probably people we know. Did you stop to think about that?"

"Hey, I didn't mean anything by it," Reggie said.

Liv dabbed her eyes. "I'm worried about my neighbor, Jennifer Wilson. There weren't many people quarantined in C Corridor. If two died and seven others were either shot or overcome with smoke, then the CWD got to most of them."

"So, don't you wonder why this group would take it to the extreme?" Reggie said. "How *do* we know health officials are tellin' the truth?"

Leo hollered from the grill. "We don't."

"Them watch dogs sure ain't buyin' it," Mort said, a toothy grin stretching across his face.

Jim Hawkins slammed his newspaper on the counter and stood up. "I've listened to this gibberish long enough! Why second-guess health officials who know more about this situation than any of you? They're here to protect us. Why don't we try letting them? The CWD can't stop this virus. And turning on health officials is the most dangerous thing we can do."

"You willin' ta stake *yer* life on it, Jim Hawkins?" Mort laughed his wheezy laugh.

George Gentry stood up. "Mark, how about us giving Mort the old heave-ho?"

"Go on. Boot him out!" Rosie said.

"And don't let him back till he learns some manners," Hattie added.

Everyone at the counter rumbled in agreement.

Mark Steele walked over and held open the door. "Sounds like a consensus, Mort. Go find another group of people to irritate this morning."

"Go ahead and throw me out. I'll be watchin' ya eat crow soon enough." He tipped his hat mockingly and left.

Jed sat at the kitchen table staring at a cup of cold coffee. The phone rang.

"Jed, it's Charlie Kirby. Any news on Jennifer?"

"She's out of surgery. But she's lost a lot of blood, Charlie. It's serious. At least she's stable."

"You know Marlene and I are praying," Charlie said. "Did Bart call you?"

"Yeah, he called and prayed with us. Man, he's tough. You know he's torn up over his grandbaby's death and everything that's going on with Blake and Melissa. I can't believe he was thinking of us."

"Our pastor's a special person, Jed. I'm grateful he and Penny weren't hurt in the attack. Do you know which two people died? The names haven't been released."

"Ellen told me, but I didn't get the names. One was a nurse found dead on the floor next to Jennifer. Shot in the upper chest. The other was one of the EMTs who had transported Blake and Melissa to the ER. Died of a gunshot wound to the head."

"Who else was shot?"

"Both ER doctors."

Charlie sighed. "As if they hadn't been through enough."

"These radicals have got to be stopped, Charlie. This thing's out of control. Who knows when they might strike again?"

"The FBI's helping us figure out a strategy for protecting the hospital. Agents are positioned around the premises, and Hal and Aaron have officers patrolling the area. The CWD isn't going to sneak up on us again."

"I'm glad you're out there, Charlie, and not stuck in quarantine. By the way, where were you and Marlene the night of Blake's reception?"

"In Ellison. I was best man at my cousin's wedding. What a break that turned out to be! I forgot to ask how the twins are doing."

"Some nice older lady is taking care of them at the Hunter Clinic. I think there were some other volunteers coming in to help. Jennifer and Rhonda seemed pretty okay with it."

"That's good. At least you don't have to worry about them. You've got enough on your mind. Listen, Jed, I need to take another call. You hang in there. Our prayers are going up."

"Yeah, I feel them, Charlie. Thanks."

When Jed hung up, he realized Rhonda was standing in the doorway.

"What are we going to do if Jennifer doesn't recover?" Rhonda's voice cracked.

Jed got up and stood facing Rhonda. He tilted her chin upward so he could see her eyes. "Babe, she's stable. Don't get ahead of this thing."

"I can't help it. I'm worried about the babies, too. Jed, what will happen to them if Jennifer can't take care of them—or if she dies?"

"A couple hundred of us felt complete peace about her taking on the role of a single mom," Jed said. "God knew this was coming. He could've given at least one of us a sense of caution. He didn't. I don't know what's going to happen, but I trust Him."

Rhonda's eyes brimmed with tears. "I'm not sure we heard God right."

"Babe, it's too late to second-guess whether or not we heard Him right. What's important now is that He is right. Either we believe God's sovereign, Rhonda, or we don't. We can't have it both ways."

On Wednesday morning, Dennis sat in the makeshift nursery at the Hunter Clinic, giving baby Number Two his ten o'clock bottle. "You little oinker. You downed that in record time."

Dennis heard a knock on the French doors. Flo answered it, and then he heard voices approaching the door to the babies' room. When he looked up, he was shocked to see the face of Nurse Sullivan.

"Hello," she said, acting as though she didn't recognize him. "I'm Martha Sullivan. I've been asked to take charge of the volunteer care of the Wilson babies. And you are?…"

"Uh, Ben Stoller. I'm Ben Stoller."

"Nice to meet you, *Ben.*" She shook his hand, gripping a little tighter and longer than was comfortable. "So, Flo tells me you're a volunteer? I don't recall seeing your name on the list."

His heart pounded in expectation of her going off on him.

"How long do you plan to stay?"

"As long as I'm needed," Dennis said.

"Well, young man, that sounds like a commitment. How do I know I can depend on you?"

Dennis was trapped in a long pause. "Uh, if you'll hold the baby for a minute, I'll show you." He gave the boy to Nurse Sullivan and then stood up. "I'll be right back."

Dennis went into the study and unzipped his leather bag. He removed an envelope containing his expired plane ticket, then went back to the nursery and handed it to Nurse Sullivan.

"You'll notice my plans are on hold so I can work this assignment," Dennis said. "I trust you'll find my credentials satisfactory." *Come on, lady. Give me a break.*

Dennis thought he saw the corners of her mouth curve slightly upward when she took out the ticket and examined it. He glanced at Flo, who seemed oblivious to the game they were playing.

"Well, yes," Nurse Sullivan said. "You seem well suited for this assignment."

Dennis sat in the rocker and she gave the baby back to him.

"I trust your accommodations are adequate?" Nurse Sullivan said.

Dennis looked at Flo and nodded. "Yes, ma'am. The hide-a-bed works fine for me. I can sack out anywhere."

"Ben's good with them babies," Flo said. "I'm mighty glad to have him."

"Flo and I have already worked out a schedule," Dennis added. "She'll do the cooking. I'll clean up and take out the trash. And when the babies squawk, we'll race to see who gets there first." Dennis flashed Nurse Sullivan his most charming smile and was disappointed she didn't respond.

"I'll arrange for someone to bring you replenishments on baby supplies and formula," Nurse Sullivan said. "And also do your grocery shopping. Keep a list. Someone will check with you several times during the week. Call me if you need something sooner or if you get into a situation you can't handle." She gave both of them her business card. "And Ben..." she said, her eyes locked on to his. "After you've finished with this assignment, maybe you'll want to consider a more *permanent* position."

Dennis felt his ears get hot.

Nurse Sullivan smiled with her eyes. "I'll leave the two of you to the task at hand. Please don't get up—I'll let myself out."

THIRTEEN

The Hunter Clinic had opened for business on Wednesday morning at eight-thirty. Through the sheers on the French doors, Dennis observed a steady stream of patients going in and out the clinic entrance. He and Flo had just put the babies down for a nap when he heard a knock on the door.

"I'll get it," Dennis said. "Probably someone looking for the clinic."

He opened the door, and a middle-aged woman stood in the hallway with a newspaper in her hand.

"Hi, I'm from the clinic across the hall. I heard the apartment was being used this week and wondered if you might like to read the paper."

"Uh, sure. Thanks."

"We're usually finished with it after our morning break," she said. "Would you like us to keep passing it on to you?"

"Yeah, thanks. That'd be great."

The woman wrinkled her nose. "Wish the news wasn't so dreadful."

Dennis closed the door and unfolded the paper. An insert fell on the floor and he picked it up, shocked at what he read. *Five shot? Two dead?*

"Flo, you're not going to believe this!" He continued reading as he walked across the living room and nearly bumped into her.

"Where'd you git the paper, Ben?"

"Some lady who works at the clinic left it. That fire at the hospital was caused by a radical group trying to wipe out the virus!"

"Land sakes!"

Flo sat at the kitchen table. Dennis laid the insert in front of her and read over her shoulder.

"Some guy told me there'd been a fire at the hospital," Dennis said, "but it was out by the time I got there. I never suspected an attack!"

"Dear Lord in heaven, what's gotten into folks? It's senseless, that's all there is to it."

"They didn't release the names of the people who were shot," Dennis said. "I wonder how we can find out if the babies' mother is all right?"

"Ain't no TV here. I suppose Martha Sullivan knows somethin'."

Dennis took Nurse Sullivan's business card out of his pocket, walked over to the phone, and dialed the number.

"Baxter Memorial Hospital, please hold." *Click.*

Dennis stretched the phone cord around the corner to the living room window. He opened the blinds and looked across the street. "Hey, Flo. Look what's been going on right under our noses!"

The hospital was teeming with agents in FBI and ATF jackets. Dennis saw a number of police officers and sheriff's deputies around the premises and a police car cruising the street.

"I'm sorry to keep you waiting. Our phones have been unusually busy. How may I help you?"

"May I please speak with Martha Sullivan at extension 1020?"

"That line is busy. Could you hold, please?"

"Sure."

Dennis turned around and leaned against the wall, his eyes scanning the fine surroundings—leather couch...wingback chairs...Oriental rug...Chinese lamps...walnut tables...hardwood floors...high ceilings...crown moldings.

"This is Martha Sullivan." Her voice startled him.

"Uh, ma'am...Nurse Sullivan, this is Ben Stoller, the one helping with the Wilson twins?"

"How are things going, *Ben?*"

"No problems with the babies. But after you left this morning, someone from the clinic brought the newspaper to us, and we were shocked to read about the firebombing and shooting. Can you tell us if the twins' mother is safe?"

"I'm sorry; I assumed you heard Dr. Rice's statement to the media this morning. Jennifer Wilson was one of the three shooting victims. She's out of surgery and in serious but stable condition."

"Can she survive that?" Dennis said. "On top of having the virus?"

"She doesn't have the virus."

"But it was on the news—"

"Speculation. A severe ear infection was causing the fever."

"Then I haven't been exposed?"

"Is that why you came back?"

"Partly. It's complicated. How serious is Jennifer?"

"I don't have any other information. Dr. Rice will give periodic updates to the media."

"There's no TV in the apartment," Dennis said.

"I forgot about that. I'll relay to you whatever information is released. I need to get back to work now. I'll be in touch."

"Thank you, ma'am—er—Nurse Sullivan."

"Why don't you just call me Martha and save yourself all that undignified fumbling for words? And just for the record: The heat of crisis can reshape your perspective—not to mention your character. That's the only reason I'm going along with this, *Ben.*" *Click.*

∽○∾

Dr. Sarah Rice stood in the doorway to Jennifer Wilson's room thinking that this young woman looked like a sleeping princess in perfect pose, her golden brown curls draped over the sides of the pillow. Even her complexion had a rosy glow, probably from the fever. How unfair that she was about to awaken into a reality worse than a bad dream. Sarah sighed. How would Jennifer handle the news that awaited her, without her parents or a husband to comfort her?

Sarah sat in a chair in the corner of the room and rubbed her tired eyes. Nothing in her medical training had prepared her for medical personnel and patients being firebombed and gunned down like helpless animals in a cage.

Sarah felt the burden of helplessness tighten her throat. She glanced out into the hallway and listened to the silence, then turned her head toward the wall and released her anguish in quiet sobs.

Special Agent Jordan Ellis had been assigned to head up the FBI's investigation of the hospital attack. He set up temporary FBI headquarters on the second story of the county courthouse and called a one o'clock meeting with those who held concurrent jurisdiction: Police Chief Aaron Cameron, County Sheriff Hal Barker, and ATF Special Agent Matt Nash.

Jordan looked at his watch. "Okay, let's get started." He stood leaning on his desk, facing the others who were seated in folding chairs. "Both the FBI and the ATF have been aware of the Citizens' Watch Dogs for the past eighteen months. After last night's call to the newspaper, we put our voice recognition capabilities to work and let the computer match the words Citizens' Watch Dogs or CWD to words spoken over the airwaves. And bingo, we got a call made from a cell phone belonging to a Mr. Bo Ritter who lives in Hannon, ten miles south of Baxter. We have him in custody. Of course, he denies any involvement. Swears he never made the call."

"Ritter's on the ATF's hot list," Matt Nash said. "Took part in the Arming America rally in Ellison last fall."

Jordan nodded. "He's involved in this, too. You should've seen his body posture. My guys'll lean on him. This bubba isn't as tough as he thinks."

"What about the rest of the group?" Hal Barker asked.

Jordan's eyebrows gathered. "There are twelve other men known to be involved with this group. We checked out their homes and work places. Nobody's seen them. We know they hang out at Ernie's Tavern on old 41, so my agents went out there and questioned the owner, Ernie Tyson. He's playing dumb. But it shouldn't take us long to find them. This group isn't real sophisticated."

"They were deadly enough," Hal said. "If you knew this group was dangerous, why wasn't I informed? This is *my* turf. I have a responsibility to the people of this county!"

"Easy, Sheriff," Jordan said. "They've never been caught in anything illegal."

Hal shot him a look. "I'm sure that's comforting to the families of the dead and wounded."

Jordan raked his hands through his hair, then started to pace in front of his desk. "We'll find them. In the meantime, we've got a big job ahead of us—protecting the hospital and keeping the peace. We'll divide up the responsibility between the police department, the sheriff's department, the ATF, and the FBI. We'll cover the hospital 24–7 with law enforcement posted at every entrance and exit, including the emergency room and receiving dock. Patrol cars will cruise the streets around the hospital's perimeter."

"Will people be allowed to visit patients in *A Corridor?*" Aaron Cameron asked.

"Only during designated hours," Jordan said. "And *only* if they've called ahead and left their name to be verified by the patient. Upon arrival, visitors will be required to show a photo ID to an FBI agent who will match it to the names on the list."

"What about the media?" Aaron said.

Jordan shook his head. "The hospital is off-limits. Period. We don't need our focus interrupted by a media circus. Any more questions?... Okay. Here're our main objectives: One, protect the hospital from further attacks. Two, make sure no one gets in unless they're authorized. Three, keep the peace. And I'll pull together everything we know about the CWD so we'll all be on the same page."

In an abandoned shack deep in the woods near Hannon, Billy Joe Sawyer sat on the floor with eleven comrades, listening to the radio.

> The FBI is about to release the names of twelve members of the militia group calling themselves the Citizens' Watch Dogs, or CWD, who have claimed responsibility for last night's brutal firebombing and shooting at Baxter Memorial Hospital. One member of the group, Bo Ritter of Hannon, was arrested by FBI agents when he arrived at his home around midnight....

Sawyer grabbed an arm that reached up and turned off the radio. "Will you lighten up, Grady? We're famous."

"So what? We're gonna starve to death! Some trade-off."

"Forget your stomach," Sawyer said. "What we did was significant."

"*Too* significant, if you ask me. This ain't what I signed up for. We never talked about killin' nobody!"

"We were defendin' our rights, Grady." Sawyer glanced at the others to see their reaction.

"Yeah? Well, you can tell that to the feds! I knew they'd trace the call."

"Someone must've got the license plate number," Sawyer said.

"Hel-lo? It was *your* truck! The only way Bo could've been ID'd was by his cell phone."

Sawyer ground his teeth, his jaw clenched. "Bo told me they couldn't do that."

"Duh. I guess they *can*. So, what now? Bo's gonna talk. He's not goin' down by himself. He didn't wanna do this anyway."

"Shut up!" Sawyer yanked off one of Grady's boots and threw it at the wall. "It's Bo's fault he got caught. I told him not to go back for that stupid mutt."

"He's gonna sell us out," Grady said.

"Doesn't matter. Bo doesn't know about this place. And Ernie'll never betray us. He'll bring us somethin' to eat and drink until I come up with a plan *B*. It isn't over."

"Sawyer, you're crazy!" Grady shouted.

"Think so? Well, I'm not about to let the feds back me down."

Sawyer pulled up the bottom of his T-shirt and wiped the sweat from his face, then stood up, suddenly feeling taller than he was. He looked at the others, moving his eyes from face to face until he sensed he was in control.

"Listen, we've got respect now. They know we mean business. But we didn't *finish* our business. We only took out two of them. The virus is still a threat, which means we *failed*, Watch Dogs. You wanna be known as a buncha losers?"

"Don't listen to him!" Grady said. "This ain't our kind of fight. We didn't sign up for killin'."

Sawyer snickered. "Too late for that."

Grady rose to his feet. "I want out."

Sawyer pushed open the door and handed him his boot. "Go

on, Grady. Let 'em throw you in jail for bein' a hero. That's just what they want."

"How do you know what they want? You don't even know who *they* are!"

"I'll tell you what I do know," Sawyer said. "People are countin' on us. And somebody's gotta wipe out that virus before it kills us all."

Grady looked at the others. "Can't any of you see what's goin' on here?"

Sawyer moved his steely gaze from one pair of eyes to another. "Somebody else have a moral problem with savin' people from the virus?"

The ten said nothing.

Sawyer looked at Grady. "You in or out?"

The dissenter had sweat rolling into his eyes. "It ain't worth killin' for."

"Like I said, Grady—too late for that." Sawyer turned and faced the others. "Ernie can get us whatever we need. He knows a ton of people and has plenty of dirt on some. Maybe it's time he collected on a few favors. Each of you has to decide for himself. But I'm not quittin'. I'm gonna finish what we started if I have to do it by myself."

FOURTEEN

On Wednesday night, Dennis lay on the hide-a-bed in the study, his hands behind his head, his legs stretched out. He was learning to prepare formula, heat bottles, change diapers, burp the babies, and catch a few winks when he could. Not that either Flo or he got more than a few hours of sleep at a time, but it was working out well. They were a good team. Flo had been napping since the last feeding, but he couldn't sleep.

Dennis looked at his watch—seven-thirty in Denver. His grandfather would be furious with him for not calling. In the rush of the day, he had completely forgotten about it. But he wasn't ready to face the wrath of Patrick Bailey and decided he'd take the coward's way out and leave a message on the machine at the insurance agency.

He got up and pressed his ear against the door adjacent to the nursery and didn't hear Flo stirring.

He walked out to the wall phone in the kitchen, entered his calling card numbers, and then the phone number.

"Hello, this is Patrick Bailey Insurance Agency. Our office hours are 8:00 A.M. until 5:30 P.M...."

Dennis pushed 01.

"This is Patrick Bailey. I'm sorry I missed your call. Leave your name, number, date and time you called, and a brief message. I'll get back to you." Beep.

"Grandpa, it's Dennis. I'm sure you're mad at me for not showing up for work and not even calling. It's a long story, and I can't go into detail right now. I'm back in Baxter. Maybe you've seen on the news that there's a quarantine down here. Well, Jennifer is involved in that, and I decided the least I could do is help with the babies until its over… Oh yeah, I forgot to tell you: She had twins—boys. They're identical. Anyway, please don't fire me. I've got three weeks vacation coming, so I'm not asking for extra time off. There's no number where you can reach me. I'll call when I can."

Dennis hung up the phone, feeling a sense of dread. His grandfather had always required a lot from him and insisted that he was capable of living up to those expectations. Patrick Bailey was a hard father figure and a rigid boss. But under the gruff exterior, Dennis got glimpses of a milder side. For some reason, the old man rarely showed it.

A demanding cry resounded from the nursery. Dennis smiled. *Number Two.* He hurried to pick up the twin that always made his wishes known. If the kid was uncomfortable or hungry, he bellowed. If Flo or Dennis failed to meet his needs, he continued to bellow until he was satisfied.

"What's your problem, bud? You sound like my Grandfather Bailey barking out orders. You're not supposed to have a bottle for another twenty minutes."

Dennis picked up the boy and got a whiff of a diaper in serious need of changing.

"Well, thanks a lot for doing this on *my* shift," he said, wrinkling his nose. "I suppose you did this on purpose, thinking it would build character. Man, with all that hollering, you sound just *like* my Grandfather Bailey. Maybe that's what I should call you—Bailey—even though at the moment you're living up to the name

Number Two. Oh, geeze…" He held his nose, fumbling to reach the baby wipes.

"What's goin' on in here?" Flo said.

"Sorry, I didn't mean to wake you."

"Ben, it wasn't you that woke me up; it was this here ornery rascal," she said, handing Dennis another baby wipe. "Well, go on. You're doin' jus' fine."

Dennis finished the cleanup and was pleased when he got the disposable diaper fastened around the boy's tiny little bottom. "Flo, meet Bailey. I've nicknamed this kid after my Grandfather Bailey who can cause enough ruckus to wake the dead. Beats calling him Number Two. What do you think?"

Flo laughed. "It's right nice. What're we gonna do about that one?" she said, nodding at the sleeping boy.

Dennis mused. "How about calling him Bear? The kid likes to hibernate and likes to be cuddled. What do you think?"

"I think we got somethin' now!"

Dennis wrinkled his nose as he held the dirty diaper with his thumb and forefinger and dropped it into a disposal bag. He pumped a dab of waterless soap on his hands and rubbed them together. "Well, Flo, how'd I do?"

"You did real good, Ben." The baby started crying again. "Now see if you can warm that bottle by yourself and get Bailey here fed so his lungs'll take a rest and not wake up this sleepin' angel."

"Okay, Bailey my boy, let's let your brother sleep a little longer while we get you situated. Yes, I hear you," he said, walking quickly toward the kitchen. "The whole *neighborhood* hears you. Grandpa, I do believe you've met your match."

Jennifer heard a knock on the door, and a few seconds later Dr. Rice was standing at her bedside.

"Did you finally eat something?" Dr. Rice asked.

"I had some broth. And a little Jell-O. I wasn't very hungry."

"The anesthetic made you groggy. This is the most awake you've seemed since you got out of recovery."

"I can't believe that nurse died."

"Me either," Dr. Rice said. "I've known Helen a long time… Jennifer, I know your surgeon told you what he had to do. Would you like to talk about it? It's got to be difficult being isolated from even your parents."

Jennifer felt the tears sting her eyes and Dr. Rice take her hand.

"The good news is you're going to be fine. Not only are you not exhibiting signs of the virus, but you're going to make an almost complete recovery from the gunshot wound."

"Sure, *almost*," Jennifer said.

"The surgeon did everything he could to repair the wound, but there was nothing he could do to restore reproductive function."

"So I'll never have more children—all because some paranoid crazies decided to attack the hospital. It's not fair!"

Dr. Rice squeezed her hand. "No, it's not. But aren't you blessed to have two beautiful children waiting for your love? As soon as this quarantine is over, you'll be able to leave here and get on with your life."

"I don't even know what my life *is* anymore! It was hard enough deciding to be a single mother. Then I get surprised with *twins,* who I don't even get a chance to bond with before we're separated by this quarantine. Then I get sent back to the hospital thinking I'm going to die of some horrible virus, which turns out to be a false alarm. And before they even send me home, I get shot, blowing any chance I had of having children with the man of my dreams! Get on with my life? *What* life?" She plucked a Kleenex from the box. "Why is God letting these things happen? Why isn't He listening to my prayers? I feel so alone being separated from everyone I love—" Her voice cracked.

Jennifer felt Dr. Rice's arms around her and tried to imagine they were her mother's. She let the pain in her heart turn to tears and wept without shame.

Billy Joe Sawyer sat on the floor of the shack, holding a flashlight with one hand, drawing plans on a yellow pad with the other. The only sound he heard was that of the others snoring.

He took a gulp of warm beer, then pushed the empty pizza boxes out of his way and stretched out his legs. It hadn't been that hard to bring these guys around: a little beer, a little pizza, a few promises. What would he have done without Ernie?

Sawyer mentally went through each detail on his diagram. This could work. Once Ernie relocated them, things would start to roll.

The youngest member of the group got up and sat beside him. "You still workin' on the plan?"

"I've about got it, Nolan," Sawyer whispered. "But I can't go forward without a *secret* partner, someone willin' to be an example of absolute loyalty. It's critical to the success."

"What about me?"

"You? You're a baby." Sawyer smiled and gave him an elbow in the ribs.

"I'm serious," Nolan said. "So what if I'm the youngest? I've got more guts than any of *them.*"

"But are you willin' to do whatever I say—no matter what? This is the big league. I'm not sure you're ready."

"Yes, I am," Nolan whispered. "Come on, Sawyer. You can trust me. I'm your man."

Sawyer stood up to hide the smirk on his face. *One down.* He grabbed Nolan's hand and pulled him to his feet. "Let's go outside and talk about it."

FIFTEEN

O n Thursday morning, Ellen Jones sat at a picnic table, looking down on Heron Lake. Cottony clouds were suspended overhead and reflected on the glassy surface. A great blue heron stalked its prey along the shoreline while a young couple looked on, passing a pair of binoculars back and forth.

Half a dozen terns flew in a random pattern over the marina, and then circled back and dove headlong into the water, shattering the glassy calm in a splashing feeding frenzy.

Ellen closed her eyes and inhaled the unmistakable scent of pine. A light breeze brushed the sides of her face and gently rearranged her curls. For a split second she was a girl again, sitting on her grandparents' back porch, watching for lightning bugs.

Ellen heard a train whistle. Her eyes flew open and she glanced at her watch. She popped the last bite of a bagel into her mouth and drank the last of the orange juice. She stood and threw her trash in the container, then hurried to her car, slipped in behind the wheel, and activated her cell phone. She started the car and pulled onto the winding road.

"Guy Langford Jones law office, how may I help you?"

"Hi, Sharon. Is that handsome husband of mine in?"

"He's been looking for you. Hold for just a moment."

Ellen took one last breath of fresh air and then rolled up the window and turned on the air conditioner.

"Ellen, where are you?" Guy said. "I called your office to find out what time you wanted to meet at the civic center. Margie said you hadn't come in yet."

"I took the *long* way."

"A side trip to the lake?"

"Uh-huh. Amazing how relaxing it is."

"Honey, the memorial service starts in thirty minutes."

"I'm almost to the edge of town. The traffic is unbelievably light. Tourists must be keeping a healthy distance."

"Not the media," Guy said. "Excuse me for saying it, but their presence might actually make up for the lack of tourism. Merchants could use an economic boost about now."

"No comment."

"Ellen, what time shall I meet you?"

"Go ahead and leave now. It won't take me long."

Ellen turned off her cell phone and drove down the main highway, and minutes later turned onto First Street. Huge shade trees lined both sides of the street, forming a leafy canopy overhead. She smiled at children racing through a sprinkler hose and waved at an elderly man in a porch swing, who seemed amused at two Scottie dogs chasing a squirrel in his front yard. The appearance of normalcy ended when she saw the barricade up ahead.

She turned right and detoured through the neighborhood near the hospital. The houses here were mostly brick bungalows and two-story structures built in the 1930s. Some had been converted into businesses, but the charming neighborhood character had been preserved.

Ellen spotted the roof of the civic center on the next block. She felt sadness for the two families whose loved ones would be memorialized today, and wondered how many more would die before the virus and the violence had run their course.

Ellen thought about Jennifer Wilson and the two ER doctors who had been wounded and survived. In the confusion and the chaos following the attack, *had* the quarantine been compromised? She didn't know if health officials were being entirely truthful. But she was sure of one thing: Time couldn't lie.

In Dr. Sarah Rice's office, health officials were meeting after a conference call with the Centers for Disease Control.

"We may never get an antibody match," Dr. Montgomery said.

"So what do we do, Lionel?" Dr. Rice exhaled loudly. "The patients aren't improving. The skin eruptions are starting to ooze, which means the risk of contamination is higher than ever."

"We continue implementing proven procedures for VHF," Dr. Montgomery said. "And let's switch the patients to Ribavirin. Antiviral drugs are typically ineffective on VHFs, but this one had some impact on Lassa fever. It's a long shot, but it's the only one we've got."

Dr. McFarland nodded. "Agreed."

"Lionel, in your opinion, how long should it take to find the baseline case?" Dr. Rice asked.

"The CDC is working with the World Health Organization to retrace the patients' journey. They can fly to the Amazon basin, land as close as possible to the village, then finish the journey by river. A lot depends on whether or not the river is passable. But we have to be prepared to see new cases any time now. Tell me again the number of people quarantined in *B* Corridor—and our capacity."

"Capacity is fifty," Dr. Rice said. "We've now got eighteen people quarantined in *B* Corridor; most of whom are not patients. Blake and Melissa Thomas, Jennifer Wilson, and Dr. Helmsley and Dr.

Gingrich are the only ones being treated."

"If we have an outbreak," Dr. Montgomery said, "we'll proceed with our plan to use the gym at the high school, where barrier nursing techniques can be easily employed."

Dr. Rice nodded. "It's also air-conditioned, and the locker rooms have shower and toilet facilities."

"What's the status of available blood?" Dr. McFarland asked.

"Surrounding communities have joined us in a massive blood drive," she said. "Our supply is at an all-time high."

Dr. McFarland stroked his red mustache. "I'm concerned about this radical group. Can law enforcement protect the school?"

"The FBI says they can," Dr. Rice said. "I keep trying to reassure my staff. Most of them trust barrier nursing techniques and would willingly work the quarantine; but they're reluctant to leave themselves vulnerable to civil unrest. One can hardly blame them."

Dr. Rice was suddenly aware of an FBI agent on the sidewalk outside her window. "Oh…I almost forgot to tell you: KJNX is running a special program tonight. Our sheriff thinks it's going to be controversial."

"Well, isn't *that* special?" Dr. Montgomery said. "A newsy spin on viral hemorrhagic fever from the blood-sucking media."

"Is that official position of CDC?" Dr. Wong asked. "Or has honorable doctor picked up colloquial term?"

Everyone laughed. Sarah thought it felt good to release the tension but wondered if they'd still be laughing after the program aired.

On Thursday afternoon, Jordan Ellis called a meeting with Aaron Cameron, Hal Barker, and Matt Nash.

"I wanted to update you," Jordan said. "Ritter spilled everything. The information is consistent with what the FBI and ATF already knew."

"So what's the CWD's plan of attack?" Hal asked.

"To hear Ritter talk, there never was a *plan*," Jordan said. "He swears the CWD is a militia group formed out of the necessity to protect themselves from government intrusion."

Hal lifted his Stetson and wiped his forehead. "What government intrusion?"

"The one stuck in their imaginations," Jordan said. "These groups have a paranoid distrust of the federal government and an obsession with weapons and explosives. Ritter kept spouting off about citizens having the God-given right to use any means necessary to protect themselves from a tyrannical government."

"Did he say whose God-given right it is to murder innocent people?" Aaron said. "What triggers a reaction like that?"

"Thanks to Ritter, we may have found the spark that lit the wick: one Billy Joe Sawyer. Ritter says the guy went off at Ernie's Tavern the other night after the Thomas baby's death. Talked the group into taking action because they believed health officials were lying about the virus threat."

"Without even confronting health officials?" Hal asked.

"There's more here than meets the eye," Jordan said. "Groups like this are not usually violent. But sometimes a leader emerges and begins to dominate the others." Jordan got up and started pacing. "We dug into his background, even beyond what we already knew. Sawyer's an explosion waiting to happen.

"He's always been a troublemaker. It didn't help that his father abused him. But his behavioral problems escalated after his father went to prison. His offenses ranged from serious vandalizing to bullying classmates to torturing a teacher's dog. He was accused of setting fires, breaking and entering, holding a toddler's head under water, and attacking a cheerleader who wouldn't go out with him. But there wasn't enough evidence to charge him. The list goes on.

"His high school counselor recorded that he had no conscience. Never showed remorse. Had no respect for authority.

"We knew he had hooked up with a neo-Nazi group when he was a junior; rubbed elbows with the KKK for about a year after that; then linked up with an animal rights group for a while. Even joined a religious cult called Armageddon that believed its members were chosen to be the sole survivors of a nuclear holocaust. Sawyer has floated in and out of groups like these for years. But there doesn't seem to be any consistency in the causes they embrace."

"Then what was he looking for?" Hal said.

"People he can dominate and control." Jordan stopped and looked at Hal. "Looks like he finally hit pay dirt."

Hal shook his head from side to side. "Since the FBI kept an eye on him, how'd you miss *that?*"

"We knew what he was doing, not what he was thinking. Ritter filled in the blanks."

"But why now?" Matt asked. "Why'd he suddenly go off the deep end?"

"Probably stress," Jordan said. "His mother died of cancer a few months ago after doctors gave her a clean bill of health. Ritter says there's no love lost between Sawyer and the medical community. Frankly, I'm concerned about what he may be planning next. I want the National Guard in here."

"The National Guard?" Hal said, looking over at Aaron. "That seems a bit extreme."

"The situation *is* extreme." Jordan sat down, his eyes moving from Hal to Aaron to Matt. "We need a minimum of two guardsmen outside each quarantined home. Plus added protection for the hospital. And if we end up with an outbreak on our hands, we're going to need more than that. I'd rather be criticized for overreacting than face the consequences if we aren't prepared."

From a muddy riverbank deep in the Amazon rain forest, field officials from the Centers for Disease Control and the World Health

Organization watched a huge fire burning in the middle of a clearing. Native South Americans carried one lifeless body after another and threw it into the flames as if to appease some pagan god of the jungle. Afterward, they lay prostrate before the fire, strips of white cloth tied around their mouths. Some were mumbling. Others weeping. All seemed afraid.

The interpreter explained that nearly a hundred people from the village had died from "the red sickness" that eight days before had begun to sweep through the tribe at lightning speed.

Worried field officials stood silent in the face of this crude crematorium, knowing the deadly virus that had provided its fuel had also traveled north to the United States.

Sixteen

On Friday morning, just as Dennis was putting Bear down after the ten o'clock feeding, the phone rang. He closed the door to the nursery and hurried to the kitchen.

"Hello, this is Ben Stoller."

"Ben, this is Jed Wilson, Jennifer Wilson's father. I understand my grandsons are being cared for over there."

Dennis's pulse raced. "Uh, yes, sir. And they're doing just fine."

"Sorry we haven't checked in lately. I'm sure you're aware Jennifer was shot in the attack on the hospital. My wife and I have been so caught up with her situation that we haven't thought of much else."

"I can imagine. The whole community's been pulling for her. How is she?"

"She's got some challenges ahead, but they expect her to make a full recovery."

Challenges? "Will she get to go home now?" Dennis asked.

"No, everyone who was in *C* Corridor has been quarantined at the hospital—just to be on the safe side."

"How's she handling everything?"

"So-so. Her relationship with the Lord is strong. He'll get her through this."

"Uh—that's good… So, Mr. Wilson, is there something I can do for you?"

"Would you fill me in on how the twins are doing?"

"They're doing great. Flo and I have their routine down to a science."

"So, how many volunteers are there?" Jed asked.

"Just the two of us. But we're here around the clock. And our only job is taking care of the babies."

"What can you tell me about them, Ben? I was with them for all of an hour."

"What would you like to know?"

"Can you tell them apart?"

"Sure. It didn't take long."

"Really?"

"Yes, sir. One of them is a little tyrant and doesn't mind pushing the envelope till he gets what he wants. He barks out orders like my Grandfather Bailey. So, that's what we call him—Bailey. The other one's good-natured and sleeps most of the time and likes to be cuddled. So we call him Bear."

Dennis told Jed all about the twins and was surprised to realize the degree of his own enthusiasm.

"I can't wait to tell Jen about this," Jed said. "Knowing the babies are in such good hands will ease her mind."

"Has she picked out names yet?" Dennis asked.

"If she has, she hasn't told us. Then again, she's been pretty out of it. Well, thanks again, Ben, for all you and Flo are doing."

"You're welcome, sir. Call any time." Dennis hung up the phone thinking that Jed Wilson didn't sound like the indifferent, detached father Jennifer had always described.

‿𝄐‿

Jed leafed through a news magazine but couldn't concentrate on anything he read. He walked out to the kitchen, picked up the phone, and dialed Pastor Thomas's cell phone.

"Hello, this is Pastor Thomas."

"Bart. It's Jed. I can't get you off my mind, so I decided to call. Hope I'm not bothering you."

"Hardly. I'm confined in B Corridor with the risk of the virus staring me in the face, the threat of another attack looming on the horizon, and Blake and Melissa teetering on the edge. I'm glad to hear your voice."

"How are you holding up?"

"A better question is, *Who's* holding me up? I'd go crazy if I tried doing this without Him."

"Yeah, same here."

"Jed, each day that Blake and Melissa and Jennifer are alive, no matter how difficult, is a gift. All we can do is sit at our Father's feet and entrust the outcome to Him."

"You're an inspiration. I'm going to hate missing church. What will you do about your Sunday radio broadcast?"

"The Lord's impressed upon me to have Charlie Kirby do it. This seems like the right time for people to hear from the mayor, especially one who packs a powerful sermon. Charlie has a way of pulling people together."

"Yeah, he does."

"Jed, did you watch last night's special report on KJNX?"

"Unfortunately."

"Didn't it seem as though they deliberately planted doubt in people's minds about the effectiveness of the quarantine?"

"Yeah, but I blow off half of what they tell us until I read the newspaper. Ellen doesn't print anything unless she's sure."

"Well, the program was misleading. I saw firsthand how heroically the medical team in *C* Corridor responded—shielding us from bullets, putting out fires, not even thinking about their own safety. Two of them died as a result. But I don't see how anyone outside *C* Corridor could've been exposed in the attack."

"I think we're all a little paranoid," Jed said. "It's unnerving waiting for new cases to start showing up. And having the National Guard called in has people on the edge."

The pastor sighed. "The National Guard...in *Baxter.* Almost defies imagination. I have to believe the Lord will use this terrible ordeal for good somehow."

"So do I, Bart. You've ingrained that in me long enough. Rhonda and I want you to know we're praying for Blake and Melissa—and for you."

"And we're praying for Jennifer. I wish they'd let me see her, but they're keeping us away from everyone else."

"How are you and Penny feeling?" Jed said.

"Fine so far. We're looking to God. There's not a thing *they* can do to prevent us from getting it."

"We'll keep praying."

"Thanks, Jed. I love you, brother."

"I love you, too, Bart. Keep the faith."

Jed was talking to Rhonda about his call to Pastor Thomas when the phone rang.

"Hello."

"Dad, what's the latest on Jen?" Mark Wilson said.

"She's going to be all right, thank the Lord. She can't come home till after the quarantine, though."

"How's she feeling?"

"Fair. But she's got an emotional hurdle to get over. Because of the gunshot wound, she won't be able to have more children."

"So...?"

"Son, could you try showing a little sensitivity? This is a big deal, especially to a woman."

"Why would she want *more* kids? She got a double whammy the first time around."

Jed sighed. "Your sister will probably marry some day. When two people love each other, having a child together can be a very big deal. It's one part of Jennifer's dream she has to let go of. Your mom explained the whole thing to me—says it's a woman thing, and that you and I probably can't know exactly how Jen feels, but we need to support her."

"Sure, Dad. Whatever. Are you and Mom going nuts being cooped up?"

"Sometimes. But I keep thanking the Lord that neither Jennifer nor anyone else has come down with the virus."

"Guess you can't thank Him for protecting Jen from the bullets."

Jed paused and counted to ten. "Son, God didn't pull the trigger. *People* did. Your mother and I are thanking Him that Jen's going to be all right."

"Whatever. Hey, you'll never guess who I ran into at the airport in Atlanta: None other than Dennis 'pond scum' Lawton. Do you believe it? We were scheduled on the same flight to Denver. The creep overheard me talking to you on the pay phone and followed me into the food court. Wanted to know if the situation in Baxter had escalated and asked how Jen and 'the boys' were doing. I told him I had nothing to say to him. Can you believe his nerve after giving Jen the shaft?"

"Well, at least he asked," Jed said, remembering how indifferent he had once been to Jennifer and Mark.

"The jerk can ask all he wants. Little brother here isn't talking. Think I oughta call Jen and give her the lowdown?"

"Not now, Mark. She's fragile. How about if you call and let her know you care?"

"Of course, I care. Can't you tell?"

Jed let that one go by.

On Friday night, after Dennis finished giving Bailey his ten o'clock bottle, the boy was wide-eyed. Flo had already put Bear down and had gone to her room to catch a few hours of sleep.

Dennis took Bailey to the study and laid him on the hide-a-bed. Then he lay on his side next to the boy, his weight resting on one elbow, and studied the baby's features.

"You're kind of cute." He stroked the baby's soft blond hair and gazed into his dark eyes. They seemed so full of questions. He took his index finger and put it in Bailey's tiny palm. The boy's hand closed around it with surprising strength.

"Don't get attached," Dennis said softly. "You need more than a father—you need a dad. Dads are cool. I never had one, but you will. Your mother'll marry some nice guy, and you and Bear will have real names and a real life." Dennis wiggled his finger, but Bailey's tiny hand gripped it tighter. "Why are you so wide awake anyhow? It's my turn to get some shut-eye. Are you going to be a night owl?" Dennis smiled. "Like I have any say-so in the matter."

Dennis had noticed from the beginning that the twins had Jennifer's mouth. Bailey's lower lip quivered when he cried—just like hers. But their ears looked exactly like his. Dennis wondered how Flo could miss it.

"Don't worry, kid. I'll be around till your mother can take over." He slipped his finger out of Bailey's grasp, then picked up his son's foot and marveled at his tiny toes. "You and your brother caught me off guard. I don't have a clue how to be a dad."

"I declare, I couldn't figure out who you was talkin' to, Ben."

Dennis rolled on his back, his hand over his heart. "Good grief, Flo. You really should warn a fella when you're up. How long have you been standing there?"

"Long enough to be sure you're playin' with the whole deck. Mercy, I thought you was talkin' to yourself." She chuckled. "But I see you got some company."

"How come you're up already? I thought you'd sleep till the next feeding."

"Just restless for some reason. Go on. Talk about whatever it is menfolk talk about. I'm gonna git me a bowl o' that raisin bran." Flo turned and left the room.

Dennis rolled over on his side and looked at Bailey. "I know you won't remember this, but at least I showed up. That's more than I can say for my father."

SEVENTEEN

On Saturday morning, the babies were down for a nap. Dennis sat at the kitchen table, eating a bowl of Rice Krispies, waiting for Flo to get out of the shower so he could run an idea by her. He smelled the fresh scent of soap and looked up as Flo walked by him and opened the curtains.

"Don't wanna miss the sun filterin' through them trees," she said. "Best part of the mornin'."

"Flo, I've had a brainstorm. How about if I videotape the boys so the Wilson family can see what they look like?"

"That's a fine idea, Ben. Have you got one o' them cameras?"

"No, but I know where I might be able to borrow one. I'd have to leave for a while, though. That means you'd be alone with the twins."

"For land sakes. I been doin' this a long time. Bein' alone with them babies ain't gonna kill me."

"You mean it?"

"Take your time and git what you need. Me and them babies'll be just fine."

"Thanks, Flo, you're a jewel!" Dennis hugged her and hoped

she didn't mind. "I'll be back as soon as I can."

Dennis walked out the French doors into the foyer and exited through the outside door. Even the hot, humid air didn't bother him after being confined in a small apartment with air conditioning. He took a whiff of fresh air and then looked across the street.

He remembered seeing a video camera in the nursery at the hospital and wondered if Martha Sullivan would lend it to him. He crossed the shady street, and walked around the hospital to the main entrance. Everywhere he looked, he saw law enforcement personnel. When he reached the front door, an FBI agent stopped him.

"Excuse me, sir. Which patient are you here to see?"

"Uh—I'm here to see Martha Sullivan. She's an RN in obstetrics."

"Is she expecting you?"

"Uh, no—not really. I forgot to call ahead, but she'll vouch for me if you call her."

"I'll need your name and a photo ID, sir." The agent's eyes were probing.

Dennis didn't see how he could turn back without creating suspicion. "Here's my driver's license."

"Excuse me while I check with the information desk." The agent dialed his cell phone and gave someone Dennis's name and stated his reason for being there.

Dennis put his hands in his pockets and started to whistle. A couple of minutes passed.

"Yeah, that's right—Denver," the agent said. He studied Dennis and then looked at his driver's license. "Yeah, it all fits." The agent turned off his phone. "All right, Mr. Lawton. You're cleared to go to the nursery. Ms. Sullivan is waiting for you there."

"Thanks." Dennis put the license back in his wallet. He walked inside and then down the hallway marked *A Corridor*.

Martha Sullivan stood in front of the nursery, her arms folded, her weight resting on one hip. "Well, well, well...Dennis 'Ben

Stoller' Lawton. That was a bold move for a man bent on conceal-
ing his identity." She sounded more amused than annoyed. "Lucky
for you I never forget a name. I assume you have a reason for being
here?"

"Thanks for getting me off the hook." He looked through the
glass and spotted the video camera on the shelf above her computer. "I may be presumptuous, but I need to ask a favor."

"Oh?"

"I thought it'd be nice if I videotaped the twins and made a tape
for the Wilsons."

"I see. And how do I enter into this?"

"I noticed you had a video camera in the nursery. I was wondering if I could borrow it? I'd be careful. I'm familiar with how
they work. I have one at home."

"In Denver, as I recall."

"Yes, ma'am—uh, Martha."

"So how long would you need to keep this video camera,
assuming it was available and I agreed to let you borrow it?"

"Just for the morning. Long enough to film the boys and...what
am I thinking? I don't have any way to make copies." Dennis
sighed. "I really wanted to do this."

"And what prompted this spurt of generosity?"

"Jed Wilson called yesterday asking about the boys. He
sounded kind of left out—like the family's having a pretty tough
time being kept away from them. He's a nice guy. Seems like the
least I could do."

"Then the video camera and VCRs will be available to you
while I'm on my shift."

"You have VCRs, too?"

Her eyes twinkled. "I do. And blank tapes. I assume you'll need
those?"

"Oh, yes ma'am—Martha. I can film the boys, then come back
here and make copies. If that's okay with you."

"Very well, then. Get on with it. Once I'm gone, no one here will authorize your admittance. Plus, you don't want to leave Flo too long, do you?"

"No. No, I don't. Thanks. I mean, I really appreciate your letting me borrow the camera and VCRs and—"

"Honestly, Ben. You do ramble on. Wait here." She unlocked the nursery door, went inside and returned with the video camera. "We usually videotape the baby with the parents and give a tape to them as a gift. But with the quarantine and Jennifer's early release, we never filmed the Wilson twins. You would actually be doing the hospital a favor."

"Sounds like we're on the same track," he said.

"Oh, I'm one step ahead of you, but you're falling in line nicely." The corners of her mouth turned up slightly. "Just be sure to get back in time to make your tapes. I'll only be here until two o'clock."

Dr. Sarah Rice was in a meeting with Drs. Montgomery, McFarland, Wong, and Roesch when they were interrupted by an emergency call from the CDC. Sarah listened intently to Dr. Montgomery's side of the conversation and pieced the details together as best she could. When he hung up the phone, his face looked grave.

"They reached the village sometime on Thursday," Dr. Montgomery said.

"And they're just now getting back to us?"

"They had difficulty with the satellite phone. They had to make the river journey back before they could get word to us."

Dr. Roesch got up and leaned against the wall. "What was the death toll, Lionel?"

"Around a hundred, according to the interpreter."

"What about other villages along the river?"

"Fortunately, the virus appeared to be isolated. The natives don't have close contact with neighboring tribes."

"Have officials determined index case?" Dr. Wong asked.

"Yes, a village boy. That's all I know. They've already gone back to do further investigation."

"When was the initial outbreak?" Dr. McFarland asked.

"Wednesday of last week."

"And they've already lost a hundred people?" Dr. McFarland tugged at his mustache. "Not terribly encouraging."

Dr. Montgomery raked his hands through his hair. "With the quarantine in effect, we won't incur that kind of loss. It's unthinkable."

There was a long pause, and Dr. Rice let the reality sink in.

"Gentlemen," she said, "I know we agreed to be open with the media, but with the CWD still threatening and KJNX using poor judgment, this sensitive information will undoubtedly provoke another attack. I don't want that on my conscience."

"Neither do I," Dr. McFarland said.

Dr. Wong nodded in agreement.

"Do you realize what you're saying?" Dr. Roesch said. "This could cost us our jobs. Maybe our careers."

Dr. Montgomery's eyebrows gathered. "It would be a serious breach of procedure—but not ethics. We must do whatever it takes to preserve the integrity of the quarantine." He moved his eyes from doctor to doctor. "Lives are at stake."

Dr. Rice exhaled loudly. "Look, it's a judgment call. The worst we can be is wrong."

"No," Dr. Roesch said. "The worst we can be is *dead* wrong."

"Flo, what've you got there?" Dennis said, zooming in with the video camera for a close-up of her holding Bailey and Bear. Both boys were wide-eyed and content. He held the camera on them for a few seconds, then pushed the standby button. "Their mother will be jazzed about this, Flo. It's turning out great."

"Don't be gittin' me in this, Ben."

"Quiet, woman. I'm going to turn this back on, so behave your-self and talk nice to me. Here we go." He pushed the record but-ton. "Flo, let me get a close up of those handsome boys...that's it."

"These here boys is different as night 'n day," she said. "This left child, he'd sleep all day if we didn't wake him up. Loves to be held and is cuddly like a teddy bear, so we been callin' him Bear. And this right child, he ain't afraid to tell you what's on *his* mind." She chuckled. "Mercy, he can squawk when he wants somethin', and won't give up till he's got it neither. We call him Bailey after Ben's grandpa, who can raise a ruckus louder 'n anyone." Flo seemed relaxed and looked right at the camera. "Mighty precious babies."

Dennis put it on standby. "That was great, Flo. You're a regular movie queen. Let me get some footage of the apartment so the Wilsons can see where the babies are staying."

After another few minutes of taping, Bear had fallen asleep again, and Bailey let out a wail, letting them all know he needed a diaper change. Dennis was pleased that he was able to capture the boys' personalities and thought it a perfect time to end it.

"Well, that concludes the film debut of the Wilson twins. So from the Hunter Clinic, this is Ben Stoller saying, 'We hope you enjoyed the show.'"

Flo let out a laugh. "They're gonna git a hoot outta seein' them babies. Heavens to Betsy, them boys surely did act like theirselves."

"If I didn't know better, I'd swear *you* were their grandma, the way you were carrying on," Dennis said.

"Me? What about *you*—struttin' around here with your chest all puffed out? Mercy, Ben, them babies is growin' on us."

At twelve-forty-five, Dennis was back at the nursery, video camera in hand. He tapped on the glass. Nurse Sullivan looked up, then got up and opened the door.

"Come this way." She led him down a connecting hallway and

into a small room. Dennis's eyes were drawn to built-ins which housed a TV and two VCRs. A rolling chair was pushed up to the work space below.

"This is cool," Dennis said.

"You know how to work all this?" Nurse Sullivan asked.

He moved closer to examine the equipment. "Sure, no problem. I didn't know hospitals had all this stuff."

"So, tell me. Did you get good footage of the babies?"

"Oh yeah. Great. Bear even fell asleep, and Bailey hollered— true to form. The Wilsons ought to get a kick out of them."

"And what about you, Ben? Do *you* get a kick out of them?"

He hated that his ears were hot again. "Uh, sure. Yeah. They're something else."

"All right. Everything you need is here. Have at it. Here are the blank tapes. How many copies do you plan to make?"

"Two—uh, maybe three."

"Three?"

Come on, Martha. Cut me some slack. "I think we should have an extra just in case something happens to the others, or in case the Wilsons decide they want another one." Dennis fiddled with the buttons on the VCR. "I can never go back and capture this time again. Seems smart not to take a chance."

"Very smart, I'd say."

Dennis turned and looked at her. The corners of her mouth gave way to a smile.

Late Saturday afternoon, Dr. Rice was finishing up some paperwork when she heard a knock at the door. "Come in." She looked up into the face of Dr. Montgomery.

"It's happening, Sarah—two patients in B Corridor with fevers. One is already starting to hemorrhage. The skin eruptions are evident."

Her heart sank. "Who are they, Lionel?"

"Clay Lindsay, the EMT who transported the patients; and Melvin Helmsley, one of the doctors who treated them."

"Not Melvin! He's still recovering from gunshot wounds. Where are you putting them?"

"Spencer and I have them isolated with the Thomas couple. These cases shouldn't surprise us. These two were the most vulnerable, having had contact with the Thomases before adequately protecting themselves."

Just then Dr. McFarland walked in. "Have you heard?"

"Heard what?" they said in unison.

The phone rang.

"Excuse me a moment. Hello, this is Dr. Rice... *What?*... *When?*... Oh, no..." She sighed. "All right... I will. Thanks for calling. Good-bye."

"What was that all about?" Dr. Montgomery asked.

"That was the Chief of Staff at Ellison Medical Center. A patient with a high fever and vomiting was admitted to their emergency room ten minutes ago."

"That's what I came to tell you!" Dr. McFarland said. "But weren't there two?"

"Where did *you* hear it?" she asked.

"Breaking news on KJNX."

Dr. Montgomery threw his hands in the air. "This is irresponsible!"

The phone rang again and Dr. Rice grabbed it.

"*Yes?* Sorry, Ivan. Things are tense over here... Yes, I just heard... Where are you?... You'll keep us informed?... Thank you. Good-bye." She hung up the phone and turned to the others. "Ivan's in his car headed for Ellison Medical Center. They called him for consultation. It's a sad state of affairs when the media reports it before health officials have been informed!"

"I just found out two minutes ago," Dr. McFarland said. "A

news bulletin came on the TV in the lounge. I hurried right over to tell you, in case you hadn't heard."

"I definitely *hadn't!*" she said. "Though I'm sure the patients and probably everyone else in town could fill me in!"

Jennifer Wilson lay in bed, her eyes tracing the flowers on the wallpaper. Why'd they have to tell her about the new virus cases? What could she do except worry that she was next? Hadn't she been through enough?

The grim news had stolen the joy from her afternoon. Nurse Sullivan had sent over a videotape of her twins, and Jennifer had watched it over and over again, imagining herself holding the boys. It was wonderful being able to see them at the clinic in such capable, caring hands.

Jennifer sighed. Maybe if she watched the tape again, the happy feeling would come back. She picked up the remote and hit "play." But the heaviness didn't go away. The smile on Flo's face and the affection in her voice caused Jennifer to feel jealous. Why did this stranger get to hold her babies when she might never see them again?

Suddenly, she was so furious with Dennis for skipping out that she actually thought Ben Stoller's voice sounded like Dennis's.

She turned off the tape and tossed the remote into the chair. She closed her eyes and tried to sleep, but the dreadful images of Ebola patients she'd seen on the KJNX news special flashed through her mind. Jennifer opened her eyes, her heart pounding, and resumed tracing flowers on the wallpaper.

EIGHTEEN

On Sunday morning, Billy Joe Sawyer sat in the family room of the CWD's new headquarters, relishing an unexpected find, when Nolan entered the room.

"Did you take care of Mumford?" Sawyer said.

"Yeah, I tied him up in the toolshed like you told me. What's in the cigar boxes?"

Sawyer smiled. "Remember all those rumors about him bein' a miser? There's thousands of dollars here."

"Whoa! Guess we ain't goin' hungry."

"You won't have time to be hungry once we get rollin'."

"We usin' Mumford's van?"

"Yep. Get the others in here."

A couple minutes later, twelve Watch Dogs were seated in the family room.

Sawyer stood up. "Thanks to Ernie, I trust everybody's enjoyin' our *air-conditioned* headquarters, though I doubt Mr. Mumford shares our enthusiasm." Sawyer snickered. "Now, listen up. There's no turnin' back from what we've already done. We need to finish it."

"Whaddya mean by *finish* it?" Grady said.

"We have a mission to complete. Here's how we're gonna do it." Sawyer held up a diagram and went through every detail. Then he turned his eyes on Grady and held his gaze. "Anyone who isn't with me 100 percent—there's the front door. Each of you will follow my orders—no questions asked. That's the only way this is gonna work." Grady shifted his posture. No one else moved.

"Nolan will demonstrate what I mean." Sawyer snapped his fingers and gave a slight nod. Nolan jumped up and left the room. Moments later a shot rang out.

Grady winced and started cracking his knuckles. The others looked around as if to size up each other's reaction. Nolan returned and flopped on the couch, a smirk on his face.

Sawyer looked at the others. "Are we clear about following orders?"

Mark Steele stepped outside Monty's Diner. July's sun had already heated the sidewalk around the town square and had begun to scorch the edges of the grass around City Park. The hum of motorboats echoed from Heron Lake.

"Mark?" Rosie Harris said. "Is something wrong?"

He turned around and shrugged. "Business is way down. We're losing the lake trade, and the boss isn't happy."

"Nobody's happy," Rosie said. "We're all scared to death—if it's not the virus, it's the violence. If not the violence, the economy."

"Yeah, I suppose."

"Well, come back inside. At least we still have Mort to entertain us."

Mark forced a smile. "Is *that* what you call it?" He put a hand on Rosie's shoulder and followed her inside where the locals seated at the counter had spent too much time and too little money.

"Oh, come on," George Gentry said. "Mort's so paranoid, he thinks he's spyin' on himself."

"It's a wonder we're not *all* paranoid," Reggie said. "No offense, Mort."

"None taken." Mort Clary looked at George and snickered. "Gittin' to ya, eh, Georgie?"

"I've lived here seventy years," Hattie Gentry said. "I don't feel safe anymore."

"Welcome to the real world." Reggie took a sip of coffee. "We've avoided it longer than most."

"Well, who needs it?" Rosie said. "I'm scared. And I don't like it."

Liv Spooner nodded. "Every time I see the National Guard on the Wilsons' porch, my heart sinks. People shot. People dead. People getting sick. If the virus doesn't kill us, the Watch Dogs will. It's enough to make you stay home with the blinds pulled."

"Them germs could still find ya," Mort said.

"Will you stop with the doom and gloom?" Mark held up the newspaper and read the headlines, "'Rumor Mill At Epidemic Level. Quarantine Under Control.' These new cases were no surprise to health officials. And things are not out of control."

Reggie flicked the newspaper with his finger. "Yeah, right. Then explain those cases in Ellison. Mort may be smarter than we think."

Mark rolled his eyes. "I don't think so."

"May I interject something here?" Jim Hawkins said. "All we've heard are unconfirmed reports. The tests haven't come back yet."

"Jim, you're the ultimate optimist," Reggie said.

"Maybe. But why borrow trouble? We've got enough to be concerned about already."

The door to Monty's burst open, and Mark turned and saw a merchant from next door rushing toward the counter. "Have you heard the latest? Blake and Melissa Thomas are dead!"

Dennis and Flo had been busy with two fussy babies earlier in the morning, but both boys were finally asleep. Dennis sat at the kitchen table reading the Sunday paper. He noticed Flo fiddling with the radio.

"Ben, I hope you don't mind if I turn on some Sunday preachin'. My week's always headin' a better direction when I pay heed to the Lord's Word."

"No. Go ahead, Flo. I'm just reading the paper."

"Are you a believin' man, Ben?"

"I guess not. I never really understood what it is I'm supposed to be believing in."

"Didn't your folks ever take you to church?" she asked.

"No. My mother raised me by herself and didn't have any use for religion. The only time my Grandfather Bailey talked about God was in vain, if you know what I mean."

"Well, you ain't no kid, Ben. Ain't you never been curious about God yourself?"

He looked up from the newspaper and caught her eye. "Not really. I've always thought people were basically hypocrites and that Christians were the worst because they act like they're better than everybody else."

"Is that how I'm actin', Ben? 'Cause I never feel thatta way."

"*You're* a Christian, Flo?"

She nodded. "Been saved since I was fifteen."

"That's what I don't get," Dennis said. "Saved from *what?*"

"From m'self first off. I got a new heart and it made me a tad more civil." She chuckled. "But it's a whole lot more excitin' than that—"

"Your program's starting," Dennis said.

She turned up the volume and sat at the table across from him.

"This is Mayor Charlie Kirby. I've been a part of the church family at Cornerstone for twelve years. This has been a difficult week for us. About half our membership is quarantined. One of our young women was shot in the hospital attack. And our pastor and his wife have suffered the pain of losing their first grandchild and watching their son and daughter-in-law in the throes of this terrible virus.

"I've had several conversations with Pastor Thomas about how helpless he feels in this situation. And I've been blessed by his willingness to accept the outcome from the hands of his heavenly Father, who has always been, is now, and forever will be sovereign over every detail of his life.

"Open your Bibles with me to 1 John, chapter three, verse one… 'How great is the love the Father has lavished on us, that we should be called children of God! And that is what we are!' Believers, what a picture of love that never fails, love that holds us together, no matter what disappointments or trials we face. When we consider the uncertainty of our world today, it's comforting to know God our Father will never change. He will never leave us. He is completely accessible to us through our Lord Jesus Christ. He knows every detail of our character and loves us more than we could ever imagine, in spite of our failings. He's there to love, protect, guide, and discipline."

Dennis looked over the top of the newspaper at Flo, who was listening with her eyes closed. Did she actually believe this stuff?

"Some of you may be asking, 'If our Father loves us so much, why doesn't He fix all our problems?' Perhaps He's concerned more with building our character than merely adjusting our comfort. If we want to be more like Him, should we not expect trials to come our way as part of the refining process? But He doesn't want us to worry about circumstances, but rather trust Him to use everything for good.

"Turn with me to Romans 8:28…'And we know that in all things God works for the good of those who love him, who have been called according to his purpose.'

"Believers, that's a hefty promise: *in all things*. That includes our current circumstances. And though we don't understand His purpose, we can trust Him with childlike faith. Our kids, seven of my own, are looking to us right now as we deal with this virus. The children aren't trying to cure it. They're not losing sleep over it. They're not trying to take it into their own hands. They trust us to take care of them.

"Wouldn't we do well to trust our Father in heaven the same way our children trust us?"

Dennis suddenly wished there was a Starbucks in town so he could take his newspaper somewhere else. He got up and went to the sink and poured a glass of water.

He wasn't sure he believed in God the Father. Or wanted to. He'd spent most of his childhood pretending that someday his dad would come get him. *That was a joke.* Why should he trust some obscure, mythical Father when he couldn't get to first base with the one he had here?

NINETEEN

Ellen Jones sat at her desk with the radio on and her Bible open, listening to the end of Charlie Kirby's sermon.

"Matthew 6:27 asks a rather poignant question: 'Who of you by worrying can add a single hour to his life?'

"Friends, worry isn't the answer. It's the problem. Worry fosters fear, which fosters doubt, which fosters trouble.

"I've thought about this all week. Perhaps what our Father would have us learn is that worry is not for Him to take away, but for us to give up. By surrendering it to Him, we make room in our hearts for His perfect peace. And that peace, no matter what our circumstances, is what keeps the vital signs of our faith healthy and strong."

Ellen admired Charlie. She admired Pastor Thomas, Jed and Rhonda, and many others from her church. She envied their faith and commitment. Why did she find it so difficult to stand up to Guy and admit she wanted God in her life? She should've been in church this morning instead of hiding out in her office to hear Charlie's sermon. But the last thing she wanted was more conflict. She looked at her watch. What was keeping Dr. Rice? Ellen's phone rang and she quickly picked it up.

"This is Ellen."

"It's Sarah Rice returning your call—and it's absolutely false!"

"I had a feeling," Ellen said. "So what's their status?"

"If anything, Blake and Melissa have made a slight improvement. These rumors are creating panic."

"I know. That's why I came straight to you for the facts. What about the case in Ellison? Do you know anything more?"

"Yes, it's been confirmed as bacterial meningitis. KJNX was irresponsible to have reported it without confirmation."

"At least they're consistent," Ellen said. "What about the doctor and the EMT who now have the virus? What's their condition?"

"Serious. But due to the high level of exposure, these cases were no surprise to us. I can't stress strongly enough the effectiveness of the quarantine. This virus is classified as Biosafety Level 4. No one sets foot in the isolation area without practicing strict barrier nursing techniques. No one outside of *B* Corridor has shown symptoms of the virus. That's very significant. Why won't KJNX report *that?*"

"Suffice it to say they have selective hearing and little conscience. They manufacture a good story and ask forgiveness later. That's their style, but it's not mine."

"I know that," Sarah said. "I appreciate this morning's headlines. Things are tense here at the hospital, but my staff's been able to convince patients there's no need to overreact. What are *you* hearing?"

Ellen leaned back in her chair and looked out the window. "Oh, I don't think you really want to know. When things get tense, people get weird. There's a lot of fear. There's even been a run on groceries. Maybe people are worried that the quarantine will be expanded to include the entire community. I don't know."

"Well," Sarah said, *"on* the record, things are under control at Baxter Memorial Hospital. And please, by all means, quote me on that."

"What's the latest on Jennifer Wilson's condition?"

"I understand she's depressed but otherwise recovering well."

"Her parents are friends of mine," Ellen said. "They told me she wouldn't be able to have more children as a result of the gunshot wound."

"I can't comment on that."

"I know. Sarah, thanks for talking to me, but my cell phone's ringing. If you'll excuse me, I need to take this call."

"Certainly. Thanks for your sensitivity. Good-bye."

Ellen picked up her cell phone. "Guy?"

"No, it's Aaron. Can you believe I'm cruising around town in my squad car, trying to keep the peace? Where are you?"

"In my office. I called in some of my staff to field calls from people demanding to know the truth about what's happening. Seems KJNX has stirred up quite a hornet's nest. How are you holding up, Chief?"

"I'm bushed. There've been disturbances all night long and we're still getting calls. People are tense, Ellen. They don't know what to believe."

"That's why I went straight to Dr. Rice. She confirmed that the case in Ellison turned out to be bacterial meningitis."

"I thought there were two cases."

"KJNX reported it wrong," Ellen said. "Also, their earlier rumors of Blake and Melissa Thomas's deaths are false."

"*What?* This is getting ridiculous!"

"It's not my newspaper putting out that garbage!"

"Yeah, I know. I didn't mean to bite your head off. But uncertainty is dangerous ground for a police chief."

"Not too swift for a newspaper editor either."

"Oh…I've got another call coming in, Ellen."

"All right. Talk to you later."

Click. "This is Aaron Cameron."

"Aaron, it's Jordan. Are your officers in place right now?"

"Yep. Everyone's tight."

"Good. Where are you?"

"Cruising the square. I just talked with Ellen Jones, and she confirmed with Dr. Rice that the case in Ellison turned out to be meningitis. Plus, the Thomas couple isn't dead. Did you know that?"

"I stopped listening to that stuff. Hey, I've got another call. Keep your antenna up, Chief."

"I will."

Click. "This is Jordan Ellis."

"Sir, it's Agent Barnett."

"Yeah, Jeff. Speak to me."

"We just broke up a fight in front of the courthouse. Two couples got into some sort of altercation—differing opinions on whether the Citizens' Watch Dogs are the good guys or the bad guys. One guy took a swing at the other, and then a few more guys joined the scuffle. Local cops made two arrests and are writing up the report right now. Small potatoes, but thought you should know."

"Yeah, thanks, Jeff. It's nice that my agents are wiping local noses. Could be the only thing running smoothly."

"What do you mean, sir?"

"Can't put my finger on it since I don't know the Ws."

"The what?"

"The Ws. You know—who, what, where, when, and why? But I'm about to jump out of my skin."

"So, you think something's going down?"

"Just stay on top of your game, Barnett. I've got another call."

"I'm gone."

Click. "This is Jordan."

"It's Hal. I just got a call from one of my deputies. Several carloads of protesters just arrived on the town square—unhappy campers who think health officials are holding out. They're carrying placards, and the media is all over them."

"How many protesters?"

"Maybe thirty," Hal said. "Doesn't surprise me. People get edgy when they hear a different story every time they tune in. By the way, you heard that Blake and Melissa Thomas aren't dead, didn't you?"

"Yeah. And Aaron heard from Ellen that the case in Ellison was confirmed as meningitis."

"What?" Hal sighed. "I rest my case."

"Frankly, I'm more worried about our pack of Watch Dogs feeding off all the media hype."

"Yeah, me too. Listen, I've got a call coming in. I'll check back later."

"Yeah. Okay, Sheriff."

Click. "This is Hal."

"Hal, it's Aaron! Can you hear me?"

"Yeah. Why is your siren on?"

"Something's going down in the neighborhood behind Saint Anthony's! I'm almost there!"

"I just hung up with Jordan. He didn't know anything about it."

"Man, black smoke's everywhere…it's hard to see…I hear gun-fire…Hal, I gotta go…"

"Aaron? Aaron! Are you there?…"

Sheriff Barker tossed his cell phone on the passenger seat. He looked in the rearview mirror and then hit the brakes, letting the rear end of his squad car swing around in the opposite direction. He turned on his siren, pushed his foot to the floor, and raced toward Saint Anthony's Catholic Church.

Ellen walked out of her office building into the sultry midday heat. She was walking toward the parking lot when she heard what sounded like the staccato of automatic weapons. She froze, her heart pounding, trying to figure out which direction the shots were coming from.

A young man ran past her down the sidewalk. "There's something going on at Saint Anthony's. Something big!"

Ellen hurried to her car and pulled onto Baxter Avenue. She saw streams of thick, black smoke and drove toward it.

When she got to Saint Anthony's, she was relieved the smoke wasn't coming from the historic old church. She saw people on the street running in all directions and Father Donaghan standing outside the rectory. She pulled over and rolled down her window.

"Father Donaghan, what happened?"

He hurried over to her car. "At first I thought it was fireworks. But people say there's been another shooting and firebombing."

Gunfire rang out and people started screaming. Ellen looked beyond the huge oak trees in the churchyard. Parked outside the wrought iron fence, which bordered the grounds of Saint Anthony's, was a white service van. A group of young men, dressed in black cargo shorts and black T-shirts, red kerchiefs tied around their heads, were firing automatic weapons into the air as they ran toward the vehicle. Ellen stopped counting at eleven when the van sped away, the last passenger's feet still dangling from the side door.

"Come inside the church where you'll be safe!" Father Donaghan opened the car door, took her hand, and pulled her to her feet.

Ellen started running, swept into the tide of terrified neighbors streaming into the church.

Jordan Ellis raced toward the scene, one hand firmly planted on the steering wheel and one ear firmly planted in his cell phone.

"Barnett, tell me what's going on!"

"A real mess, sir. *Seven* houses burning, soldiers down, people running in all directions."

"Did anyone see who did it?"

"It's pandemonium, sir. But from what we've been able to determine so far, somewhere between eight and twelve men with automatic weapons opened fire and threw firebombs at homes in the neighborhood behind Saint Anthony's. We don't know the details of how it went down, but the men reportedly left in a white van that was parked near the church. We've got the license number. Our agents are on it."

"Good work, Barnett. Where are you?"

"Standing outside a burning home on the 200 block of Elm Street. Firefighters have rescued the family, but the house is completely engulfed. There's not enough manpower to fight this many fires simultaneously. Volunteer units from surrounding areas are on the way."

"Barnett, the family that was rescued, were they being quarantined?"

"That's my guess. We've got seven fires. And seven homes in this neighborhood were designated as District 4 of the home quarantine."

Jordan dialed his cell phone and waited for four rings. *Come on, pick up!*

"Hello, this is Dr. Rice."

"It's Special Agent Ellis. Have you heard about the attack?"

"I hear sirens. What happened?"

"All seven residences in District 4 have been firebombed, and the families driven from their homes. I assume that means the quarantine has been compromised."

"Tell me exactly what you know!" she said.

"Firefighters have rescued at least one family from a burning home. I have no word on the others yet. Special Agent Barnett is gathering all survivors who were quarantined, plus everyone who came in contact with them or entered the burning homes. Firefighters, law enforcement, neighbors—everyone. We need you to get over there and tell us what to do."

"Where should I go?" Her voice was shaking.

"Start with the 200 block of Elm Street. Special Agent Jeff Barnett will find *you*. Have some official ID on you. The area is being secured."

The white van swerved sideways in the middle of Hawthorne Avenue and came to a stop. The doors flung wide open and men jumped out, scattering in all directions.

Squad cars barricaded all surrounding streets. In a matter of minutes, the members of Citizens' Watch Dogs were apprehended and searched, then made to lie down, hands cuffed behind them, in the grassy easement along Hawthorne.

Jordan parked his car and ran up to Agent McCullum. "Fill me in."

"Sir, we've apprehended eleven male Caucasians and a white van loaded with automatic weapons and firebombs. Eyewitnesses say that a band of men with red kerchiefs tied around their heads and dressed in black shorts and T-shirts, spread out over several blocks behind the Catholic church, then opened fire with automatic weapons, and firebombed homes that had a quarantine notice on the front door. They fled in a white van with a license number matching the vehicle here. The van belongs to a Percy Mumford in rural Norris County. Agents are checking out the residence."

"Which one of these clowns is Sawyer?"

"The suspects aren't talking, sir."

"Find out," Jordan said. "And don't make me wait long."

Ellen sat in the fourth pew at Saint Anthony's, her hands shaking, her pulse racing. Why hadn't she thought to bring her cell phone when she fled the car? She looked around the church and guessed there to be about forty people there, all sitting near the front.

"Thank God none of you dear people were injured," Father Donaghan said.

A young father spoke up, his voice emotional. "Two of the men pointed their guns at me and my son. Thank God they didn't shoot us."

The man's wife nodded. "One of them had the letters CWD written in black down his legs."

Their little boy about four years old was whining. "The man...the bad man...the bad man..."

"It's all right, Dylan; they're gone now." His mother held him and rocked, but the child kept on.

"The bad man...the bad man...the bad man..."

"They can't hurt you now, son." The father took the boy into his arms.

"I can identify two of the men," an elderly man said. "They shot a soldier from the National Guard in cold blood, then stood in front of my neighbor's house and chanted, 'The virus can fry. We're not gonna die,' and threw firebombs at the house."

"The bad man...the bad man..." The child reached for his mother, clutching at her blouse. "The bad man...the bad man..."

All at once, a man jumped out from behind the altar and pointed a pistol at Father Donaghan's head. "Somebody shut that kid up!"

"*The bad man!*" The little boy buried his head in his father's chest and started to cry.

"Shut him up!"

The father held his son tightly to his chest and whispered something in his ear, but the little boy whimpered. The man with the gun held the barrel to the father's head. "I said, shut him up!"

Ellen felt her temples throb, her neck tighten. The father whispered something to the boy and rocked him back and forth until he finally quieted down.

The man was dressed like the others who had fled in the van. He had a wild look in his eyes. "You wanna turn me in?" He pushed the gun barrel against the back of Father Donaghan's head. "Those people at the hospital are lyin' to you! That's what this shootin' and bombin's about. It's self-defense—pure and simple. If we don't wipe out the virus, it's gonna kill all of us. Don't you get it?"

Ellen felt herself trembling. She had never seen this young man before, and hoped he didn't recognize her as the newspaper's editor.

"Sit down." He shoved Father Donaghan toward the front row. "I didn't come in here to kill anybody, but if that's what it takes to get outta here, that's what I'll do. Sit there and keep your mouths shut. I need to think and cool off."

"Would you like some water?" Father Donaghan said.

"Now, Father, why would you be kind to a man holdin' a gun on these nice people? You aren't tryin' to divert my attention, are you?" He waved the gun in the priest's face.

"I just thought you might need some water. There's a water fountain in the hallway, just outside that door."

"Yeah, right. You must think I'm a real dupe." He pointed the gun at a girl about seven. "You. Get up here. You're goin' with me. You, too." He grabbed the arm of a boy about the same age.

Ellen held her breath as the parents wisely stifled their protest. One mother whimpered.

The man ordered the children to hold hands. He grabbed the little girl by the arm and slowly backed up, keeping the gun on the children and his eyes on the people in the pews.

"I got nothin' to lose here. Don't make me use it."

TWENTY

J ed and Rhonda Wilson sat in the living room, watching live reports on KJNX.

"As of now, five members of the National Guard have been transported here with gunshot wounds. It is unknown whether or not there were fatalities. This is Heather Montoya reporting live outside the Ellison Medical Center. Monica..."

"Getting back to a story that broke just minutes ago, sources told KJNX that a third *new* case of the virus has been reported in the quarantined *B* Corridor at Baxter Memorial.

"Dr. Allen Gingrich, the second emergency room physician who treated Blake and Melissa Thomas, began exhibiting symptoms of the virus early this afternoon and is being isolated with the other patients confirmed to have the virus. The hospital's Chief of Staff, Dr. Sarah Rice, maintains that these new cases are not surprising to health officials since these individuals had close contact with the infected couple prior to barrier nursing being initiated. However, sources told KJNX that more cases of the virus likely would be reported within the hour.

"Let's go to Marcus Payne, who is on the scene in the 200 block of Elm Street in Baxter, where just hours ago the militant group calling themselves the Citizens' Watch Dogs, or CWD, made a swift and brutal attack in a residential neighborhood designated as District 4 of the home quarantines. Marcus, what's going on there?"

"Monica, things are tense here after at least eleven members of the CWD launched a surprise attack in this residential neighborhood. Witnesses say the men, dressed in black jumpsuits and red berets and armed with automatic weapons, seemed to appear out of nowhere and began to open fire on the residences displaying quarantine notices, wounding five soldiers from the National Guard.

"Witnesses at the scene said the men chanted, 'The virus can fry, we're not gonna die,' as they threw firebombs at the homes and then fled on foot. Sources told KJNX that members of the quarantined households were forced out of their homes. And at least one family had to be brought to safety by fire rescuers. No injuries were reported.

"Dr. Sarah Rice was on the scene in the aftermath and had this to say: 'Let me stress that the bunker gear and oxygen masks worn by firefighters would have been as effective as the protective clothing required in barrier nursing. In addition, not one of the individuals involved in home quarantines is showing symptoms of the virus. It is doubtful that any exposure resulted from this attack. The families who lost their homes in the fire are being quarantined in the gym at Baxter High School. There is no reason for the community to fear an outbreak.'

"Monica, as you know, that statement by Dr. Rice was made before KJNX learned that another case of the virus has been reported at Baxter Memorial. Sources now tell us there may be numerous cases reported within the hour.

"I've talked with residents in this neighborhood, and they're worried about the risk of the virus spreading now that the quarantine has been compromised. And there's still another question looming: If the National Guard can't protect them, who can? Back to you."

Jed put the TV on mute. "I can't listen to any more of this." He noticed the tears trickling down Rhonda's face.

"Why is this happening?" she said. "Why does the Lord seem deaf to our cries for help? I can't take much more."

Jed put his arm around Rhonda and sighed. "I don't know, babe. But Charlie's sermon made sense. Right now, we're like children. We have no control over our circumstances. But just because there's nothing we can do doesn't mean God's abandoned us."

"But I'm still scared."

"Me, too. I hate not having control. But it's not like He hasn't answered any of our prayers. We're still in one piece. Jen's going to be fine. The babies are doing great. And you have to admit, Ben and Flo were custom-made for the job."

"I know." Rhonda dabbed at her tears and took a deep breath. "Why can't I just remember what the Lord has done, instead of what He hasn't done?"

"He's been good to us during the eight months we've known Him."

She nodded. "I was thinking about that this afternoon—right before I started worrying again."

"Well, if worrying won't change things and there's nothing we can do, then let's agree to be strong together and ride this thing out as King's kids. Isn't that what we signed on for? Besides, I hear the *family* benefits are really *out of this world*. And that any day now, we could get *caught up* in a vacation package with unlimited days in *paradise*."

Rhonda started to smile. "So, you think paradise is going to be a better deal, huh?"

"Pure *rapture*," he said, nuzzling her neck.

Rhonda laughed and pushed him away.

Jed was glad to see her smile. He got up and put the tape Ben Stoller made them in the VCR. "Let's watch the babies again. In a few days they'll be home, and all this will be history."

∾∾∾

Ellen glanced at her watch. The man with the gun had been in the church over three hours. He seemed more threatening each time he returned from the water fountain with the children.

The minutes ticked by slowly. He paced at the communion rail, talking to himself, sweat streaking his face and soaking through his shirt. The tension was almost tangible.

Three squirming toddlers were becoming a handful for their parents, and Ellen knew they couldn't be restrained much longer.

Suddenly, the man stopped, his eyes fixed on something in the back of the church. Ellen turned to see what had stolen his attention, but she didn't see anything.

"Don't even think about it!" he shouted. "Just turn around and leave the church and nobody'll get hurt."

Ellen turned again toward the back of the church. What was he looking at?

"Leave or I'll shoot. I mean it. I'll kill them all!" His eyes were crazed, his gun pointed at some children in the front pews. "Don't come any closer! Stop right there! Stop!" He raised his gun and began firing toward the back.

The sound was deafening. Ellen dropped down between the pews, her heart racing, and covered her head. People were screaming. Seconds later, the side door opened. She peeked around the end of the pew in time to see it close. Did he leave?

Time seemed to stand still. One by one, people stood and turned toward the back of the church.

"Who was he shooting at?" said the man holding the little boy.

"No one could've come through that main door," Father Donaghan said. "It's locked."

"Well, no one came in the side door," the man's wife said. "We would've seen them."

"Someone was back there," Ellen said. "You saw his face. He wasn't shooting at nothing."

Ellen walked through the archway in the back of the church and looked around the vestibule. She tried the door. It was locked.

Dennis heard the doorbell ring. He opened the French doors and looked through the beveled glass on the front door and saw Martha Sullivan standing outside. He walked to the door and opened it.

"May I come in out of the heat?" she said.

"Oh, sure. Sorry." Dennis stepped aside and let her in. "Let's go sit down."

"No, this is fine. I promised to keep you updated on news developments." She looked solemn. "Something awful's happened."

She told Dennis about the attack on the residential neighborhood and about the incident at the church. "The FBI has put the city on a high state of alert. The man is still out there, armed and dangerous."

"I never expected trouble like this here."

"None of us did, Ben. It's almost beyond comprehension. But that's not all…there've been three new virus cases in B Corridor—all of them medical personnel who treated the Thomas couple. Those cases were somewhat anticipated, but people are in an uproar."

"So the twins' mother is still all right?"

"Yes, as far as I know."

"Were you able to get the videos to her and her family?" Dennis asked.

Martha nodded. "I had one delivered to the Wilsons' home and gave the other to a friend of mine who's working B Corridor… I hope you don't mind, but I played it once through, just to be sure it recorded properly."

"Turned out good, didn't it?"

"You did a first-class job, Ben. I'm sure they appreciated it. It can't be easy for them being away from those babies—especially with these new developments."

The sound of Bailey's demanding cry filled the foyer. Dennis glanced at his watch. "Well, his little highness is right on time."

"In more ways than one," she said.

"What's that supposed to mean?"

Martha opened the front door and then turned around, her eyes planted right on his conscience. "You'll figure it out."

Guy Jones opened the kitchen door for Ellen. She went inside, hung her keys on the hook, then took a bottle of water from the refrigerator and sat at the table. She heard the cuckoo clock strike seven. Guy sat down and took her hands in his.

"Do you want to talk to me about it?" he said.

"Guy, you heard everything I had to say to the FBI. What happened today is as close to death as I care to get, all right? What else do you want me to say?"

"That you're not fostering this angel theory Father Donaghan and the others are throwing around."

"I never said I was."

"You never said you weren't… Look, Ellen, the FBI will figure out what happened."

"Good," she said. "Then they can explain it to me."

TWENTY-ONE

On Monday morning, a line had formed outside Monty's Diner by the time Mark Steele turned on the Open sign and unlocked the door.

"The newspaper's not here yet," Mark said. "But the coffee's ready."

"I need my caffeine." Mort headed straight for the counter.

"Rosie, the coffee's on me," George Gentry said. "Maybe Mort'll be civil. Things are too serious for his kiddin' around."

Rosie Harris stood at the counter, her fingers holding six mugs. "What's the latest? Do we know whether anyone was killed in the attack?"

Reggie Mason shrugged. "All I heard was five guardsmen were wounded. But KJNX keeps implyin' there're more virus cases at the hospital than they're tellin' us."

"Well, it's on the cable channels now," Mark said. "We don't have to rely on them."

"Why don't we wait for the newspaper," Jim Hawkins said. "Isn't anyone else tired of speculation?"

"I sure am," Liv Spooner said. "But I've got to tell you, I'm plenty scared. There are a couple of quarantined homes in my neighborhood. We could be next."

"Nah, they got most of those guys yesterday." Reggie blew on his coffee.

"Most ain't all," Mort said.

Hattie Gentry pointed her finger at him. "Be good, mister. George is buying your coffee."

"There's only one Watch Dog still out there," Mark said. "With the rest of the pack locked up, he's probably running scared."

FBI Special Agent Jordan Ellis called another meeting of law enforcement officials.

"Quite a showdown yesterday afternoon," Jordan said. "I commend you for working as a team. We got eleven more of these losers before they killed anyone else.

"One of the suspects, Grady somebody, fingered the kid who shot Mumford and admitted the group seized the house and turned it into CWD headquarters. According to him, Ernie Tyson, our buddy the tavern owner, arranged it—gee, what a surprise. This Grady also said the same thing Ritter said: Billy Joe Sawyer is the idea man."

"Any clue where he is?" Police Chief Aaron Cameron asked.

Jordan shook his head. "Not yet. But we'll look under every rock until we find him. There are sixty-three other quarantined households out there. And I don't want a repeat of what happened at Saint Anthony's."

"That was close," Aaron said. "Ellen Jones said there's no explanation for why the guy ran. Some of the other folks seemed convinced it was supernatural—angels or something. Go figure."

Jordan produced a phony smile. "As long as they're on *my* side, I don't care what they were."

"Where have you looked for Sawyer?" Sheriff Hal Barker asked.

"We've torn apart the woods around Mumford's house. We found the shack this Grady character told us about. No sign of Sawyer." Jordan got up and started to pace. "But we haven't seen the last of him. The guy's finally got a cause. Who knows how many others he may recruit? My agents are breathing down the neck of anyone who even knows how to *spell* his name."

Dr. Sarah Rice leaned back in her chair. She closed her eyes and massaged her temples.

"Are you taking something for that headache?" Dr. Montgomery asked.

"What I need to *take* is a vacation."

"Well, as I was saying, it could've been worse. At least no one died in yesterday's attack. And no one was exposed to the virus."

"But they had to send the wounded to Ellison Medical Center because we're at capacity! Any more attacks and we'll have to set up a MASH unit!" She got up and looked out the window.

"I'm completely baffled by what happened yesterday," he said. "I thought we had our protection in place. How the CWD was able to sneak in and do that much damage I'll never know."

"That's because you don't live here, Lionel. People don't know what to watch for. We have no experience with this sort of violence."

"At least now there's some kind of a pattern."

"The Baxter I grew up in was a safe, peaceful place. It seems as though we've imported the worst disease and crime in one fell swoop. It's hard to take."

"I suppose it is. But you've had problems here before. Wasn't there a kidnapping that made the news last winter?"

"Yes, it was awful. But this is more all-encompassing. This time, each of us is at risk."

There was a knock on the door.

"Excuse me…" Dr. McFarland stood in the doorway, his nose red, his mustache quivering.

Sarah's heart sank. "Spencer, what happened?"

There was a long pause.

"Blake Thomas has regained consciousness. His fever's broken."

Billy Joe Sawyer sat cross-legged on the floor of a boathouse, his shirt soaked with sweat, his stomach growling. He picked up a plastic bucket and took another swig of the lake water he had drawn the night before. What a break to have found an open padlock.

He patted the gun in his waistband and the switchblade in his pocket. He wondered if the others had been caught, but really didn't care. They were morons he could manipulate into doing whatever he said. But their response had been passionless, especially Grady's. They weren't committed to this cause.

He had planned to ditch them after the attack, at which point they would have either died in the exchange of gunfire or outlived their usefulness. They would only get in the way now. The last phase was personal. And he wasn't taking any chances.

This place was stifling! Sawyer stood and breathed in fresh air from the small, open window. He spotted a row of white T-shirts hanging on a clothesline about twenty yards up the hill. Was it worth the risk? He decided it was.

Dr. Sarah Rice stood with Pastor Thomas and his wife in front of the glass room and watched as Drs. Montgomery and McFarland stood on either side of Blake's bed. Dr. Montgomery looked in their direction and nodded, assuring them that Blake was awake. Dr. Rice reached up and turned on the intercom so they could hear.

"Blake, I'm Dr. Montgomery. You're in the hospital with a serious virus. But you're past the danger point. If you remember, squeeze my hand."

Dr. Montgomery looked at them and shook his head. "That's all right. Short-term amnesia is normal under the circumstances. Don't be alarmed. Your memory should return soon. Blake, if you understand, squeeze my hand."

Dr. Montgomery looked up and nodded.

"I'm going to let you rest now, but I wanted to personally welcome you back. You've survived an almost unbelievable ordeal. You are one very strong and very lucky young man."

"Thank you, Lord," Pastor Thomas said, his hand squeezing his wife's.

Dr. Rice blinked to clear her eyes. She touched his shoulder and then moved to the opposite wall to give them privacy. She stood looking at Blake. The young man's face was drawn, his eyes hollow and sunken. The skin eruptions were starting to form scabs. But all that would heal.

She could hardly believe Blake Thomas had survived. And if his fever didn't return by nightfall, he would be taken out of isolation.

Sawyer peeled off the sweaty black T-shirt and slipped on the clean white one he had snatched from the clothesline. He spotted an Atlanta Braves cap hanging on a hook and adjusted the strap, then tried it on. Not bad. He reached for the sunglasses he had found in a tackle box and put them on.

He spotted something on a high shelf—a sort of satchel. He took off the sunglasses and put them in his pocket, then pushed a step stool next to the shelving and stretched until he finally grabbed the object of his curiosity and pulled it down, realizing as the straps hit him in the face that it was an old backpack.

He jumped down, unfastened the flaps, and found that his gun fit perfectly inside. He took two of the four extra clips from the pockets of his cargo shorts and put them in the backpack.

Someone was turning the doorknob! He sprang to the wall by the door, leaned his back against it, and opened his switchblade.

The door to the boathouse slowly opened, and a little boy poked his head in the door.

Sawyer put the knife in his back pocket and stepped away from the wall. "What do you want, kid?"

The little boy looked startled. "Whatcha doin'?"

"Uh—rearranging things for your mother."

"Oh," the boy said, matter-of-factly.

"Look, kid, what can I do for you? I'm kinda busy."

"I need my sailboat."

"There's no sailboat in here. I've been all over these shelves, and I didn't see it."

"I left it here."

"No, you didn't. Now beat it."

"But it's in here; I *know* I left it here." The boy's voice was getting louder.

"Okay, kid." Sawyer pulled him all the way into the boathouse and shut the door. "Show me where you left the sailboat."

The little boy shrugged. "I'm not sure."

"What do you mean you're not sure?"

"I'm sure I left it here. But I don't remember where."

"If you left it here, this *is* where." Sawyer pointed to the open shelves above the workbench.

The boy looked confused.

"Look, it's not here."

"Uh-huh."

"Unh-unh. Now beat it!"

"It's my boathouse! You're not the boss of me! I'm gonna tell my mommy you're not bein' nice!"

Sawyer grabbed the kid by his hair and shoved him to the floor. "Fine. It's all yours, you whiny brat."

Sawyer picked up the backpack. He opened the door and poked his head outside. *Not a soul.* He stepped out and pulled the door shut, laughing as he closed the padlock and left the muffled cries of the little whiner locked inside the boathouse.

Dennis took two cans of Coke out of the refrigerator and sat at the kitchen table opposite Flo.

"There you go," he said. "A well-deserved break is in order."

"Them babies sure do keep a body hoppin'," Flo said. "I ain't cut out for this like I was when I was young. But this quarantine's gonna be over day after tomorrow. And I sure am gonna miss them boys."

"What do you do the rest of the time?"

"Oh, I get along just fine. Too old to hold down a job, but I do volunteerin' at the hospital. That's how I come to know Martha."

"Sullivan?"

"Uh-huh. She's a tough ol' bird, but she's got a heart o' gold when it comes to babies. Fiercely protective, that one."

"Yeah, I noticed."

"What about you, Ben? Volunteerin' is one thing, but it don't pay the bills."

"I don't worry too much about bills."

"Ain't you got a job?"

"I don't have to work. My dad's wealthy so I can do what I want. For now, it's volunteering my help here. Next week, I think I'll go to Colorado and visit my folks."

"You jus' do what you want without nothin' holdin' you back? Sounds like the life o' Riley, it surely does."

"It's not quite that simple." Dennis saw Martha Sullivan coming up the walk. He heard the outside door slam, then a knock on the French doors.

"I'll git it this time," Flo said, and she headed to answer the door. "Why, hello, Martha. Come on in here where it's cool. Ben and I was out in the kitchen havin' us a Coke."

Dennis stood when Martha entered the kitchen.

"I have some encouraging news," she said. "Blake Thomas regained consciousness. If he doesn't have a fever by tonight, they'll take him out of isolation."

"That's great," Dennis said. "What about his wife?"

"She's stabilized. If there's going to be a change, the doctors believe it'll happen in the next twenty-four hours."

"Then, if no one outside the hospital develops this virus by Thursday, will the home quarantines be over?" Dennis asked.

"Should be. A few of those in *B* Corridor will have to ride it out longer because they came in contact with blood from the shooting victims who now have the virus. But the home quarantines should be lifted."

"Me and Ben was just talkin' about what we'll be doin' after all this. Ben's headin' for Colorado to visit with his rich kinfolk. He don't hafta work." Flo laughed. "Don't that beat all?"

"Oh?" Martha turned and looked at him.

"I haven't decided what I'm going to do after I'm not needed here anymore."

"Ben's done a marvelous job, hasn't he, Flo?"

"That he has. The boy's got somethin' special with them babies. I expect he outta try it hisself one o' these days—bein' a daddy, I mean. Why, I don't think them babies woulda got any better lovin' if Ben *was* their daddy."

"No, I'm *sure* they wouldn't have," Martha said.

"Come on, I didn't do any more than Flo. I just happened to be available."

"Well, since you don't have to work, it was generous of you to *be* available," Martha said. "By the way, Jennifer Wilson loved the video."

"Really?" Dennis said.

"I also heard she's decided on names for the boys: Bailey and *Benjamin.*"

"Well, ain't that somethin'!" Flo said.

"She told one of the nurses that the boys' father could learn a lot from Ben Stoller."

"She did?" Dennis said. "Uh—well—maybe the guy will someday. Maybe he just needs a little space. He's probably not all bad."

"Let's hope you're right," Martha said.

Jennifer heard footsteps and then a knock on the door. She put the video on pause.

"Come in," she said.

Dr. Rice walked to her bed, a smile on her face. "Are you ready for some *good* news, young lady?"

"I heard everyone cheering. What happened?"

"Blake Thomas is wide awake. His fever's gone, and we're taking him out of isolation. He made it!"

Jennifer laughed and cried at the same time. "Oh, my! That's—that's so great! What about Melissa?"

"Not yet, but we're hopeful. This is the most encouraging thing that's happened. I wanted to deliver the news personally."

"Thank you, Dr. Rice!"

"I'll check back later. I have to be in a meeting in five minutes."

"Don't they ever let you out of here?" Jennifer said.

Dr. Rice smiled. "Maybe now I can spend a little more time at home."

Jennifer couldn't sleep. Her mind raced with possibilities and her heart with renewed hope.

She watched the video again and could hardly wait to hold Bailey and Benjamin. She wondered if she'd get to meet Flo and

Ben when the quarantine was over. Why couldn't her boys have a father who cared—that's what they needed. *That's a laugh!* All Dennis cared about was himself.

Jennifer remembered the first time she met Dennis...

"You're the prettiest lady at the party and we still haven't met. I'm Dennis Lawton."

Jennifer sized him up in an instant—tall, blond, handsome, charming—and a ladies' man. Not a woman in the room had failed to notice.

"Nice to meet you. I'm Jennifer Wilson."

"I know." Dennis sat down beside her. "Would you like to go have coffee? Starbucks is around the corner. We can walk."

Jennifer looked into his eyes and tried to read them. Half the gals at the party had been all over him. Why was he interested in *her?*

"I'm not usually this forward," Dennis said. "But truthfully, you seem like someone I don't want to get away. I've been watching you all evening. Not only are you attractive, you're a real *lady.* There's not many of you left."

"Oh, really?" she said. "And you base this on?..."

He glanced at a group of young women across the room. "The *un-*ladylikes."

"The what?"

He smiled. "Never mind. I just don't come across a class act very often. I'd be flattered if you'd accompany me to Starbucks, Jennifer." His eyes melted into her soul.

Jennifer's instincts told her to run, but insecurity had already pushed her to her feet in acceptance of his invitation.

Things were good in the beginning, but it didn't take her long to realize that what she valued in a relationship didn't mean anything to Dennis...

"Sorry, Jen. I made plans to watch the Broncos game with the guys. You know I never miss a kickoff."

"But you said we could spend the weekend in the mountains. I've got this wonderful dinner planned, and—"

"I'll make it up to you." He slipped his arms around her and started kissing her neck.

"That's not what I'm talking about, Dennis. We never talk any more."

"What do you want from me? We're together almost every night."

She sighed. "Maybe that's the problem."

"You've never complained before."

"I guess I didn't realize that's all we had."

Soon after that, she broke it off. Then the pregnancy test came back positive…

She studied the twin faces on the TV screen. Bailey…and Benjamin. So perfect. Yet so fragile. Jennifer remembered the misery of growing up as an unwanted child, wishing her dad would love her. Why did her boys have to grow up feeling the same emptiness? *Dennis, you're such a jerk. Lord, forgive me, but he is.*

After the 6:00 P.M. feeding, Flo and the boys were asleep, and Dennis stood looking out the kitchen window. Things were quiet across the street. Jennifer would recover soon. In just a couple of days her parents would come get the twins.

Jennifer didn't need to know he was Ben Stoller. But Dennis felt good that, for once in his life, he'd done something worthwhile. Better that she live with the illusion that some nice guy had come to help. Maybe it would renew her faith in men.

He closed the kitchen blinds and walked to the study. Now that Flo and the boys were asleep, he decided to run over to the Quick Stop and use the pay phone to make his airline reservation for Thursday.

Dennis picked up his wallet and checked to be sure he had his credit card. He flipped over to Jennifer's picture. He remembered the night he took this. They had known each other about a week, and she was curled up on the couch, looking at the sketches he had done at Larimer Square…

"Dennis, these are unbelievable. Why aren't you showing your work in a gallery?"

"I don't know. I've never taken it that seriously."

"Well, if you ever get tired of selling insurance, you might be sitting on a gold mine."

"Come on, Jen. They're not *that* good."

"What do you mean? Look at this face. The woman's eyes…her expression…you captured her soul. It's amazing."

"I'm glad you like them. I've got a whole closet full of this stuff."

"I want to see them all."

Jennifer sat admiring the sketches in her lap, her golden brown hair falling in soft curls down the sides of her face to her elbows.

"Hold it right there," he said. He squatted down in front of her and snapped a close-up.

"Why'd you do that?"

"I liked you in that pose. Maybe I'll do a charcoal."

Dennis sat beside her and relished her enthusiasm about his work. Her compliments seemed as genuine as the glow in her cheeks.

He turned her face toward him and studied the outline of her lips, the shape of her nose, and then gazed into the most beautiful hazel eyes he had ever seen. All at once, it was as though she was looking into his heart. He shuddered.

"What's wrong, Dennis?"

"Nothing. Uh—why don't we get ice cream or something? There's a new Ben & Jerry's around the corner."

Jennifer looked at him questioningly, her eyes probing. "Okay."

They went to Ben & Jerry's, and then took a long walk in the park. Afterwards, Jennifer came home with him and spent the night…

Dennis closed his wallet and put it in his back pocket. He didn't know why, but every time he let himself feel anything for Jennifer, that weird thing happened—and that was the end of it. He was better in relationships that were physical, noncommittal.

Dennis left the study and listened outside Flo's door, and then at the nursery. He walked through the living room and out the French doors, suddenly realizing he had been happy this past week for the first time in his life.

TWENTY-TWO

Dennis stood with his back to the brick wall of the Quick Stop, the pay phone to his ear, and waited for the call to go through.

"Patrick Bailey here."

"Grandpa, it's me, and before you start yelling, let me explain."

"This better be good, Dennis."

"I assume you got your voice mail and know I'm in Baxter."

"And I've also been watching cable. Are you out of your mind?"

"I'm fine, Grandpa. I came back here because Jennifer was in the hospital with symptoms of the virus. I'd been with her the day before and was scared I was at risk. But then I figured since I'd already been exposed, I might as well help out with the twins since they'd been exposed, too. Turns out I overreacted. Jennifer didn't have the virus, and only three more people have come down with it. The home quarantines should be lifted on Thursday. That's when I'm coming home."

"What about the twins?"

"Jennifer's parents will take them until she's out of the hospital."

"The hospital?"

"Yeah, she was shot in the hospital attack. But she's going to be all right."

"Jennifer got caught in that? I heard there was another fire-bombing on a residential neighborhood. It's all over the TV."

"Bad, too, from what I hear. Flo and I are pretty cut off from the real world right now."

"*Flo?*"

"It's not what you think, Grandpa. She's a nice elderly lady that's helping me with the boys at the clinic."

"The clinic?"

"Well, the apartment in the clinic. It's across from the hospital."

"Well, Dennis, you certainly are full of surprises."

"You still mad?"

"I haven't had time to digest it. This is uncharacteristic of you."

"I know. I did some quick soul-searching when I thought I was at risk for the virus. I was ashamed to admit what people would remember me for if I died. That's when I decided to come back here and help with the boys. And I'm actually enjoying it."

"Are you?"

"Yeah, they're a kick—identical, except for their personalities. One is particularly resourceful at getting what he wants, and you'll never guess what I named him?"

"*You* named him?"

"Well, temporarily. But Jennifer decided to make it permanent. Flo and I called him *Bailey*—after you, Grandpa."

"Bailey, huh? And the other boy?"

"Benjamin. We called him Bear, but Jennifer decided to call him Benjamin after Ben Stoller, who's really me. It's the phony name I'm using so Jennifer won't know I'm here."

Dennis could feel the question mark on the other end of the receiver. "Grandpa, let me back up and start at the beginning…"

Dennis quickly put the events in sequence, beginning with the canceled flight in Atlanta.

"Dennis, if I didn't know better, I'd say you're hooked on those boys."

"Uh—not really. I just did what I had to. It's time for me to leave. Like I said, I'll be home on Thursday. Do I still have a job?"

"Far be it from me to fire my own grandson. I chalked it up to vacation time; you had quite a bit accumulated. So, you're really going to leave?"

"Yeah. Like I said, Jennifer doesn't even know that I'm the one who's been helping out. I'd rather leave her believing this guy was a real sweetheart."

There was a long pause.

"Dennis, promise me you'll come home Thursday."

"Is something wrong?"

"It'll keep till then."

"Okay, Grandpa. My flight leaves Atlanta around 7:00 A.M."

"If I'm not at the house, I'll leave you a note…and could you bring a picture of the twins? I'd like to at least see what these namesakes of ours look like."

"I don't have a camera with me, but I've got a copy of a video-tape I made for the Wilsons. And I've already done a ton of sketches."

Dennis sat at the kitchen table, putting the final touches on his pencil sketch of Flo holding the two babies. "It needs just a little shading right here…all right…that should do it." He held it up and smiled, then gave it to Flo.

"I declare. It's amazin', Ben. How do you git your hands to show what your eyes are seein'? It's a talent from the Lord, sure enough."

"That one's for you, Flo. I've got these others I've been playing around with all week."

"You mean I can keep this one?"

"Please. As a keepsake of our week with the twins."

"Oh, Ben. You know I'll cherish this long as I'm breathin'."

"I'm glad because I'll always remember you. I consider it an honor to have known you." Dennis got up and kissed her on the cheek.

"Land sakes."

"I mean it. It's been a great week for me."

"I've enjoyed it, too, Ben."

"You know something else? You're the first *real* Christian I've ever known."

"You're embarrassin' me now."

"I'm serious. You live what you believe. I've watched you, Flo. Most Christians I've known are two-faced—not you."

She got quiet, her dark eyes looking into his. "You know, Ben, ever'body's got two faces. Bein' a Christian's about narrowin' it down to one. It's about becomin' free."

"What do you mean?"

"Didn't you ever pretend to be somethin' you ain't?"

"Well…sure. Hasn't everyone?"

"That's all I'm sayin'. Ever'body's got two faces. We just hafta learn which one we was meant to keep. Till we do that, we ain't never gonna be happy."

Dennis looked at the sketches on the table. "Faces tell a lot about people."

"But what counts ain't what *we* show, Ben. It's what's deep down inside. Only the Father in Heaven Hisself can draw it outta us."

"Are you saying God's the only One who knows who we are?"

"Now you're talkin'. Try givin' *Him* the pencil and see what He does with it."

"Flo, it boggles my brain, thinking about all this stuff."

"Land sakes. I don't remember no one ever sayin' that to me before. I ain't real smart; I jus' know some things that's helped me."

All at once a demanding cry resounded from the nursery. Dennis and Flo looked at each other. "Bailey!" they said at the same time, then burst into laughter.

On Monday evening, Billy Joe Sawyer walked down the sidewalk on First Street, wearing the stolen backpack, sunglasses, and Atlanta Braves cap. He laughed out loud, thinking about the box of fried chicken he'd stolen from a picnic table while some parents took their kids to the john. At least he wouldn't have to think about his stomach again for a while.

He saw the hospital up ahead and cut through some yards until he was across the street from the visitor parking lot. He stood behind a tree and observed. The National Guardsmen were posted at the barricade, while a law enforcement officer checked IDs of people pulling into the parking lot.

He noticed a family getting out of their car in visitor parking, and he quickly made his way over to them.

"Nice evening, isn't it?" Sawyer removed his sunglasses.

"If you like hot," the man said.

"Cute kids."

"Thanks." The woman stroked her daughter's ponytail.

"Can I ask you folks a question? Some guy asked me for a handout and then grabbed my wallet. That's the only ID I had. Does that ruin my chances for visiting my grandmother?"

"Afraid so," the man said. "After the firebombing, they've made getting in here a ritual. I don't think they'll break the rules—unless, of course, your grandmother can come to the main entrance and identify you."

"Oh." Sawyer let his face drop. "That won't be possible. She's in ICU. That's why I walked here." He sighed. "Oh, well. Rules are there to protect us. I just hope she doesn't think I don't care about her."

"Tough break," the man said.

Sawyer looked at the couple's children, then squatted down to eye level. "What's your name?"

"Lindsay."

"Lindsay? What a pretty name…and what's your name?"

"Trevor."

"Trevor. Now that's a man's name if I ever heard one. Let me feel those muscles…Wow, mighty impressive." He stood up. "Well, nice meetin' you folks. You have a real nice family. Guess I'll be headin' back to Ellison."

"Ellison?" the woman said. "You walked all the way from Ellison?"

"Yes, ma'am."

"Wait…" the man said. "Why don't you come with us? We can tell them you're my little brother or something."

"I can't ask you to do that," Sawyer said.

"Well, what's the harm?" the woman said. "You walked all this way, and it's not your fault you had your wallet stolen. You should be able to see your grandmother. The rule's intended to protect the hospital from militants, not from folks like us."

Sawyer shook his head from side to side. "You folks are so nice." It was all he could do to keep from laughing.

"We're here to see Oscar Holmstead," the man said. "He's my father. What's your name?"

"David Smith."

"Okay, David, for tonight you're a Holmstead. I'm Jason and this is my wife, Linda. You've met our children. Let's see if they'll let you in with us."

Sawyer followed the Holmsteads to the front entrance of the hospital. *Buddy, you just made the lousiest character call of your life!*

～∞～

Jordan Ellis sat in Sheriff Hal Barker's office, listening to him question Gerrad Bennigan about what had happened at the boathouse.

"Gerrad, can you tell us what the man looked like?" Hal said.

"Big. And mean."

"Do you remember what clothes he had on?"

"A white T-shirt."

"Did he have a beard or a mustache?"

"No."

"Was he shorter or taller than your daddy?"

"I dunno."

"Was he older or younger than your daddy?"

The little boy shrugged.

"What color was his hair?"

"I couldn't see. It was under my daddy's baseball cap."

Jordan shifted in his chair. *Bingo!*

"What kind of ball cap?" Hal asked.

"Atlanta Braves," Mr. Bennigan said. "It's missing from the boathouse."

"Gerrad, do you remember anything else about this man. Think, son. Anything?"

"Um...he took my Granddaddy's pack."

"Gerrad's referring to a brown leather backpack," Mr. Bennigan said. "It's ancient. Hasn't been used in years."

"Son, I'm going to show you a picture now. I want you to tell me if it looks like the man you saw." Hal held up the picture so Gerrad could see.

"Kind of." The boy's eyes welled with tears. "He pulled my hair and pushed me down and I couldn't get out. It was real hot and I kept yelling, but Mommy couldn't hear me."

"I knew something was wrong when Gerrad didn't come right back," Mrs. Bennigan said. "I let him go to the boathouse to get his sailboat, but he was taking too long, so I went down there. When I found the door padlocked, I thought he'd found his boat and gone down to the water to sail it by himself. I ran to the house and called the Lake Patrol, and then called my husband and he came right home."

Mr. Bennigan nodded. "We looked for hours. Then out of sheer desperation, we went back to the boathouse to retrace our steps and noticed the window was open. I looked in and saw Gerrad lying on the floor! We got in there as fast as we could. He'd cried himself to sleep and was lethargic from the heat. But other than a bruise on his back and a few scratches, he wasn't hurt. Not physically anyway."

"Thank God the window was open," Mrs. Bennigan said, fighting the emotion. "He could've died in that heat. What kind of a man does something that cruel to a little boy?"

Jordan loosened his collar. He would like to have laid the guy out.

"I don't know, Mrs. Bennigan," Hal said. "But we're going to find out. Gerrad, thanks for being brave and telling us about this man. We're going to find him so he can't scare any more little boys."

"Is that a *real* gun?" Gerrad asked, looking at Hal Barker's holster.

"Yes, it's real."

"Are you going to *shoot* the man, Sheriff?" he asked, wide-eyed.

"I hope not. We don't shoot unless we have no other choice. But we'll get this guy so he can't scare any more little boys." Hal turned to Mr. and Mrs. Bennigan. "You folks did exactly the right thing. Thanks for reporting this. I'll walk you to the elevator."

Jordan sat at his desk, hands behind his head, and waited for Hal to come back.

The sheriff walked in and sat down. "Could be Sawyer. What do you think?"

"I'll put out the word," Jordan said. "Let's see if this *baseball cap* sticks his head out. If he does, we'll throw a noose around his neck."

Hal didn't say anything.

"Lighten up, Sheriff," Jordan said. "It's just wishful thinking. I hate guys who hurt kids."

"That's all right. I was thinking the same thing."

Sawyer stood with the Holmsteads at the main entrance to Baxter Memorial Hospital, where FBI Special Agent Adam McCullum was checking IDs.

"Did you folks call ahead?" McCullum asked.

"Yes, I called," Linda said. "I explained that our whole family would be coming."

"What's the name of the patient you're here to see?"

"My father, Oscar Holmstead," Jason said.

"May I see a photo ID, sir?"

"Certainly." Holmstead took out his license and handed it to the agent. "This is my wife, Linda, my brother, David, and my children, Lindsay and Trevor."

"I'm going to need to see some ID on the two of you," McCullum said, looking at Sawyer and Linda. "While you're getting that, let me call the information desk and make sure they're expecting you. You understand it's for security purposes? I apologize for any inconvenience."

"No problem," Jason said.

The agent took out his cell phone and dialed. "This is Agent McCullum at the main entrance. I have some visitors to see Oscar Holmstead…she called?… Yes, that's what she said—the whole family…thanks." McCullum turned off his phone. "All right. I just need to see a photo ID on you two and then you can go in."

Linda took out her driver's license and handed it to the agent just as his phone rang.

"This is McCullum…" He lowered his voice and turned his head. "Chinese takeout? Man, I'm starved…hold on." He handed Linda her driver's license. "You folks can go in. The lady at the desk said she got a call from Mrs. Holmstead."

His heart pounding, Sawyer walked past Agent McCullum and followed the family down A Corridor. He thanked them for their kindness, and then they parted ways.

Sawyer walked toward ICU; and when he was sure he wasn't being followed, he slipped into an alcove. He poked his head into the hallway and looked both ways, then walked the other direction, wondering if what he was about to do would create as much commotion as Agent McCullum's critical slip of protocol.

TWENTY-THREE

C ome on, McCullum, answer your phone…" Jordan Ellis put his chewing gum in a Post-it note and pitched it in the waste can. He tapped the desk with a pencil and looked at his watch.

"This is Adam."

"What took you so long, McCullum? I expect you to be on your toes."

"Sorry, sir. I had another call when I heard you beeping in."

"Keep your eyes peeled," Jordan said. "Sawyer may have surfaced. A couple out at the lake reported their five-year-old son bumped into a stranger in the family's boathouse. The guy got rough with the kid and left with an Atlanta Braves ball cap and a brown leather backpack and—"

"Sir, I'll call you back!" *Click.*

"McCullum?… Don't you dare hang up on me! McCullum?…"

Jordan slammed the phone down and raked his hand through his hair. *Who does he think he is?* He pushed his chair back and stood up, then grabbed his keys and headed out the door.

✧

Dr. Sarah Rice picked up her briefcase and turned out the lights in her office. She pulled the door shut and heard footsteps running in the hallway. She turned in time to see two men run into a patient's room.

"FBI, freeze!" a male voice shouted.

Sarah stood frozen, her heart racing, and listened intently.

"Where's the man who came in here with you? We believe he's armed and extremely dangerous."

"Oh, my gosh, Jason!" a woman exclaimed. "Tell them!"

"Look, the guy said he was here to visit his grandmother in ICU. He didn't have an ID and we felt sorry for him! We didn't know—"

The two agents ran out of the room and down the hall in the other direction. One of them was on his cell phone. "This is McCullum. Knowles and I need backup. We think Sawyer's in the building…"

Sarah opened her office door, went back inside, and locked it. She picked up the phone, her hands shaking, and dialed the nurses' station in *B* Corridor.

Sawyer saw the quarantine notice and looked through the window on the double doors. He saw two people, each outfitted with gown, surgical mask, goggles, and gloves. He spotted what appeared to be a linen cart in the hallway. He waited until they were gone, then pushed open the double doors. He ran to the cart and grabbed what he needed, then ducked into a restroom and locked the door.

Sawyer laid the items from the cart in the sink, then slipped off his backpack and laid it on the floor. He patted his pockets and made sure he had two of the extra clips. He slipped on a gown over his clothes, tied a surgical mask around his face, then put on the goggles and surgical gloves. He reached down and removed the Glock .45 from the backpack.

He cracked the door to the restroom and listened intently, then stepped out with his arms folded, his gun concealed under his arm, and began walking down the main hallway, looking for the glass room he had heard about on TV.

The double doors at his back suddenly burst open. He heard footsteps running and quickly turned into one of the patient's rooms as two armed men raced by.

Sawyer waited a few seconds, then turned around and saw a young woman patient, surprised that she didn't seem very sick. He pulled her out of bed and held the gun barrel to her head.

"Don't make a sound."

He walked her to the door, then poked his head into the hallway and looked in both directions. "Okay, lady. There're FBI agents at both ends of the hall. You're goin' with me."

Sawyer forced her into the hallway, the gun to her head, his arm tightly around her neck. The scent of her hair reminded him of his mother, and he felt a surge of anger.

"I'll kill her if anyone makes a move! I got nothin' to lose!"

He moved along the wall toward an alcove about halfway down B Corridor, firing shots in one direction and then the other, his left arm clasped so tightly around the young woman's throat that she began to whimper.

When he reached the arrow that pointed to the emergency exit, Sawyer shoved her to the floor and darted for the door.

Dennis had just gotten Benjamin to sleep when the popping sound of gunshots shattered the quiet. He stood and gently laid Benjamin in the crib. He glanced at Bailey, who was still asleep, then walked out and closed the nursery door behind him.

He hurried to the living room, where Flo had pulled back the lacy curtain and was peeking through the blinds.

"That was gunfire," Dennis said, looking over her shoulder. "I'm going to see where it's coming from."

"Don't be gittin' yourself in the line o' fire, Ben." More shots rang out, and Flo clutched his arm. "Lord, have mercy."

"I'm going to stick my head out the front door and see if I can tell where it's coming from. Don't worry. I won't go outside."

Dennis walked toward the front entrance. Through the lacy panels and beveled glass, he saw what appeared to be a surgeon run up the steps and pound on the glass.

Must be a shooting at the hospital! Dennis quickly unlocked the door and opened it—and in the next instant was looking down the barrel of a gun.

Jordan Ellis slowed as he approached the barricade on First Street, surprised when one of his agents motioned him to stop.

"Sir, there's been a shooting. It just happened."

"Inside the hospital?"

The agent nodded. *"B* Corridor. I don't have details, but agents have a suspect trapped in the Hunter Clinic—behind the hospital."

The agent let Jordan pass. His tires screeched as he accelerated down First, then turned on the street behind the hospital. Halfway down the block, he spotted FBI agents standing on the sidewalk outside a white picket fence. *McCullum!*

Jordan parked along the curb and ran over to him. "I assume this is why you hung up on me?"

"Yes, sir." McCullum leaned forward, his hands on his knees, trying to catch his breath. "I had just seen the suspect...you described...my instincts kicked in."

"What'd you do?"

"I knew which patient he'd come to see...so Knowles and I ran to the patient's room. When he wasn't there, I figured he'd gone to B Corridor." McCullum drew in a slow, deep breath, then stood up straight. "We would've had him, but he was holding a female patient with a gun to her head. He fired at us, then made a run for the emergency exit."

"Why didn't you take him out?" Jordan said.

"Knowles and I were at one end of B Corridor; and by the time we ran out the exit and started to chase him, we couldn't get a clear shot. We saw him enter the clinic. The door's locked. The place is surrounded."

Jordan glanced up at the clinic and then at McCullum, his face hot, the veins in his neck throbbing. "How did he get by you in the first place?"

"It's a long story, sir. You can skin me alive later, but I don't want to lose this guy."

Dennis stood in the foyer at the clinic, a gun pointed at his chest, hoping Flo would stay where she was until he could figure out what to do.

"Is the door behind me locked?" the man said.

"Yeah. Locks automatically when the clinic's closed." Dennis looked through the sheer panels at FBI agents outside.

"What are you doin' in here?" the man asked.

"I'm working late."

"Where?"

"Uh, there." Dennis nodded toward the clinic door across from the apartment. "Just catching up on some paperwork. I was about to leave for the day."

"You're not goin' anywhere. Anyone else here?"

"No, I'm the last one." Dennis saw someone outside holding a bullhorn.

"Sawyer, this is the FBI. We have the building surrounded. Put down your weapons and come out with your hands up."

Dennis's heart pounded. *Billy Joe Sawyer?*

"Yeah, right, " Sawyer said. "They'd love to take me out!"

Dennis heard the French doors open.

"Ben, are you out there? Oh, my…"

"Get over here, ol' woman!" Sawyer grabbed her by the arm. "You're my ticket outta this place!" He looked at the French doors. "What's in there?"

"Nothin' special," she said.

"Well, how about the two of you take me to nothin' special." Sawyer prodded them into the apartment, the gun at their backs. "Well, looky here. A regular house…with air conditioning, no less."

The bullhorn sounded again. "Sawyer, this is the FBI. We know you're in there. Put down your weapons and come out with your hands up."

"They're wastin' their time." Sawyer took off the surgical mask and the goggles, then untied the gown and threw it in the corner. "You two turn around and keep your hands on the wall."

Dennis heard Sawyer peel off the surgical gloves one at a time. He glanced at his watch. How much longer would Bailey sleep?

"Turn around and tell me your names. You first, Grandma."

"I…I'm Flo Hamlin."

"What about you, pretty boy? What's your name?"

"Ben Stoller."

"Anyone else livin' here besides the ol' woman?"

Jordan Ellis took the bullhorn from Agent Knowles.

"Sawyer, this is Special Agent Jordan Ellis of the FBI. This is your last warning. Come out with your hands in the air, or we're coming in after you."

A lady came rushing across the street from the hospital. "Who's in charge here?"

"I am, ma'am," Jordan said.

"There are four people in there, including newborn twins! Tell your men to back off."

"Two babies? Lady, are you *sure?*"

"Positive. My name's Martha Sullivan, senior RN of obstetrics at the hospital. See those windows to the right of the front door? Two of my volunteers are in there caring for the newborns while their mother is quarantined."

Dennis stood in the kitchen next to Flo, his eyes fixed on the Glock .45, imagining what it would feel like to beat the tar out of Sawyer.

"All right, Grandma" Sawyer said. "Show me the rest of it."

Dennis's heart pounded as the man herded them toward the bedrooms.

Sawyer poked his head in Flo's room, and then moved on to the doorway of the study. "Wait a minute…whose stuff is this?" He glared at Flo. "I thought you lived here alone."

"Well, I—"

"I'm staying with Aunt Flo," Dennis said. "That's my stuff."

Sawyer's eyebrows gathered. He nodded toward the nursery door. "Show me what's in there." Sawyer opened the door and flipped the light switch. "You two go first and stand over against the wall."

Dennis did as he was told.

"Well, looky here!" Sawyer bellowed. "Two little rug rats to buy my freedom!"

Bailey woke up screaming.

"Shut up, kid!" Sawyer shouted.

Benjamin started crying.

Dennis took a protective step forward, but was stopped by the barrel of Sawyer's gun.

"Now you listen to me," Flo said, her face livid. "Them babies don't take kindly to *loud*. And there ain't no way to force them babies to do whatcha want. You gotta be gentle with 'em."

Sawyer seemed amused by her grit. "Fine, Grandma. *You* handle the little squawkers. But get 'em calmed down!" He pushed the gun barrel harder into Dennis's chest. "So, you're the last one here, eh? Leaving for the day? What else are you holding back?"

"Nothing," Dennis said. "I didn't want to involve Aunt Flo in a hostage situation. These are my sister's kids. We're watching them while she's out of town."

Dennis felt the butt end of Sawyer's gun bash his cheekbone. He fell backward against the wall, feeling light-headed and nauseated. He blinked several times until his eyes focused.

"Lie to me again," Sawyer said, "and it'll be the last time."

Jordan Ellis stood outside the clinic. He activated his cell phone and dialed the number Nurse Sullivan had given him. "Come on, somebody, pick up…"

"Hello. This is Ben Stoller."

"This is Special Agent Ellis of the FBI. Stay cool, Ben. Let me talk to Sawyer."

"It's the FBI—for you."

"Stand over there by Grandma so I can keep an eye on you both. This is Sawyer. Who's this?"

"Special Agent Ellis of the FBI. We need to talk."

"What for? You won't listen."

"We both want the same thing, Sawyer—the truth."

"You don't want us knowin' the truth! You think we're too dumb to know what you're tryin' to pull?"

Jordan took a slow, deep breath. "Blake Thomas is awake, Sawyer. He pulled through. No one has died of the virus. All the worry was for nothing. There's no reason to pursue this anymore."

"Yeah? That's what *you* think!" *Click.*

TWENTY-FOUR

Jordan Ellis redialed the number of the apartment.

"Yeah."

"Tell me what you want," Jordan said, aware of a baby crying.

"I want the truth! I want those liars at the hospital to admit on camera they're not tellin' the truth about the threat to the rest of us."

"Anything else?" Jordan asked.

"I want the oncologist who treated my mother to lose his license. He told her she was cured. He lied to her just like they're lyin' now!"

"Is that everything?"

"No. I want a pilot and a plane full of fuel. And some cash— twenty thousand dollars. If you try to pull something, I'll take everyone in here down with me. I swear it."

"It's going to take hours to pull all that together," Jordan said.

"You've got till midnight." *Click.*

Jordan motioned to the SWAT team leader. "Send your best shooter in through the back. See if he can get a clear shot at Sawyer. Go!"

∽o∾

Jennifer's sedation took only the edge off her anguish. She had tried talking to her mother, but it had gotten too emotional, and her father took the line.

"Dad, I can't handle any more!"

"Jen, Sawyer didn't hurt you. I doubt if he's out to hurt the boys either."

"Why is God allowing this?" she said. "What good can come of it? After all I've been through, now the twins are being held by some madman! It's like I'm on a merry-go-round that's out of control and I can't jump off."

"I don't have all the answers, but this Sawyer isn't in control, the Lord is. And no matter how bleak things look, we need to trust Him and keep praying."

"I am praying, Dad. Where *is* He? I'm still new at this, and I'm wavering here."

"Honey, if we can't trust *Him* with the boys, who can we trust?"

"I'm trying. It's just so hard to accept what He may decide to allow. Look what happened to Blake and Melissa's baby…" Jennifer plucked a Kleenex and blew her nose.

"I'll never believe He turned a deaf ear to all those people who were praying for them. He'll use even that sad circumstance for—"

"I don't *want* any more sad circumstances! What if that horrible man kills my boys? They're all I've got!"

"Jen, honey, calm down…listen to me…the Lord knows exactly how many heartbeats He planned for them. Those boys are *His*."

"I don't want to hear that!"

"The whole church is praying. Put the boys in His hands, and let God be God. He's still in control, no matter how things feel. He'll give you the grace to get through this."

"I believe He'll give me the grace. But if anything happens to the boys, I'm scared I won't be willing to accept it."

❧

Dennis sat at the kitchen table, Benjamin asleep in his arms. Flo sat across from him, trying everything she knew to pacify Bailey, who would not be consoled. He had reacted to each of Sawyer's erratic outbursts, which were becoming more frequent.

Sawyer stood with his back against the kitchen wall, his gun held on the four of them, and peeked through a crack in the curtains. "What's takin' so long? How hard can it be to get a few doctors on camera and get a plane here? They're messin' with me!" he shouted, his voice booming across the kitchen.

Bailey let out a wail, and Flo got up and started to walk with him.

"Why's that kid screamin' again? Can't you shut him up?" Sawyer said.

"All this loud talkin' just keeps him upset," Flo said softly, her arms wrapped around Bailey.

Dennis glanced at his watch. It was after eleven. What would Sawyer do if his demands weren't met?

Jordan put his walkie-talkie to his ear. "Yeah."

"It's a no-go," the shooter said. "Repeat: a no-go."

"Have you spotted the suspect?" Jordan said.

"Negative."

"Stay in there. Keep looking for an opening. I'll see if I can lure him out into the foyer." Jordan took out his cell phone and dialed the phone to the apartment.

"Did you do what I said?" Sawyer asked.

"We're still working on it," Jordan said. "Can we get you a pizza or something?"

"Okay. A large pepperoni with black olives and green pepper. A six-pack of Budweiser, too."

"All right. I'll let you know when it's here. Hang in there, Sawyer. We're getting close."

Dennis felt as though his neck were in a vise. He sat at the kitchen table, holding Benjamin with one arm and rubbing the back of his neck with his free hand.

"Get that brat to shut up!" Sawyer shouted at Flo.

Her eyes filled with desperation. "I'm afraid he's got the colic."

Dennis stood up and walked to where Flo was standing. As he took Bailey and gave her Benjamin, the telephone rang. He cringed when Sawyer picked it up. The decibel level was already unbearable.

"This is Sawyer, who's this?"

Dennis used hand gestures to indicate to Sawyer that he and Flo were taking the boys to the nursery.

Sawyer stood in the kitchen doorway, not taking his eyes off them. "Forget it, I've lost my appetite. I can't hear myself think with that brat screaming!" *Click.*

Sawyer barged into the nursery where both boys were getting a diaper change. "Why can't you shut that kid up?" His voice thundered over the cribs, causing Benjamin to start crying.

Flo turned to Sawyer, her eyes wide with indignation. "Now, mister, it's *your* yellin' them babies is reactin' to! Maybe if you could stop hollerin' we could git these tired young'uns to sleep! And it might help you think better."

"You don't know how I *think!*" His dark eyes were threatening.

"Yessir, that'd be a true statement," Flo said in a softer tone. "But I do know about them babies, and they ain't gonna settle down 'less we give 'em breathin' room. The sooner they stop cryin', the sooner we can *all* hear ourself think."

"Do whatever it takes!" Sawyer squeezed Flo's arm until she cried. "But shut those brats up, or I'm goin' to!" He held the gun to

Bailey's head. "If that kid doesn't stop crying, I'm going to hurt him! I mean it, I'm—"

"Why don't you let Flo and the babies leave?" Dennis said. "Hold *me* hostage. It's obvious that something's wrong with him, and you can't just make a baby stop crying. Why not let them go, and just keep me? It'll be less trouble for you."

"You think I'm *stupid?* That ol' woman and those babies are my ticket outta here. Maybe I'll just put that loudmouth kid outta his misery!"

Dennis's heart raced with fear. "What about keeping the three of us and releasing just him?"

"I'm not releasing any hostages! I'll kill you all before I compromise. And that loudmouth kid's gonna be first."

Dennis picked up Bailey and held him snugly against his chest. He felt the boy's legs draw up as he continued to scream. *Okay, God. I don't know if You're really there and You sure don't owe me anything. But Jennifer seems to think You've promised to take care of her and these babies. Please do whatever You can to keep these boys from getting hurt.*

Dennis glanced down at Flo, terror racing through him. "What should I do?" he mouthed.

"Here…lemme try walkin' with him, but I don' know if it'll help just now. This poor child may need to cry it out. There now, Bailey. Don't be carryin' on so."

Outside the apartment, Jordan Ellis had assembled the SWAT team, and they were ready and waiting.

"Jordan, what do you think?" Sheriff Hal Barker asked.

"We can't wait much longer. The tension's going to drive him over the edge. Listen to that baby screaming." Jordan took a handkerchief and wiped the anxiety from his forehead. "Our inside shooter says it's a no-go."

"Any family or friends who can plead with him?" Hal said.

Jordan shook his head. He glanced at his watch. "We can't find his brother. And the only friends he has are his comrades who're behind bars. Man, I'd like to take this guy out! I'd give anything if those babies weren't in there."

The phone rang in the kitchen. Dennis and Flo walked into the living room when Sawyer answered it.

"This is Sawyer. Time's up. Where's my plane?"

Dennis stood holding Benjamin against his chest, glad that he was asleep. Flo had finally gotten Bailey quieted down. She hummed softly as she stood holding him in her arms, gently rocking him from side to side.

"I'm tired of your lame excuses," Sawyer shouted. "Maybe I should kill all four hostages and show you at least *I* do what I say I'll do!"

Bailey started crying again. Then Benjamin woke up.

Sawyer threw the receiver at Bailey and hit Flo squarely on the shoulder. She choked back the tears as her trembling hands put the screaming baby in Dennis's arms and took Benjamin into her own.

Sawyer pulled the long phone cord across the floor until he had the receiver in his hand again. "Look, I can't stand this anymore! I gotta get off this phone and put an end to the racket once and for all!"

Sawyer slammed down the receiver and turned his wild gaze on Bailey. "Put the kid on the couch."

Flo began to whimper. Dennis didn't move.

"You deaf? I said, put him down, pretty boy. Or would you rather I shoot him right out of your arms?"

Dennis turned and put Bailey in Flo's free arm, then turned and stood between Sawyer and the others. "They're leaving. Flo, stay behind me, and let's move toward the French doors."

Sawyer seemed dumbfounded for a moment. "Don't be stupid, man. It's just some rug rat."

"You'll have to kill me first. Flo, let's go." Dennis side-stepped toward the French doors, Flo and two crying babies behind him.

"Hold it right there! I'll shoot. I swear I will." Sawyer took a step forward, his arm extended, his finger on the trigger. "You think I'm bluffin'? Get outta the way, or you're *all* gonna die!"

Dennis gauged the distance between him and the gun…then let out a loud shriek and kicked Sawyer's right hand with all the force he could deliver.

The gun fell to the floor, and Dennis dove for it. He had it in his hand when Sawyer jumped on his back, knocking the gun loose. They grappled for it until Dennis finally slid it under the coffee table.

Sawyer lunged at Dennis's throat and started to strangle him. Dennis pushed him off, then rolled him face down on the floor and straddled him, delivering one angry blow after another until Sawyer stopped fighting. Then Dennis pulled Sawyer's arms behind his back and yanked until he begged for mercy.

Dennis was suddenly aware of the boys' crying. He looked up and saw Flo, a baby in each arm, tears streaming down her face, and realized it was over. He struggled to keep his composure. After that, everything was a blur until he saw the SWAT team burst into the living room.

TWENTY-FIVE

It was 3:30 A.M. Dennis sat in the dark on the side of the hide-a-bed, his bag packed, his emotions on overload. The FBI had stayed long enough to get statements from him and Flo and to take pictures.

Dennis got up and walked into the living room and stood by the window. He pulled back the lacy curtain and looked outside. The media presence was growing. If he stayed until morning, he would be inundated with questions, and his picture would be taken and plastered across the news. Nothing he had done felt heroic. He didn't see how anyone could have stood by and watched Sawyer murder two helpless babies and a sweet old woman.

He sighed. Leaving Flo this way would be harder than he thought…but not as difficult as what he was about to do.

Dennis walked across the hardwood floor to the nursery door and peeked in at the two tiny boys in blue sleepers. He tiptoed over to the cribs and ever-so-gently picked up Benjamin. He held the child warmly against his chest, memorizing the moment, feeling his son's heart beating against his own. His eyes brimmed with tears. Dennis looked down at Bailey, knowing he would wake up if he were moved, and imagined for a moment that he was holding him, too.

Dennis pressed his lips to Benjamin's cheek. *Please don't hate me for this. I'm just not ready to be your father. You deserve better. Someday you'll understand.*

But even as he thought the words, Dennis realized he had never understood or come to peace with why his own father had left.

Dennis gently laid Benjamin in the crib and touched his cheek one last time. He stood studying his two sleeping sons and sketched the moment in his memory, then wiped the tears from his face and left the nursery.

He went back to the study and rummaged through the desk until he found a pen and some paper and left Flo a note propped against a stack of books.

Dennis stepped over to the window and twisted the rusty lock until it finally gave way and he was able to raise the window. He picked up his leather bag and dropped it on the ground outside, then squeezed through the opening and landed on his feet in the alley. He walked down the alley and then cut through a side yard toward the curb where he had parked the rental car.

Dennis stole a last look at the old house-turned-clinic, where the media vigilantly waited outside for an interview with Ben Stoller. He got in the car and slowly pulled away from the curb, relieved that he wouldn't be around to face the fanfare.

Mark Steele turned on the open sign at Monty's Diner and then held the door as Tuesday's early-morning customers filed in.

"Did ya hear what that Sawyer fella nearly did?" Mort said.

"It's on the front page." Mark handed him a newspaper and herded him toward the counter. "Come on in, everybody. Rosie's got your coffee poured."

"Everybody want your usual?" Rosie Harris asked.

A half dozen heads nodded, then the early crowd sat at the counter and buried their heads in the *Daily News*.

Mark Steele stood behind George Gentry and read over his shoulder.

"BIG BEN" STRIKES ON TIME
Hostage-Turned-Hero Seizes the Moment

Mark read every detail of last night's hostage ordeal and could hardly believe the drama that had unfolded. "Anybody heard of this Ben Stoller?" he finally said.

"Nope." George Gentry took a sip of coffee. "But I'm impressed. It took guts to put himself in front of a loaded gun to protect that woman and those babies."

"A guy threatening to shoot a defenseless little baby..." Rosie said. "Gives me cold chills to think he's walked down the same sidewalks as us."

"The guy did wrong," Mort said. "But he was tryin' to save all of ya from the worst."

"Sawyer and his kind *are* the worst," Jim Hawkins said.

George nodded. "You got that right. We have more to fear from violence than from any virus. They've already killed three, shot eight, burned a whole wing of the hospital, firebombed seven homes, held hostages, and almost murdered an innocent baby."

"And that doesn't begin to cover the emotional scars," Jim said. "Mort, *none* of this would've happened if the CWD hadn't taken things into their own hands."

"Well, Jimbo, they mighta saved *yer* life."

"Oh, gimme a break," George said. "A couple of days ago you were tryin' to tell us they were bioterrorists *spreading* the virus. You just like to hear the sound of your own voice."

A grin spread across Mort's face. "Keeps things interestin'."

Jim looked at George who looked at Mark.

"You want to give him the boot again?" Mark said, trying to keep a straight face.

"Come on now," Mort said. "I ain't had my pancakes. Let's call a truce till we're full up."

"Oh, let him stay." Rosie winked at Mark. "This place wouldn't be the same without Mort's rabble-rousing, and you know it. You guys eat it up. Been that way as long as I can remember."

Jennifer Wilson sat in bed, her breakfast tray in front of her, listening to the morning news on KJNX.

"There are unconfirmed reports that the mother of the infant twin boys may be the woman Sawyer used as a human shield before making his escape from the hospital. Though the identity of the twins is not being released, KJNX has learned that their first names are Bailey and Benjamin...."

Jennifer sighed. It was just a matter of time before she would have to struggle with another kind of isolation: trying to keep herself and her boys from being exploited by the media.

"We have not yet been able to speak with Ben Stoller, the young hostage who, authorities tell us, kicked the gun from Billy Joe Sawyer's hand and then overpowered him, ending the five-hour nightmare.

"Stoller would not talk to KJNX, but Flo Hamlin, the other caregiver at the clinic, told KJNX that Stoller put himself between Hamlin, who was holding the two babies, and Sawyer, who held a gun and threatened to kill them. Ms. Hamlin said she was crouched behind Stoller when she heard the gun go off and believes it's a miracle that Stoller was not hit.

"Unfortunately, that's all the information we have right now. Things are quiet this morning inside the clinic, and we're hoping soon to interview Ben Stoller and find out firsthand exactly what he was thinking. Jonathan, back to you...."

Jennifer's eyes filled with tears. *Thank you, Lord.* She was amazed that a stranger would risk his very life for her boys when their own father couldn't be bothered to give even a tiny part of his.

At the far end of *B* Corridor, Blake Thomas sat up in bed, awaiting a reunion with the parents he couldn't remember. He stared at his reflection in the mirror that folded out from the rolling table at his bedside. He looked ghastly…his face gaunt and covered with circular scabs, his eyes hollow, his lips cracked and sore. He heard footsteps and looked up.

A gray-haired man and a petite woman walked into the room, accompanied by Dr. Lionel Montgomery from the CDC. Blake's heart pounded.

Dr. Montgomery approached his bed. "Blake, your parents are here to see you. Remember what we talked about. Don't worry if this feels awkward and foreign right now. Your memory will come back."

Blake nodded.

The gray-haired man stepped forward. "Do you remember anything at all, son?"

Son? How strange that sounded. Blake studied his father's face. "No, not yet."

"It's all right, Blake," the woman said. "We're just so grateful you're alive. God answered our prayers."

Blake watched his mother's gratitude turn to tears and lamented that he could remember nothing about either parent when it was obvious they cared very much for him.

"I'm sorry…I just can't remember," he said weakly.

His mother touched his hand. "We're going to leave and let you rest. We'll be back later."

Blake's eyes remained fixed on his parents, hoping that something would register. But only one incident played over and over in his mind. Without knowing anything about himself or the details of his life, even that made no sense.

Ellen Jones sat at her desk at the *Baxter Daily News,* sipping coffee and rereading the front page. She was pleased with the reporting of last night's near-tragedy and could see the potential for a good human-interest story once she gained access to Ben Stoller. If there was ever a time this community needed a hero, it was now. She was startled by the sound of the phone ringing.

"This is Ellen."

"Ellen, it's Sarah Rice. I wanted you to be the first outside the hospital to know that Melissa Thomas has regained consciousness. Her fever's broken. She's pulled through."

"Oh, Sarah, I'm so happy for her…for the whole family…well, for all of us! Does she remember anything?"

"Very little. She remembers being in labor, but doesn't remember the details of what happened. She can't remember being married to Blake either. We feel confident all that will come back. Temporary amnesia for those who survive hemorrhagic fever is not uncommon."

"Isn't that a blessing for now?"

"We think so," Sarah said. "Heaven knows how Melissa will handle it when she does remember. We're just grateful she pulled through. But we're quite concerned about Drs. Helmsley and Gingrich. Their condition is deteriorating."

"That's not good news. Do you think it's because of their weakened state after being shot in the attack?"

"Maybe. But the EMT isn't improving either. Ellen, there's something else you should know—off the record."

"I'm listening."

"We learned on Saturday that in the village where Blake and Melissa were exposed to the virus nearly a hundred people have died."

"What!"

"I know we agreed to be open with you, but we decided to wait because the scenario here was completely different and we didn't want people to overreact—"

"And you think they *won't* after you've held back?"

"Ellen, our patients were being given supportive care in a sterile environment—a far cry from the primitive conditions in the village. We weren't looking for a high number of casualties."

"Then why didn't you just say that?"

"We were afraid information that sensitive would provoke another attack. And we didn't want that on our conscience. Can you imagine what KJNX would've done with it?"

"KJNX isn't the only game in town," Ellen said. "And frankly, I'm tired of paying for their transgressions. Besides, your withholding the truth did nothing to prevent the second attack."

"At least I can say with a clear conscience that it didn't happen because the CWD reacted to the death count in the village."

Ellen let a steely silence register her disapproval.

"Look," Sarah said, "surely you can appreciate what a tough call this was? How can one ever be sure of the right choice until after the fact?"

"I guess you're about to find out."

"Ellen, what good would it have done to worry the public over a hundred deaths that resulted largely from ignorance and inadequate medical facilities? We had every reason to believe the care we were giving the Thomas couple was the reason they were improving. Our ability to provide fluids, oxygen, and blood kept them from going into shock."

Ellen sighed. "And now?"

"Well, in spite of all that, things are suddenly looking grim for our virus patients."

Ellen was silent for a moment. "Sarah, I appreciate your candor 'off the record.' But you can't keep this out of the news."

"I know. That's why I called. Now that this Sawyer character is off the street, we feel we can be forthcoming with information. So, day after tomorrow, when the home quarantines have been lifted, we'll address the hard facts publicly in more detail. People will be less nervous then."

"Sawyer may be off the street, but KJNX isn't. And if they get wind of this, they won't wait to air it."

"There are only six people who know about the village, and you're one of them. Give me until Thursday; that's all I ask."

Dennis leaned his head against the window as the 747 began its descent into Denver on Tuesday afternoon. Except for the Rockies off to the west, the flat terrain around the Mile High City looked browner than he remembered and was quite a contrast from where he had just come.

He closed his eyes and could see the lush green hills and thick woodlands of the countryside around Baxter. Sketched in his mind were the rows of enormous shade trees overhanging the streets like leafy green awnings, insulating everything beneath them from the July sun.

A baby began to cry as the plane lost altitude, and for a moment, he almost forgot he didn't have to respond. He ignored the aching he felt and was vaguely aware that the Fasten Seatbelt sign was turned on.

Dennis yawned, his eyelids heavy. His grandfather wasn't expecting him until Thursday, so he decided until then just to go home and crash.

On Thursday morning, he would resume his life in Denver, letting his actions in Baxter serve as a ten-day penance. At least there was finally one unselfish deed to his credit. He wasn't a total loss.

TWENTY-SIX

When it was time for Thursday morning's press conference, Dr. Sarah Rice emerged from the hospital with Dr. Lionel Montgomery, Dr. Spencer McFarland, Dr. Yo Wong and Dr. Ivan Roesch. She spotted Ellen Jones and one of her reporters standing near the front. An impressive crowd had gathered, and there was also a sizeable media presence, including KJNX and the cable TV networks, which were carrying the press conference live. Security was tight.

At precisely 9:00 A.M., a hush began to fall over the crowd as Dr. Montgomery stepped up to the mike. He waited for the silence to settle, and then began speaking.

"Ladies and gentlemen, it is with the utmost degree of gratitude and satisfaction that I announce the home quarantines are officially over."

Cheers and applause resounded. Dr. Montgomery held up his hands and waited for the applause to subside.

"Members of all seventy households, including the seven involved in last Sunday's firebombing, continue to be symptom-free after a reasonable incubation period. Even as I'm speaking, safety monitors are taking down the quarantine signs and welcoming these families back into the community—healthy and safe."

Applause and shouts and whistles rose from the crowd.

"On behalf of the Centers for Disease Control, I cannot thank you enough as a community, and especially those of you who have personally endured the tedious days of the quarantine, for your cooperation and willingness to help prevent the spread of this virus. I am proud to say there has been no outbreak of the virus beyond B Corridor. That, my dear friends, was our goal, and we *have* succeeded."

Again applause resounded throughout the hospital grounds. Sarah looked at Ellen and smiled.

"At the same time, I want to reiterate what most of you already know: that Blake and Melissa Thomas have indeed survived the virus, and both are fully conscious. They are still recovering in B Corridor, but they are no longer at risk from the illness. They have fought the hard fight, and they have won."

The applause exploded and went on for quite some time.

"I want to take a moment to thank those who trusted the effectiveness of barrier nursing procedures and volunteered to help those in B Corridor. Your brave and unselfish efforts were a comfort in this horrible ordeal. You were the merciful ones, and I want to personally acknowledge you.

"And for those who reacted courageously during the surprise attacks on the hospital, your quick thinking enabled us to keep the virus securely quarantined. All of us owe you a debt of gratitude."

Another round of applause echoed through the crowd, and the five doctors joined in.

"Even though the home quarantines have been lifted, we are extending the quarantine in B Corridor because we began that ten-day quarantine over again after the firebombing and shooting. Therefore, those in B Corridor not exhibiting symptoms of the virus will be free to go home on Saturday morning.

"The other three patients in B Corridor, Dr. Melvin Helmsley and Dr. Allen Gingrich and EMT Clay Lindsay, continue to receive therapy. But since the CDC has been unable to identify the virus, there is no vaccine, and each patient must rely on his own natural ability to fight the virus. As you know, Drs. Helmsley and Gingrich are also recovering from gunshot wounds sustained in the hospital attack. Unfortunately, their injuries may have weakened their immune systems.

"I want to make public what the CDC has learned from the investigative team that traced this virus all the way back to the Amazon basin in South America. Our team, joined by field officials from the World Health Organization, journeyed to the river village where Blake and Melissa Thomas spent time in their missionary endeavors, and found the virus had claimed nearly a hundred lives."

A rumble went through the crowd, but Dr. Montgomery held up his hands and continued.

"But here in Baxter, we do not anticipate an outbreak of this nature. We immediately quarantined the virus and all persons exposed. We have maintained barrier nursing to prevent the spread of this virus to medical personnel. We have provided fluids, oxygen, and blood as part of our patients' supportive therapy. None of this was available to the people of that remote village. If they'd had what is available to us, I'm confident there would've been few victims.

"That's the bad news. The good news is that no other people in the tribes along the river have become symptomatic, and it appears the virus is nonexistent anywhere else in the region. The remains of those who died in the village were burned, and there have been no new cases reported. CDC and WHO officials now feel that the virus there is no longer active.

"The host is believed to have been a rare breed of Mahat monkey called a Magondallias, which a young native boy trapped and attempted to tame. The monkey bit the child several days before Blake and Melissa Thomas left the village. The boy developed a high fever, and the Thomas couple went to visit him the day of their departure, which we believe was their point of exposure. A few days later, the boy died and the virus quickly swept through the village. The rest is history.

"Thanks to our strict adherence to the conditions of the quarantine, both in homes and at the hospital, *we* have had no casualties from the virus, and what could have been catastrophic, appears to be contained. Thanks to those of you who endured the ten-day quarantine, we have prevailed."

Applause spread throughout the crowd. Cameras flashed. People whistled.

Dr. Rice felt a tap on her shoulder. Her secretary whispered something in her ear and she felt the blood drain from her face. She looked out at the jubilant faces of those who had embraced Dr. Montgomery's words. Was this the time to say something? She decided it wasn't.

Dennis had watched the hospital news conference on CNN while he downed his fourth cup of coffee. He sat at the breakfast bar staring at Martha Sullivan's business card. He might as well get it over with. He picked up the phone and dialed.

"Baxter Memorial Hospital."

"Would you connect me to the nurse's station in OB?"

"One moment."

Dennis felt like a kid in the principal's office. *Come on…be there.*

"This is Martha Sullivan."

"Martha, this is—"

"Dennis?"

"Uh, yes, ma'am."

"Where are you? Why did you disappear like that?"

Dennis couldn't remember what he planned to say, and the only thing between him and Nurse Sullivan was dead air.

"I should've known," she said. "I had you figured right in the first place."

"Martha, please don't tell Jennifer. Isn't it better that she thinks Ben Stoller was real? The truth will crush her. She doesn't need that."

"You've left me in a very awkward position, Dennis. Just how do you think I'm going to justify having let a *stranger* care for two newborns when I don't even have an address on him? The media is all over this."

"I'm sorry."

"Sorry doesn't cut it."

"It's better this way."

"For *whom?* Look, I've got work to do."

"So, you won't tell Jennifer it was me?"

"I'll try to dance around it for her sake. But I'm not going to lie for you." *Click.*

Dennis hung up the phone. He felt the sting of her disapproval but felt sure she wouldn't say anything. He went into the bathroom and stood in front of the mirror. He picked up his razor and started to shave, carefully avoiding the bruised and swollen cheek that had encountered the butt end of Sawyer's gun. When he finished, he wiped the shaving cream from his face and looked at his reflection. *Some hero.*

He stepped into the shower and let the warm, soothing water cascade over him, hoping to wash every ounce of guilt down the drain. Jennifer would have no trouble stealing the heart of a respectable man who would stay committed to her and help her raise the boys.

Dennis stepped out of the shower and dried off, then walked into his room and slipped on a pair of khakis, a striped shirt and a tie. As he combed his hair and splashed on some cologne, it occurred to him that he hadn't missed his job or his life while he was in Baxter.

Dennis grabbed his keys, the video, and the sketches, then headed out the front door. Playing the part of Ben Stoller had been a great starring role, but that's where the credits ended.

Jed Wilson took Rhonda's hand and walked up the steps of the Hunter Clinic. He and Rhonda showed their IDs to the FBI agents posted there. When they were cleared, Jed opened the door, and they entered the foyer and walked to the French doors.

"This is it, babe." Jed knocked on the door. "We're really going to take the boys home."

"My knees feel like rubber," Rhonda said. "After what happened the other night, I just want them out of here."

The door opened and an elderly woman with curly white hair appeared, donning a big smile.

"Flo!" Jed said.

"Well, you must be the Wilsons. So nice to make your acqain- tance. I been expectin' you."

Rhonda threw her arms around Flo. "We're so glad you're all right. What a horrible ordeal you've been through."

"It was somethin' awful, sure enough. Praise the Lord, them babies is fine."

"We're grateful to you and Ben. Wish we could've met him," Jed said. "We feel as if we know you both."

"You folks woulda liked that young man. He's a fine fella. Loved them babies, too. You shoulda seen how he took to bein' a daddy. Why, you'd a thought them babies was his own, the way he carried on."

"I'm dying to see them!" Rhonda said.

"Where's my manners?" Flo said. "Come on in, them babies is bright-eyed and bushy-tailed like they knowed you was comin' for 'em. They're in here," she said, leading the way to the nursery. "They're already fed, dressed, and sittin' in their infant seats... Looky, boys, who's here to see you. It's your grandmama and granddaddy."

"Uh, Flo," Jed said. "Who's who?"

Just then one of the babies started to cry.

"Betcha can figure it out now!" She chuckled, her dark eyes twinkling.

"Bailey!" Rhonda said. "Can I pick him up?"

"Go on now," she said. "He's probably needin' a diaper change."

Rhonda picked him up. "Well, hello, Bailey. Oh, dear, now I know why you're raising such a *stink*. You really could've waited until we got to know each other better." She laid him on the changing table.

"So, this one's Benjamin." Jed said. "How in the world do you tell them apart?"

"Oh, they're different as night and day, but you just gotta be around 'em to tell it. Bailey don't mind tellin' you what he wants. I expect he'll be runnin' for president one o' these days." She chuckled. "Now Ben there—he don't make much fuss about nothin'. You hafta watch after him a li'l more 'cause he don't always know what he needs."

"You're really going to miss them, aren't you?" Jed said.

"I suppose I am." Flo blinked to clear her eyes.

"We hope you'll come visit them, don't we, Rhonda?"

"Absolutely! In fact, why don't you come see Bailey right now and make sure I've got this thing fastened so it won't fall off."

"Oh, them newfangled things is real easy once you get used to 'em. I kinda like 'em now. Sure beats wringin' out them ol' cloth ones."

Jed heard a knock on the door and then footsteps walking toward the nursery.

A middle-aged woman stood in the doorway. "Hello, I'm Martha

Sullivan. I don't know if you remember me, but I was working the shift the morning your daughter delivered the twins."

"Sure I remember you." Jed extended his hand.

"Me, too." Rhonda put a dab of waterless soap on her palm and rubbed her hands together.

Martha smiled. "Flo has the boys ready to go, I see. She's done an amazing job with very little help since Ben left."

"What can you tell us about him?" Jed asked.

"Not much," she said. "He showed up right after the hospital was firebombed, able and willing to help. Flo assumed he was from the agency and let him in. All her volunteers had backed out because they thought your daughter had the virus. By the time we knew it was a false alarm, Ben was already in place and working out very well."

Flo nodded. "Can't imagine nobody better with them babies."

"We'd sure like to thank him," Jed said. "Do you have his address and phone number?"

Martha blushed. "I can't seem to locate any paperwork on Ben."

"He left me a note," Flo said. "Read it for yourself and see if it tells you anythin'." Flo took the note from her apron and handed it to Jed.

He read the note out loud.

Dear Flo,

I hope you'll forgive me for slipping away like this. My work here is essentially done, and I don't want to face the media. I don't see myself as a hero. But if the babies' mother does, she'll be proud of the names she gave her sons and this will make a great story to tell them someday. She doesn't have to meet me for that to happen.

This week working with you, I felt like I had found the grandmother I never knew. I'll always remember the kind and unselfish way you took care of Bailey and Benjamin.

You're a good person, Flo, and you brought out the best in me. I'll never forget you.

Your friend,

Ben

"Such a nice kid," Jed said.

The old woman's eyes brimmed with tears. "Them media folks is still tryin' to find out where he is. They ain't givin' up nohow, but nobody seems to know anything about him. I ain't got nothin' to tell 'em neither. Ben Stoller come here as an answer to my prayer for help and ended up savin' our lives."

Jed handed the note back to Flo. "Yeah, it was no accident he happened to be here. Did he ever say where he's from?"

"Oh, he said somethin' about rich kinfolk in Colorado, but best I can tell, he come to me straight from God."

TWENTY-SEVEN

Dr. Sarah Rice sat at her desk, her face in her hands. She heard footsteps and looked up into the eyes of Dr. Lionel Montgomery.

"Nothing like having someone drop a bomb on you while you're in front of the cameras," he said. "How's your headache?"

"Throbbing." Sarah rubbed her temples. "I'm still in a state of shock. Dr. Helmsley dead? Dr. Gingrich in a coma?"

"You hid your reaction well. I saw a replay of the press conference."

"I wasn't about to rain on your parade, Lionel. The crowd was so excited that this thing was almost over."

Dr. Montgomery pulled up a chair and sat down.

Sarah searched his eyes and grimaced. "What now?"

"The EMT has taken a turn for the worse."

"Oh, no…"

"You can't let this get to you. We're doing everything we know to do, but these people were high risk."

"I know, Lionel. I was just ready to get out from under the stress."

"Spencer says morale is down in *B* Corridor," he said. "Perhaps we should have a meeting to reassure the healthy ones that the degree of risk hasn't changed."

She nodded. "Sounds like a good idea. The last thing we need now is paranoia *inside* the hospital."

Dr. Rice and Dr. Montgomery held a meeting with those still quarantined in *B* Corridor, each of whom was outfitted in gown, mask, goggles, and gloves.

"I want to emphasize that these unfortunate developments have not increased the risk factor," Dr. Rice said. "All of you remain healthy well into the incubation period. The death of Dr. Helmsley and the worsening condition of the other two patients has been a setback to our emotional well-being, but certainly not to our procedural effectiveness. These medical professionals came into direct contact with the virus at its most dangerous stage and were at high risk. The odds of your leaving Baxter Memorial on Saturday morning are still excellent."

Dr. Montgomery nodded. "Even if the results of your blood tests come back showing antibodies for this virus, that doesn't mean you'll develop it. False positives are not uncommon. So, if you're symptom free on Saturday, you can go home."

Dr. Rice noticed that one of the nurses seemed dazed. "Beverly, do you have a question?"

"Uh, no," Beverly Stein said. "I think you've answered everything."

"All right then." Dr. Rice stood up. "Let me encourage all of you to be patient for just a couple more days."

As the group dismissed, Dr. Rice noticed that Beverly was still seated. She started to go back and say something to her, then noticed the time and remembered she had promised to call Ellen Jones with an update.

❦

Jennifer Wilson held the receiver to her ear and listened to her parents' excitement.

"Jen, they're beautiful!" Rhonda said. "I can hardly wait for you to see them."

"Tell me everything, Mom. Do they look like they did on the video?"

"Well, yes and no. I can tell they're the same babies, but their features look more defined. They're darling!"

"They take after their grandfather," Jed said. "Spittin' image."

"Really?" Jennifer said.

"Honey, they don't look a thing like Jed. Actually, they have *your* mouth. When Bailey fusses, his lower lip quivers just like yours."

"Oh, like *that's* adorable!"

"Actually, it is," Rhonda said. "Just think, Jen. By this time on Saturday, they'll be in your arms."

"Mom, I'm so ready. After everything that's happened, I just want out of here. It's so depressing. They've assured me that my going home won't pose any risk to the boys—or anyone else."

"Well, we've talked to Dr. Harmon," Rhonda said. "He got released from quarantine today, too. No physician has more of a stake in the boys' well being than the man who brought them into the world. He says we can trust everything the CDC is telling us concerning quarantine procedures. He's very comfortable with your coming home Saturday."

"Jen, have you thought of middle names yet?" Jed asked.

"Actually, I have. I think you'll be pleased, but I don't want to make the decision final until I actually see them. I love their first names."

"Me, too," Rhonda said. "I'm telling you, these boys are absolutely beautiful. Oh, listen to me...I used to run from grandmothers who talk this way!"

"Hey, Mom, it's music to my ears. Brag all you want. I can hardly wait to get home."

"We're so anxious to see you. I know what you've been through has been horrible, but you're going to be all right, and you have these two adorable little lives to share yours with."

"It's weird, but having such 'near misses' all week, and the twins almost killed…" Jennifer paused to gather her composure. "I finally stopped worrying about how it's going to work out raising two boys. I'm so grateful that all of us survived that I'm ready to take on the challenge. God will show me how to manage if I'll just trust Him."

"Sounds like you've got a better handle on things," Jed said.

"I'm just so ready to get on with life. By the way, have either of you heard from Mark?"

"He's in Nashville for a meeting," Rhonda said. "But he called when he heard about Sawyer and the whole hostage thing. He sounded pretty shook up. He's coming home this weekend."

"That's a shock," Jennifer said.

"Oh, you know your brother," Rhonda said. "It might be a while before he warms up to the babies, but he cares about *you.*"

"Where are we going to put him?" Jed asked. "His old bedroom's a nursery."

There was a long pause and Jennifer could feel the wheels turning on the other end.

Rhonda laughed. "Ohhh…what a great opportunity for some *male bonding.* Maybe it's time Uncle Mark got with the program."

Dennis drove his black Toyota 4Runner down the wide, shady avenue of the old Denver neighborhood and turned into the driveway of a three-story gray stone mansion. He spotted the name on the mailbox and smiled. *Bailey.* A little twinge reminded him that the name had now taken on a double identity.

Dennis got out of the car and started up the stone walkway lined on both sides by neatly trimmed privet hedges. The manicured emerald green lawn was shaded with cottonwood, oak, and maple trees. The flower beds along the front of the house held a menagerie of colorful summer flowers. Everything about this place reflected the personality of a man in charge. Dennis smiled. Not one leaf had dared to fall on his grandfather's freshly mowed lawn.

Dennis rang the bell and waited, and then remembered Thursday was the housekeeper's day off. He put his key in the lock, opened the front door, and disarmed the security system. An envelope with his name on it was propped on the entry hall table. He opened it and began reading.

Dennis,
I've checked in to Patrick Bailey Memorial Hospital. Please see me before you go back to work. There's something I need to talk to you about.
Grandpa

Dennis laughed out loud. *Patrick Bailey Memorial Hospital.* His grandfather had given so much money to East Side Hospital in the thirty years since Dennis's grandmother died that he was determined it would be named after him someday. *I wonder what's going on.*

Dennis called his mother's house and got no answer, so he tried her car phone. Still no answer. He hadn't bothered to return even one of the numerous messages she had left on his machine, but he wondered why she hadn't at least mentioned there was something going on with his grandfather.

Dennis reset the security alarm and locked the front door. He began walking swiftly down the front walk to his SUV, wondering if he should be scared or mad.

∽o∾

Beverly Stein ran her finger round and round the smooth rim of the glass and realized the ice had melted. She looked up at the clock and decided she couldn't stand it any longer. She picked up the phone and dialed Dr. Rice's extension.

"This is Dr. Rice."

"Dr. Rice, this is Beverly Stein."

"I was going to call you. You seemed concerned earlier. Is something wrong?"

"Do you think I could talk with you in person? I wouldn't ask, but something's come up that might be important. And since I can't leave *B* Corridor, I need you to come here as soon as possible. I apologize for the inconvenience. I'm not sure where to turn." Her voice was shaking.

Dr. Rice looked at her watch. "I have a conference call in fifteen minutes, so it might be forty-five minutes or so. Is that soon enough?"

"Yes. Thank you."

Dennis walked to Room 782, where the lady at the information desk had told him he could find his grandfather. He knocked and peeked inside. The room was vacant and had been made up. Dennis heaved a sigh of disgust and went back to the nurses' station.

"Excuse me, ma'am, but could you tell me where I can find Patrick Bailey? The lady in the lobby said Room 782, but he's not there and his name's not on the door. We must've gotten our wires crossed."

A nurse looked up from her paperwork. "I'll help this young man." She pushed back her chair and walked out to where Dennis was standing in the hallway. "Mr. Bailey was just moved to another room and gave us strict instructions not to publicly post his room number."

"I'm his grandson. What's the deal?"

"Oh, then you're Dennis? He said you were coming."

"So, would you please tell me what's going on?"

"There's no need to be alarmed, but your grandfather had a stroke just after checking in yesterday morning."

"What?"

"Mr. Bailey's blood pressure has been dangerously high. He waited too long before coming to the hospital. The doctor will need to explain the details, but he's being carefully monitored. We have him in a special suite. I use the term loosely, but it's much more like home than a hospital." She motioned Dennis to follow her. "He's able to talk, but you'll notice his left side has been affected."

"What do you mean *affected?*" Dennis said.

"The paralysis could've been much worse. And he'll probably regain most of the lost function. But there's a bigger problem: We need to get his blood pressure down and keep it down so he doesn't have another stroke. With his temperament, that's been a real challenge."

"Yeah, I can imagine." Dennis felt numb as the nurse stopped in front of a dark wood door with a fancy brass handle.

"Your mother just left to run some errands and said she plans to be back in an hour. Mr. Bailey needs to rest, so ten minutes is the limit, all right?"

"Uh, sure. I can't believe this. My grandfather's a control freak. This must be awful for him."

"I'm sure it is. I've never known a stroke victim who enjoyed feeling helpless."

"Yeah, but you don't understand, my grandfath—"

"Oh, I've *dealt* with your grandfather. I think I *do.*" Her eyes widened and she gave Dennis a knowing look. "Ten minutes, okay?"

Dennis nodded. He put his hand on the brass handle, and looked over at the nurse. "Is he going to pull out of this?"

"We need to get his pressure down, Dennis. He's in the best possible hands, but no one can play God."

Dennis raised his eyebrows. "How long have you known my grandfather?"

Beverly Stein sat in her room, aware of footsteps coming down the hall. The door to her room opened and she looked up.

"Dr. Rice…thank you for coming. I know how busy you are."

Dr. Rice pulled up a chair and sat down. "What's this about?"

"You're aware I suffered from smoke inhalation after the attack and have been quarantined with the others?"

"Yes, of course."

"Well, something may have happened last night. I keep hoping I'm imagining it, but I don't dare take a chance."

"What do you mean?"

"Dr. Rice, I'm a sleepwalker. That's never been an issue on the job before, and I honestly didn't give it a thought. But last night I may have entered the isolation area. I have this sense that I was in there without protective clothing and don't know if I was dreaming or if it really happened."

"Surely someone would've seen you."

Beverly sighed. "You'd think so. But what if I did enter the isolation area? Every unprotected person who treated Blake and Melissa Thomas is either dead or dying—plus a hundred people in that village. I'm scared. What should I do?"

"Well, for starters, let's not panic. Pastor Thomas and his wife haven't developed the virus even though they were in close proximity to both Blake and Melissa. Neither have the nurses who were in the ER. What we need to do is keep you away from the others who are essentially out of the woods. Beverly, look at me…we'll monitor you carefully. Perhaps you were dreaming and this never happened. But if it did, be encouraged that Blake and Melissa survived it. You're healthy. Don't look for trouble. It may never happen."

"Dr. Rice, my husband and I don't have children. I'm all he's got. He won't be able to handle it if something happens to me. I can't die. I just can't…"

"No one says you're going to. You did the right thing by coming forward when you did. I'll call Dr. Montgomery and advise him of this development, but you couldn't be in better hands."

Dennis slowly pushed the heavy wooden door open just enough to see one end of the hospital suite where his grandfather was being treated. What he saw through the crack in the door looked more like a bed-and-breakfast than a hospital room. A cherry armoire stood angled in the left corner. A long, cherry dresser was centered on the back wall, and above it hung a framed oil painting of Pikes Peak. The colors were rich and tasteful. Dennis had never seen a hospital room this nice.

When the door was all the way open, he saw his grandfather lying in a traditional hospital bed, hooked up to all sorts of ominous looking machines. His heart sank.

Dennis knocked gently and entered the room. "Grandpa?" he said softly. "It's me."

His grandfather's steely blue eyes opened wide, and he looked directly at Dennis without saying anything.

"I told you I'd be home on Thursday, so here I am…they told me what happened."

There was silence for a half a minute or so. His grandfather seemed to be concentrating on how to make the words come out. "Glad…you're home." His voice was weak.

"Grandpa, don't try to talk now. We'll have plenty of time for that later. I just wanted you to know I came back like I said I would."

His grandfather seemed to be focused on the black-and-blue knot on Dennis's cheek. "TV says…Ben's…a hero." He seemed to push the words out.

"Not really. Anyone else would've done the same thing. But I'm home now. Ben Stoller's history."

His grandfather's gaze felt intrusive. "Did you…bring the sketches?"

"Uh, yeah sure. They're out in the car."

"Get them," he whispered.

"Grandpa, they told me I could stay only ten minutes. How about if I bring them next go-around?"

"Now." His eyes were more demanding, though his voice was weak.

"All right. Can I get you anything else?"

"The…video."

"Okay, Grandpa. I'll be right back."

Dennis hurried down the hall and into the elevator. He got out on ground floor and ran to his car. He grabbed the sketches and the video but doubted that his grandfather had the stamina at the moment to appreciate either.

Beverly Stein sat picking at a cold dinner tray, the telephone receiver held to her ear. How was she supposed to console her husband?

"Frank, we have to wait it out, that's all. What choice do we have?"

"This is a rip, Bev! I don't know why you hadda work this assignment in the first place."

"I can't undo what's done."

"I hate this. Why didn't someone stop you?"

"No one saw me; what can I say? Besides, I've worked so many shifts in *B* Corridor, who would pay attention if they saw me walking around?"

"Well, they're sure payin' attention now!"

"Be nice, Frank. They're doing what they can. Plus, I'm in the hands of the Great Physician like Pastor Thomas says. Don't I wish I had faith like that?"

"Why, what good did it do him? He still lost his granddaughter. Plus his son and daughter-in-law have been to hell and back. Not that I believe in hell, but fighting fires is as close as I wanna get."

"Well, it's amazing. Pastor Thomas got a little emotional during the ordeal, but he was like a rock. He said all along that God had a plan and that He was in control."

"Oh, well, that makes me feel a lot better! This is all God's fault, for cryin' out loud?"

"Pastor Thomas didn't say it was His *fault*—just that He wouldn't waste the opportunity to make something good out of all this."

"That's beautiful, Bev. But I doubt if God cares much about what's goin' on down here. If He did, He'd certainly do a better job."

"Frank!"

"Well, why'd all this hafta happen? And why to us? What makes God decide who's a schlemiel and who isn't? What'd we do to make Him mad anyway? I wonder if your pastor friend can answer that one. You know I think religion's a crock. I won't go to the synagogue either, so don't get mad at me. At least I'm consistent."

"I'm not mad, Frank; I'm scared. I'm just trying to be as positive as I can. It's not easy being here without you either." She started to cry.

"Aw, honey, I'm sorry. I've been so busy worryin' about myself that I wasn't even thinkin' how you must be feelin'. I just can't believe this is happenin'."

"Listen, Frank, I can't talk anymore right now. I'm planning to come home in ten days. If you want to help, keep the laundry caught up."

"That's another reason you needa come home," he said. "One lousy red sock turned all my underwear pink. I'm humiliated."

"Pink?" She laughed. "You've got on pink boxer shorts under your bunker gear?"

"Yeah, I'm gettin' dressed in the bathroom at the station. If the guys find out, I'll never live it down. Don't leave me, Bev. I'm no good with a washin' machine."

"For cryin' out loud, Frank. Try using bleach. Might help you save face till I get home." There was a long pause. She knew he was getting emotional. "Don't worry. I'm not going anywhere. I just thought of something scarier than the virus: *your mother,* rest her soul, chasing me all over the hereafter, reminding me I had the gall to die and leave her son the brave firefighter in wrinkled, pink shorts. She had enough trouble already when she found out I didn't iron them—but *this?* I'd never live it down, not even in death."

Beverly started to laugh and then laugh harder at the image of Rachel Stein waiting in the hereafter with an iron in one hand and a bottle of bleach in the other. She and Frank laughed until they cried, and then an aching silence filled the space between them.

"I love you, Frank. I'm not leaving. We're just not ready."

"I'll never be ready," he said. "You're my life."

As Frank said the words, Beverly considered how uncertain life had become. And for the first time, she seriously wondered what was on the other side of death's door.

TWENTY-EIGHT

When Dennis got back to the hospital suite, his grandfather was asleep. He set the pencil sketches on the bedside table and stood looking at a frail version of the man he knew. The stroke had affected his grandfather's left side, but the distortion to his face was actually minor.

Dennis could have sketched him from memory. The old man had a full head of unruly white hair that reminded Dennis of uncombed cotton. His aging skin was lined and flawed like fine leather, and his nose sharp like his disposition.

Patrick Bailey was a powerful moneymonger who exercised little tact or sensitivity. Yet everything his grandfather touched seemed to turn to gold—except for the people, who often turned sour. If pretty women were Dennis's weakness, financial profits were his grandfather's.

The Patrick Bailey Insurance Agency was nothing more than an investment toy to his grandfather, who had hired the most congenial and ambitious agents he could find. Within five years, it became so successful that there were now sixteen on staff, including Dennis, and the agency was doing millions.

At the moment, this crusty financial whiz seemed anything but fierce, and it was unsettling to Dennis seeing him so weak. He glanced at the digital numbers on the machine next to the bed. His grandfather's blood pressure was still way too high.

The old man stirred and his eyes opened. He seemed to focus for a few moments before he spoke. "Did you…bring them?"

"Yeah, they're right here." Dennis picked up a stack of pencil sketches and put them in his grandfather's right hand.

The old man squinted, studying the sketch on top. "Is this…my namesake?"

Dennis looked on the back where he had written the name. "No, that's Ben."

The old man's eyes remained fixed on the sketch. "*Your* name-sake."

Dennis felt his ears get hot. He fumbled through the stack, pulled out a different sketch, and put it on top. "Uh, this one's Bailey, Grandpa. He's the resourceful one. Jennifer won't have to worry about this kid. He'll find a way to get whatever he needs."

His grandfather mused. "Kid needs a dad."

Dennis felt the tears sting his eyes. Past and present hit head-on, and he rushed from his grandfather's room toward the restroom he had seen in the hallway. He closed the door and turned the lock. By then everything was a blur. Dennis leaned his hands against the door, hung his head, and let the tears go.

Blake Thomas lay in his hospital bed, thinking back on the trip home from South America and the welcome reception at the church. He remembered feeling both exhilarated and exhausted when he went to bed, and then waking up achy and hot, unable to focus.

It had all come back to him…Melissa's fever…blood on his pil-low…blood on his fingers…standing…stumbling…falling…retching…spinning…vomiting…shaking…praying.

But Blake vividly remembered something else. It must have been a dream, but it seemed so real…

He looked up into the penetrating eyes of an enormous being clothed in light with magnificent wings. The angel's arms held a lifeless baby who suddenly turned into a young woman and stood up. She smiled at Blake and Melissa, her eyes exuding love, even without words. The angel took her hand and they disappeared into the heavens, leaving a golden cordlike strand dangling from above.

Blake took hold of the loose end and examined the heavy strand, finding its texture peculiar, unlike anything he had ever seen or touched.

Woven on the strand were facial images of people he didn't recognize. And though the circumference of the strand was only several inches, the faces were distinct. He had an overriding sense that it was part of a huge, divine tapestry and was somehow being threaded through the circumstances of their baby's death…

When Blake had regained consciousness and was told their daughter had been stillborn, his heart seemed strangely insulated from the grief. And had he not recognized the unmistakable sense of God's peace from times before, he might have thought he was in denial. But he knew this was different.

Though Blake remembered almost nothing of the physical world during the time he was sick with the virus, he could see in his mind every vivid detail of this strange encounter.

Dennis splashed cold water on his face and waited for the splotchy redness to go away. Tears were not high on his grandfather's list of strengths.

Dennis looked at his watch. He'd been gone fifteen minutes. He combed his hands through his hair, then unbolted the lock and slowly pushed open the door, relieved that no one was waiting outside. He walked down the hall to the dark, wooden door.

He knocked gently and walked into the room, surprised to see his grandfather still holding the sketches. Dennis stood beside the bed. "Sorry, Grandpa. I'm not feeling well. Must be something I ate."

"Or something you *left*."

"Did you see the sketches I did of Flo? She was really something."

But his grandfather held the sketch of Bailey and continued to study it. "So this one's pushy?"

"I didn't say that, Grandpa. I said he's *resourceful*."

One side of his grandfather's mouth turned up slightly. "Same thing. What's their mother like?"

"What difference does it make? I'm not going to see her again. She can't stand me."

His grandfather turned his steely blue eyes on Dennis and held his gaze. "She liked Ben Stoller."

"He doesn't exist. It was act."

"That was some acting, Dennis. You could've won an Oscar," His voice sounded weak.

"Look, Grandpa, this is wearing you out. Why don't we talk later?"

"Might not be a later…let me finish." He sounded determined. "When your father skipped out, I knew Catherine needed my help to raise you, but I resented the intrusion. I didn't want you."

"Grandpa, I don't want to hear—"

"And I'm ashamed to admit…it was easier to bully you…than to build you up. But somewhere along the line, I started to care about you…a lot."

"You never told me that."

"Didn't know how." His grandfather's eyes dropped down to the sketch of Bailey. "Remember you said…you were ashamed of what people would remember about you if you died?"

"Yeah."

"Well, I'll tell you something, Dennis… I'm proud of what you did."

"It was an act, Grandpa."

"No, it wasn't. Without this pushy old goat breathing down your neck, you had room to be yourself."

Dennis's heart pounded. His face felt flushed. He swallowed the emotion, holding on to every word his grandfather said.

"We should both behave more like Ben Stoller." A tear rolled down his grandfather's cheek.

"Grandpa, you need to rest—"

"Let me say it…you have to ride herd on Bailey or he'll end up like me. And you have to build up Ben's confidence so Bailey won't run over him the way I did you."

"No! You told me to make this go away! I'm out of their lives now!"

"I didn't give you enough credit…why not *really* be…their hero?" His grandfather ran out of wind.

Dennis had no idea how to respond, and couldn't have anyway. The intense feelings were caught in his throat. He was startled by the sound of someone entering the room.

"Dad, I'm glad to see you're awake," Catherine Lawton said. She glared at Dennis. "So nice you could make it."

Blake sat at Melissa's bedside and held her hand, his thumb slowly moving back and forth across her wedding band. Her face was gaunt like his, her skin covered with the same unsightly ring-shaped scabs. Her eyes were closed, tears rolling down the sides of her face.

Blake had insisted on being the one to tell her about the baby. But he had expected her to say *something*. Her silent suffering was almost more than he could bear.

Melissa opened her eyes, wet with tears, and looked into his. He thought his heart would break.

Blake kissed her hand and held it to his cheek. This was not the time to tell her about the dream.

Blake slowly pushed the wheels of his chair down to Beverly Stein's room and saw the door was open. He knocked gently.

"Nobody here but us lepers," she said.

"It's Blake Thomas, Mrs. Stein. Mind if I come in?"

"Not if you cut the Mrs. Stein and call me Beverly."

He wheeled the chair next to her bed. "I hope you don't mind my barging in on you. I wanted to meet you."

"You did?"

"My dad told me they just put you in isolation, and I feel somewhat responsible. I'm really sorry."

"I don't blame you, Blake. It's just a random roll of the dice. Who can figure why such things happen? On the bright side, working in here has given me a chance to get to know your father. I like him. He's a strong man."

"My dad's amazing. I have such respect for him."

"Then you've got your memory back?"

"Yes." He noticed her staring at him and read the fear in her eyes. "Beverly, I know I look ghastly. I hope my being here isn't upsetting."

"Not at all. It's lonesome at this end of the hall. Besides, you're the only one who'll come near me without all that protective gear on. I don't like being the patient. How are you feeling?"

"Run-over," he said, "but grateful to be alive. I can't imagine how hard it would've been for Melissa to go through this alone."

"How's she doing?"

"So-so. Losing our baby was a real blow, of course."

"I'm so sorry for your loss," Beverly said.

"Thank you. Everyone's been kind. How're you holding up?" Blake was surprised to see the Gideon Bible on Beverly's nightstand.

"Me? I'm scared out of my skull that I'm going to die. But then, you and Melissa made it. Who knows?"

Dennis was in no condition for a confrontation with his mother and couldn't excuse himself fast enough. He snatched up the sketches and left his grandfather's room. He was waiting for the elevator when he heard footsteps.

"Oh no, you don't," his mother said. "I've been trying to get you to answer my phone messages for days. Where've you been?"

"I was busy, Mom. You never said anything was wrong with Grandpa or I would've called back."

"Couldn't you return my messages out of common courtesy, Dennis? Or were you holed up somewhere with one of your bimbos?"

"Mom, I'm not a kid anymore. Don't lay a trip on me because I don't call you every day. You should've left a message that something was wrong."

"Well, for your information, your grandfather's blood pressure was sky-high all weekend. Of course, *he* decided on Monday that if *he* couldn't get it under control by Thursday, *he* would check into the hospital. Well, I was frantic. I could've used a little support!"

"Then you should've said so."

"When he finally admitted he'd had tingling and numbness in his left hand, I nearly came unglued. Of course, my nagging didn't faze him."

"Mom, the nurse said he was already checked in when he had the stroke. What happened?"

"The obstinate old goat finally got scared enough to call me at five o'clock Wednesday morning. Twenty-three minutes after I got him checked in, he had a stroke. All I can say is it's a good thing he was already in the hospital when it happened—or it would've been much worse."

"Yeah," Dennis said. "I'm surprised he can talk as well as he can."

"Well, if they can't get his blood pressure down, he could have another one. And the only way I could get him to calm down and stop tormenting the staff was to have him put in the VIP suite. Of course, they were more than accommodating. If his condition declines, so will his contributions…" She put her hand to her mouth and turned away.

"Mom, don't cry. I'm here now."

"When you and your grandfather are a handful at the same time, the entire burden falls on me. I'm wearing out with it!"

Blake sat in his room for a few minutes after Dr. Lionel Montgomery left, letting the news sink in. He got in his wheelchair, pushed himself down the hall, and stopped outside Beverly Stein's room. He knocked gently. "May I come in?"

"Suit yourself." She sounded despondent.

He wheeled up to Beverly's bed. She was crying.

"I guess you heard Dr. Gingrich is dead," she said. "That leaves just me and one EMT."

"Dr. Montgomery told me. I feel bad that Melissa and I started this whole chain of events."

She turned to him. "You didn't ask for this any more than we did."

"I know. But that doesn't make me feel any better."

Beverly reached out and took his hand. "Let's blame it on the monkey." She smiled slightly.

"Yeah, the monkey."

"Health officials say that's what started it all, but I've never asked how you got exposed."

Blake set the brake on his wheelchair and stared at the tile on the floor. Was he ready to talk about this? "Uh, a ten-year-old boy named Abosiah."

"From the village?"

Blake nodded. "He caught this unusual monkey and brought it home, hoping to make a pet out of it. I can still see his face…he was so proud. Things went well for a couple of days until he tried to feed the monkey, and it bit him. A few days later, the boy started running a high fever. His hand was infected, so his mother applied some kind of leaves to the wound. But it didn't help."

"How'd you get exposed?"

"Our last stop before leaving on furlough was to see Abosiah. The poor kid was half-delirious. We prayed for him, and then Melissa held him in her arms, and I put cool cloths on his forehead." Blake blinked to clear his eyes. "We had to leave when the boat arrived and had no idea that's the last time we'd ever see him. I'm not sure it's hit me yet."

"So he was the baseline case?"

"That's what health officials think."

"And no one who had the virus survived it, right?"

Blake gazed into her worried eyes, praying for a suitable answer.

"I didn't think so," she said.

Dennis lay on the couch, a cushion under his head, his legs up over the back, thinking about what had happened at the hospital. Dennis had always longed for his grandfather's approval, and today the old man made up for thirty years of not caring.

If the truth were known, Dennis had resented his grandfather as much as the old man resented him. It would have been impossible to count the embarrassing moments his grandfather had put him through, or the feelings of abandonment he had left him with.

Patrick Bailey had been an authority figure to endure—and little else.

Why was his grandfather suddenly softening and pushing him toward the very situation he had been insistent that Dennis "take care of"? Dennis felt no more ready to be a dad than he did before he went to Baxter.

The phone rang and he grabbed it, hoping for a female distraction. "Hello, this is Dennis the debonair, who's *this?*"

"Sorry to disappoint you, Romeo," said his grandfather's attorney. "I need to talk to you about something. I've been trying to reach you all afternoon. After you left the hospital, it was my understanding you'd be *working,* but no one at the agency had heard from you. What a surprise."

"You should've left a message, Clark."

"I had other things to do," he said bluntly. "I need to get this out of the way. Are you available?"

"You mean *now?* This *minute?*" He loved to aggravate the man who had despised him since he was a kid.

"Look, if you're entertaining…"

Dennis laughed. "Lighten up, Clark. I'm just hanging out. Come in. I assume you're in the driveway." *Click.*

Dennis got up and peeked through a crack in the drapes and saw the silver Mercedes. As soon as Clark Rogers reached the front door, Dennis opened it.

"Hey, Clark. Nice to see you."

"Good evening, Dennis."

"So, what brings you to the prodigal grandson's house?"

"Business. May I sit down?"

"Sure. Sit anywhere you like. What kind of business?"

"Serious business, Dennis. That's s-e-r-i-o-u-s—in case you want to look it up. Shall I get right to the point?"

"I'm all ears."

"For some reason I will *never* understand, your grandfather has requested that I give you this letter involving a sizable sum of money."

"You're kidding? How sizable?"

"See for yourself." Clark gave a sigh of utter contempt, and handed Dennis an envelope. "Off the record, I think your grandfather has lost his mind."

TWENTY-NINE

D ennis lay in bed and turned on one side and then the other, the top sheet a tangled mess, the thermal blanket in a heap on the floor. What a night! He sat up, peeled off the sheet, and swung his legs over the side of the bed. He raked his hands through his hair and noticed a pink glow on the horizon. He moved his head from side to side until he heard his neck crack, then stood and stretched, glad to smell the coffee brewing.

He reached down to the nightstand and picked up the letter Clark Rogers had given him and walked out to the kitchen. He poured a cup of coffee, sat at the breakfast bar, and read the letter for the umpteenth time.

Dennis,

I'm giving this because I want to and don't have to justify it to anyone. The amount is $3,000,000. If you haven't fainted, let me explain how this is going to work.

Separate trust funds have been established for Bailey and Benjamin in the amount of $1,000,000 each, and may be accessed by their mother or legal guardian only for the express purpose of covering college expenses. When each boy graduates from college, and not before, he will be entitled to the remaining money in his trust fund, and may withdraw up to $50,000 per year until he turns thirty. After that, the remainder plus whatever interest accumulates is all his.

The other $1,000,000 is for you, and that will be the amount *after* taxes. Clark and I have worked out the details so that the entire million is yours whenever you want it. Consider it a reward for heroic behavior, or just another way for an old man to say he's proud of you.

There's one stipulation, and it applies only to the trust funds for the boys. *You* must explain it to Jennifer Wilson in person and get her signature notarized on the papers before July 31. After that, the deal's off the table. Clark thinks I've got a screw loose, but I've decided to entrust that responsibility to you. Seems appropriate that you be the one to deliver the good news.

I'm not good at saying it out loud, but I love you, Dennis.

Grandpa

Dennis stared at the last line, his chin quivering and his heart racing. He blinked to clear his eyes, and then read it again. *Why did you wait all these years to tell me?*

Jennifer Wilson sat next to the window in her hospital room and looked outside. She took in everything—the bluebird sky, the shade trees, the flowers, the butterflies, the birds. She could almost smell the fresh air that awaited her tomorrow and didn't even mind that it would be humid. She could hardly wait to hold her boys!

A baby squirrel climbed up on the window ledge and put its front paws on the glass.

"Hi, cutie." She eased her face closer to the glass when a knock on the door startled her. "Come in."

"It's me again," Blake said. "Am I disturbing you?"

"Are you kidding? I've been in here so long I'm tired of *myself*. Don't you dare leave!"

Blake wheeled his chair next to hers. "One more day and you'll be home with those twins."

"Uh, yes, I—"

"You don't have to hide your excitement. Melissa and I are happy for you."

"I know how badly you wanted your child."

"God knows that, too," Blake said. "He had other plans. I don't understand it, but I have a real peace that it's going to be all right."

"Is Melissa feeling better?"

"We had a good cry this morning, but she's accepting it. We both believe strongly that God's in control of what happens."

"I believe that, Blake. So why do I struggle to trust Him?"

"It's something we have to learn. I haven't got it mastered yet."

Jennifer leaned her head against the back of the chair. "Would you believe that after all I've been through, I'm still having trouble trusting Him to take care of things?"

"What do you mean?"

"Well, you know my story… I'm a single mom and was planning on a single baby. God decided to double my joy, but I'm responding by worrying twice as much. I've never had this kind of responsibility before, and I'm concerned about how I'm going to manage. I know it's useless to worry, but how do I not?"

"Maybe you're concentrating too hard on what *might* happen. Those 'what ifs' will drive you crazy."

"As a missionary, you're used to living by faith," Jennifer said. "You're light-years ahead of me."

"But the solution's the same for both of us," Blake said. "It boils down to faith. The more I reflect on who God is and what He's already done for me, the less I worry about how He'll do it again. He controls every aspect of my life, not just the finances."

"I'll be glad when I get to the place where I'm comfortable with that. It's so hard to accept why bad things happen to good people. Look at what happened to you and Melissa."

Blake paused, his eyebrows gathered. "Jennifer, do you believe everything in a Christian's life happens for a reason?"

"Yes, but it doesn't make sense to me."

"Would it surprise you that we believe the baby we lost had a purpose? And that she accomplished it?"

"Wow, I don't know if I would've ever considered it."

"Well, Melissa and I have. She wanted me to share something with you before you go home."

"Really?"

"Melissa's pretty intuitive…since you're a new mother, she figured you'd have a hard time with our baby's death. What I have to say is extremely personal, but we'd like to share it with you."

Jennifer listened intently while Blake told her the dream. She could feel his joy, and when he was finished, she dabbed her eyes and tried to process the implications.

"You think it was from God?"

There was a long pause.

"I say this cautiously: I believe it was. I feel wrapped in perfect peace, and I've never experienced this kind of peace any other way."

"Did you recognize any of the faces on the golden strand?"

"No. But I don't know that I'm supposed to. Maybe all God wants me to know is the child we never got to see had a purpose."

By eight o'clock, Dennis was standing in the hospital elevator, on his way up to see his grandfather. He knew his mother had a hair appointment and wouldn't be there until ten.

The elevator stopped on the seventh floor, and Dennis walked down the hall to the dark wood door. He stood outside and knocked gently, then slowly opened the door. His grandfather appeared to be asleep.

"Grandpa, are you awake?" he whispered. "Grandpa?..."

The old man's eyes opened. "I've been expecting you."

Dennis suddenly felt as if he had a mouthful of cotton. He shifted from one foot to the other and forgot everything he had planned to say. "Grandpa, I, uh—"

"You're welcome, Dennis."

"It's far too generous. I wasn't expecting it."

"Until I die, anyway."

"I didn't say that."

"You were thinking it."

"Grandpa, how can I thank you enough? Jennifer will never have to worry about Bailey and Benjamin's future."

"You mean *you* won't."

"Okay, I won't. Isn't that why you're doing this?"

"They won't get a penny until they're out of college."

"That's when they're really going to need it," Dennis said, immediately realizing the flaw in his reasoning.

"The way I see it, they're going to be entirely dependent till they're twenty-one."

"I see where this is going...forget it, Grandpa. I'm not equipped for it."

"Explain Ben Stoller."

"Will you stop? I played a part. That's all."

"Dennis, look me straight in the eye and tell me you were faking the feelings. You told me yourself you enjoyed it and were glad you went back."

"Because no one knew I was the father! They didn't expect much. I don't know how to be a dad. I never had one. I've never hung around one. And I don't handle commitments well."

"There's a first time…for everything."

"Look, Grandpa, you're not strong enough to argue about this. I really appreciate the trust fund for the boys and the generous amount you've offered me, but I'm not going to play dad. If that's what I have to do for the money, then I can't accept it."

"I may be a pushy old goat…but I'm a man…of my word." He looked exhausted and weak. "Just get the papers signed."

"Once I do that, will you let me get back to my life? No strings attached?"

"I won't bring up the money…I did that…for *me*…everything I do is for me…remember?"

"What about my job?"

"I've covered your tail often enough…if you have to take some time to get this done…I'll take care of it."

"Grandpa, you're exhausted. It's not a good idea for me to leave town right now."

"Go…I'm doing better…blood pressure is back…to normal. Going to take…a while to come out of this." His eyes were full of the Bailey determination Dennis didn't want to tangle with.

"Okay, Grandpa. I'll go talk to Jennifer and get the papers signed. I should be back by Tuesday at the latest."

"What's the hurry?"

Dennis was sure the right side of his mouth turned up slightly.

Beverly Stein sat in her room and started to file her nails, then realized there was nothing left to file. She sighed. The wait was maddening. She heard a knock on the door.

"Beverly, may I come in?" Blake said.

"Oh, sure. Welcome to death row with no chance for appeal."

"It can't be *that* bad."

"No? Since Dr. Gingrich died, feels like I'm in solitary confinement. Everyone hurries out of here. Makes me feel real secure, you know?"

"Yeah, I do," Blake said. "When they see my ugly scabs, they walk the other way. People are afraid of what they can't control."

"When everyone leaves tomorrow, this place will be a virtual morgue."

"But look on the bright side. None of those people got the virus, and you may not either. Besides, Melissa and I survived it."

"I might not be so lucky."

"Beverly, I don't believe luck had anything to do with it. God's in control of my life. He must have more for me to do. It wasn't time."

"So, what do you think: Is it *time* for me?" She blinked to clear her eyes.

"Only God can answer that, but I do know that worrying won't add a single hour to your life. Trusting the One who can give you peace makes more sense than worrying about something you have no control over."

"Easy for you to say. You just came through it."

"Our baby didn't."

"Oh…I'm so sorry. I wasn't thinking. How could I have said such a thing?"

"You're scared."

"Blake, I don't know how to handle it. Your father has amazing strength. You're just like him. I don't know where you get it."

"It's not that it's always easy, but as Christians we believe we weren't made for this world. What happens here is only temporary, and whether we live or die is up to the One who created us. The strength comes from knowing that because of Jesus Christ and His sacrifice on the cross, we're going to spend eternity in the very presence of God, so death itself isn't a fearful thing—though the dying *process* has to be reckoned with."

Beverly let the words sink in. "You sound a lot like your father, too. He was a rock the whole time you were out of it, determined that God knew what He was doing. I really respect him. The man has chutzpah."

"*Chutzpah?*" Blake chuckled. "I love it. Pastor Bart Thomas has chutzpah."

"Well, he'd have made a good rabbi. Oops…maybe I shouldn't say so. You probably don't think so much of the Jews."

"Beverly, why would you say that? I love the Jews. My Jesus was a Jew."

She felt the heat scald her face. "I figured you blamed us for killing Him."

"Actually, we're all to blame, since we're all sinners. But Jesus laid down His life voluntarily."

"You're telling me He did it on purpose?"

Blake nodded. "It was part of the plan of salvation. He was born to die."

"But you believe he was God's son. What are you saying?"

"Think of everything you understand about the Passover lamb…what I'm saying is that Jesus chose to become the one, unblemished and final sacrifice. The perfect Lamb of God took the sins of everyone on Himself and died on the cross, once and for all. It's His blood that covers us and saves us from eternal death."

"I never heard that before."

"Christianity's roots are in Judaism, Beverly. It was all part of the plan."

Her heart raced, but she didn't know why. "You know, Blake, sometimes I wish Jesus hadn't come so long ago. I look around the synagogue and I see stale people who need something fresh. There's so much fighting and division and liberal thinking. My husband Frank won't even go with me anymore. If Jesus had waited until now to come, who knows? Maybe we would listen."

∽o∾

On Friday night, Blake sat in his wheelchair, looking through the glass wall surrounding the isolation area, and wept. Clay Lindsay had just been pronounced dead.

He knew this man was one of the EMTs who had transported him and Melissa to the hospital. He also knew that he was no more responsible for Clay's death than he was for his own survival. But it hurt him that somewhere outside these walls, a widow and young children would be grieving, and relatives and friends would have to say good-bye to someone they loved. The passing of a life was always solemn to Blake, and he wondered if Clay had died a believer.

As he watched the staff unhook the IV, his thoughts turned to Beverly. How would she handle being the only one left quarantined in *B* Corridor?

"Hello, Frank. It's me…"

"Bev, you don't sound so good. What's wrong? Are you—"

"It's not me," she said quickly, regaining her composure. "It's Clay Lindsay, the EMT that brought in the Thomas couple. He just died."

Hearing herself say the words shattered any hope she had. There was a long pause.

"I wanna see you," he said.

"You can't. You know that."

"I *don't* know that. Why can't I cover up in all that hospital stuff like the people who are taking care of you? Did anyone ever ask?"

"I don't know."

"Well, I wanna find out. Who do I talk to? If they won't let me cover up in hospital stuff, I'll wear my bunker gear. You said yourself the firemen weren't exposed in the attack because they had gear on."

Beverly plucked a Kleenex from the box and held it to her mouth until the quivering stopped.

"I don't think there's anyone to ask tonight, Frank. But Dr. Rice and Dr. Montgomery will be here in the morning. I'm sure there's going to be some sort of media fanfare when they let the others go. I can ask them then."

"Bev, I'm *gonna* see you. Be sure you tell them that. Are you hearing me? If I have to make a scene, I will. If they think I'm just gonna sit by while you…"

"While I what, Frank—die? You might as well say it."

"It's not gonna happen, Bev. I won't let it." He sounded determined and unemotional.

"It's not our call, Frank."

"Don't come at me with the God thing again. I don't wanna hear it."

"I've been having some long talks with Blake Thomas."

"The missionary responsible for all this?"

"He's no more responsible for this than I am. Blake's a real nice kid. Smart, too. Maybe even a little wise. He's been good company, Frank. Everyone else is polite enough, but they treat me like I've got the plague and can't wait to beat it out of here. Blake's been coming in to see me. He's been a real godsend."

"Now that's funny. How could a Christian missionary from the Amazon be a godsend to a Jewish nurse from Baxter? What could you possibly have in common?"

"You might be surprised. It's amazing how you listen differently to people when the rules change."

"What do you mean?"

"Well, let's face it. I'm at high risk for developing the virus, and the chances of surviving it aren't too good. Suddenly I'm not so narrow-minded."

"About what?"

"About beliefs I've been unsure about for years. Look, Frank, at first, I figured the kid probably hated me because I'm Jewish. Well, I couldn't have been more wrong. Then he tells me he actually loves the Jews, and reminded me that Jesus was Jewish. Then he tells me something I never heard before. He said Jesus became the Passover Lamb, who was sacrificed for sin—and that His blood covered us *all*—Jew and Gentile. If Jesus really was the Son of God, then we don't need more sacrifices to cover our sins."

"Bev, you actually believe Jesus was the Messiah?"

"I don't know. Maybe I just want to so badly that I'm grasping at straws. But it's all making sense to me. What if there is a new covenant?"

"Well, you know I don't buy any of it."

"I know, Frank. But you aren't the last one sitting in *B* Corridor either."

THIRTY

On Saturday morning, Jennifer saw a long line of cars parked along the street and a big "Welcome Home!" banner across the front of the house.

"Dad, what's this all about?"

Jed smiled. "This is one of the happiest days of my life. I hope we don't wear you out, but half the people in the county wanted to be here for this." He reached over and hugged her. "I don't think I realized how much I love you until I almost lost you—" Jed choked on the words. "Come on, you've waited long enough to see those boys."

Jed helped Jennifer out of the car and escorted her up the steps. Rhonda was at the door with a baby in each arm.

"Oh, I can't believe it," Jennifer said, her eyes flooded with tears. She heard voices and laughter and felt a hand guide her over to the rocking chair.

"I'm putting Bailey in your left arm," Rhonda said, "and Benjamin in your right."

Jennifer blinked to clear her eyes. Had she ever felt such joy? "Look at you two! You've changed so much! You're even more beautiful than I remember… Mom, am I being partial, or am I right?"

Rhonda laughed. "You're asking me?"

"So ask me," Mark said.

Jennifer was surprised and pleased to see her brother. "Well, what's the verdict?"

He grinned. "Sorta cute for a couple of squawkers."

"Are you hungry?" Jed said. "Monty's sent over a brunch tray with all kinds of goodies on it."

"Maybe in a while," she said. "I don't want to let go of these boys."

The house was filled with well-wishers from church, and with friends and neighbors and family. The babies seemed content, and Jennifer was sure she was running on adrenaline. The love and support she felt was overwhelming.

"Are you going to tell us what you've named the babies?" Pastor Thomas asked.

"Actually, I'd like to," she said. "Heaven knows I've had plenty of time to think about it."

The room got quiet and people gathered around.

Jennifer looked down at Bailey. "My oldest is Bailey Christopher. His first name means 'stewardship.' Christopher means 'carrier of Christ.' So, to me his name means *entrusted with the Word*. Maybe someday Bailey will use his determined nature to tell people about the Lord. Maybe God spared his life for just that reason…" She blinked away the tears and kissed him on the cheek.

"I love it," Rhonda said.

Jennifer looked at the baby in her right arm. "This child is Benjamin Casey. Benjamin means 'son of my right hand,' and Casey means 'valorous.' To me, his name means son of *strength and courage*…" Jennifer's voice cracked and she paused to regain her composure. "I hope he grows up to be like Ben Stoller, willing to put the welfare of others ahead of his own." She kissed Benjamin and wiped her tears off his cheek.

Jed stood up. "Some of you know Casey is also the name of the mentally-challenged young man who introduced me to Christ eight months ago. Having Jennifer choose that middle name adds another dimension for me. Casey Lasiter's simple courage sent me all the way to the cross—which saved my marriage and brought our family together."

"Guy, what's wrong?" Ellen said. "You haven't said a word since we left the Wilsons'."

"Does something have to be wrong just because I'm quiet?"

"Yes."

"I don't know, Ellen. I just can't get into the whole 'Christian' thing, that's all."

"It was a homecoming for Jennifer. What Christian 'thing' are you referring to?"

"The whole atmosphere with people from your church makes me uncomfortable."

"What are you talking about? Jennifer came home and we all supported her. What's bothering you?"

"All right, the twins' names, for one thing. Why do they have to have such a religious significance? What ever happened to just naming the kids whatever you like just because you like it?"

"I think it's kind of nice that the names have significance."

"*Entrusted with the Word?* Give me a break."

"That has a lot of significance to a Christian."

"I'm sure it does, Ellen. But it turns me off."

"You don't like *son of strength and courage* either?"

"Look," Guy said, "I'm sure it's important to Jennifer and Jed and Rhonda. It just makes me uncomfortable, that's all."

"And?"

There was a long pause.

"And the more you're around those people, the further apart we seem. I'm worried it's hurting our marriage."

"What do you mean by 'it'?"

"Ellen, stop playing newspaper editor and get real with me, okay? I don't believe there's a God. I'm not a Christian. I don't want to be a Christian—"

"And you don't want to be married to a Christian?"

"Your words."

Ellen felt a ripping in her heart. "Guy, I love you. Nothing's changed between us except the wall you've put up. I can't ignore the amazing things I've seen over the past months. What if there is a God who wants a relationship with us? Are you willing to throw it away without even investigating?"

"How late is Abernathy's open?" he said.

"Six o'clock. Why?"

"I promised you I'd fix the basement door."

Ellen looked at him, dumbfounded. "It's been broken for six months."

"Well, then, it's time I fixed it."

Late Saturday evening, Beverly Stein sat waiting for Frank to arrive. Since she was the only one quarantined, permission was given for her husband to visit. What would she say to him? She heard footsteps approaching the door and looked up at the outline of a man outfitted with scrubs, mask, goggles, and gloves.

"Frank?"

"Who else would wear this dorky costume?"

Beverly stood up. He walked to her and threw his arms around her, holding her close until a nurse accidentally intruded on their privacy.

"Come sit down," Beverly said.

"This place is like a ghost town."

"Blake's been keeping me company."

Frank took her hand with his gloved one. "Wish I could take this thing off."

"Don't you dare," Beverly said. "You got enough trouble already."

She looked past the reflection on Frank's goggles into his eyes and tried to read his mood. He looked terrified. And lost. "It's gonna be okay, Frank."

"What if it isn't? Bev, I can't lose you."

"Don't talk like that. I'm still doing all right. No symptoms."

"It hasn't been five days yet. That's the magic number, right?"

"There's no magic number, Frank."

"Seems like the others started in with symptoms after about five days."

"Do we have to talk about it?"

"No." Frank kissed her hand, a surgical mask over his mouth. "I love you, Bev. That's what I came here to talk about."

Beverly fought back the tears as she sat quietly, Frank holding her hand. The love exchanged in the silence seemed far more effective than anything they could say. Her mind wandered back to their courtship and all the years they had meant everything to each other. How would he survive without her?

An hour passed. Then two. Frank finally went home. Beverly felt as though her heart would break when he walked away.

She wished she had the peace Blake Thomas had. She knelt beside her bed and rested her head on her hands. "God, I'm a little confused, and since I'm probably going to die, could You make it clear to me if Jesus is who Blake says He is? I know I haven't been a good Jew. My parents, rest their souls, would turn over in their graves if they knew how much I've compromised what they taught me. Something's been missing for a long time. I don't know what it is. Frank won't even go to synagogue anymore, and I got tired of trying to be spiritual for both of us. All I have are poor excuses, but I really want to get things right. So, if Jesus was Your Son, and if He was my Messiah...I really need to know."

Jennifer sat at the kitchen table listening to the end of Pastor Thomas's radio sermon, vaguely aware of her parents feeding the babies, and Mark devouring a second helping of scrambled eggs and bacon.

"It's over now. Turn it off," Mark said.

"Wow, what a testimony to God's faithfulness." Jennifer dabbed her eyes.

"Why get worked up over a sermon?" Mark said.

"Because she's lived through what he's talking about," Jed said, poking him on the shoulder.

Jennifer felt privileged that Blake had shared his dream with her and wondered how their church family would react if they knew the whole story.

"Jen, you seem far away," Rhonda said.

"Huh? Oh, I'm just thinking back on all that's happened. I'm grateful to be home. Sorry you couldn't go to church today. I know you wanted to be there."

"Right now we need to help you," Rhonda said. "But can you imagine the celebration when Blake and Melissa and you are back in church?"

"I can hardly wait," Jennifer said.

"By the way, son, how'd you sleep last night?"

"Very funny, Mom. I ended up on the couch."

"You didn't like camping out with the boys in your old room?"

"I don't know how mothers do it. How do you sleep with all that racket? Babies either cry or make weird noises."

Jennifer smiled. "Right now, I don't care if I ever sleep again. It's just great being with them."

"Okay, how about *you* sleep in the nursery and let me have your room?"

"And deprive you of the privilege of male bonding? Not on your life!"

"Wasn't all that bad," Mark said. "I didn't think I was gonna like them at all. But they're cool."

Jennifer looked at her mother and father, and then at Mark. "Then it's okay to call you Uncle Mark?"

His cheeks turned red, and a grin stole his face. "Whatever."

Beverly Stein had been up most of the night. She read through the Psalms, then wandered around the New Testament until her eyes fell on the book of Hebrews. She devoured every word. She waited until after breakfast, then picked up the phone and called Blake and Melissa's room.

"Hello."

"Blake, it's Beverly. I read the Bible all night. And I found the book of Hebrews! Can you come to my room?"

"Be right there. On foot!"

Beverly sat on the side of her bed, feeling like a kid on the first day of school. Blake walked through the door, a smile on his face, his eyes alive with joy. She sprang to her feet.

"Blake, I have to make a choice to believe that Jesus died for me—or that He didn't." Her eyes filled with tears. "With all my heart, I believe He did!"

Beverly felt his arms around her.

"I love the way God works," he said. "A preacher's son and a rabbi's daughter. Who would've thought?"

"An unlikely pair, eh?"

"Beverly, do you want to accept Jesus?"

She nodded. "Tell me what to do."

They knelt together on the shiny tile floor and Beverly repeated the words after Blake, asking Jesus into her heart. She finished with her own words, and with a conviction she never dreamed possible. "So Jesus, *my* Messiah, the perfect spotless sacrifice for all my sins, thank You for coming to dwell in my heart, a temple not made with hands."

The words tugged at Beverly's heart like helium balloons so full they could hardly be held. She was aware of Blake staring at her. "What? You've never seen such a happy face before?"

His eyes welled with tears. "I saw your face in a dream. I just didn't realize it till this moment."

Beverly sat in her hospital room and reveled in the joy. How could Blake have seen her face on the golden strand unless God had shown him? And how could God love her that much? It was overwhelming. She picked up the phone and dialed.

"Hi, Frank, it's me again."

"Bev? Are you all right?" His voice sounded tense.

"I'm *wonderful*. Something's happened…" She was choked with emotion.

"What happened, Bev?"

"*Jesus* is what happened, Frank. I'm just going to tell you right out. I'm not sure I could keep it in anyway!"

"What're you talkin' about?"

Beverly told him everything, hoping the contents of her newborn heart would somehow spill over into his. She laughed that her sentences ran together, but loved the freedom of telling him what she'd discovered.

"Don't you see, Frank? Jesus fulfilled the prophecies given to the Jews!"

There was a long, uncomfortable pause.

"How in the world did you come to this conclusion just sittin' over there in that hospital? What did this Blake Thomas say anyhow?"

"I don't know that it's so much what he said as who he *is*. I admire his strength. I got to know this family, and they have something special. The more I listened to Pastor Thomas and then his son, the more my eyes were opened. When I read the book of Hebrews, it suddenly made sense. I'm not sure if I can explain *how* I know, but I just do."

"Does this mean you're a Christian?" Frank said.

"I know what you're thinking—that Joshua and Hannah Goldman are turning over in their graves."

"Don't tell me your mother's not ticked!"

Beverly smiled. "She'll forgive me… Frank, thanks for not letting this come between us. I need the joy and strength right now. Would you believe I'm not afraid to die?"

"What? Now you're ready to leave me?"

"Frank. I love you. *I* wouldn't choose this time to die, but if that's what God has in mind, I'm ready."

Beverly sat in silence, the receiver to her ear, her heart pressed to Frank's. But the salty streams coming from her eyes no longer contained a drop of fear.

Dennis got out of the car and walked up the steps to the front porch. He took a slow, deep breath and rang the doorbell. When the door opened, Mark Wilson stood staring him in the face.

"What are *you* doing here? If I were you, Lawton, I'd make an about-face and beat it. Or maybe you'd like me to bruise the *other* side of your face. Nobody here wants anything to do with you."

"They'll want to hear what I have to say," Dennis said. "Look, Mark, I'm not here to cause trouble. I just need to talk—"

"Who is it, Mark?" said a middle-aged man.

"Mr. Wilson? I'm Dennis Lawton. You have every right to throw me out, but what I have to say is something all of you will be pleased about. May I come in?"

Dennis felt Jed Wilson's eyes sizing him up.

"Mark, let me talk to him for a moment—alone." Jed stepped out on the porch. "Look, Jennifer's been through more in the past ten days than you'll probably go through in a lifetime—all that on top of the pain you already caused her. Your reason for coming here had better be good. Why should I let you speak with her?"

"I have a financial offer for the boys. I'm not here to hurt Jennifer or to confuse her thinking. I just need to talk with her for a few minutes, then I'll be on my way. I promise not to upset her."

Jennifer appeared in the doorway. "What are *you* doing here? I don't have anything to say to you, Dennis."

"I was telling your father I have a financial offer that I think you'll want to hear. I just need a few minutes. I'm not here to hurt you, Jen. I'm really not."

"What kind of financial offer? I told you I don't want your money."

"May I come in? Look, your dad can throw me out if you think I'm out of line. But you're going to want to hear what I have to say."

Seated at the dining room table, Dennis tried to keep his emotions locked in business mode, but found it impossible to ignore the boys. Bailey was in Mrs. Wilson's arms and Benjamin was in Jennifer's. He felt his heart stir, and the fear of unwelcome emotions motivated him to concentrate on the facts. He explained everything Clark Rogers had told him about the trust funds and how they were going to work. He could tell Jennifer and her parents were surprised and pleased.

"So, when they turn thirty," Dennis said, "everything remaining in the trust funds—interest and all—will be completely accessible to them. They're not going to have to worry about their financial future."

"Your grandfather is a generous man," Jed said. "He didn't have to do this."

Rhonda turned to Jennifer. "Are you going to accept the offer?"

She wiped her eyes. "Of course. How can I not?"

"Jen, I know you aren't asking for anything, but I also want to work out something regarding child support," Dennis said. "I had our family attorney draw up some papers." Dennis handed them to her and waited for her reaction.

"Four thousand dollars a month?" She stared at him in disbelief.

"The boys are going to need you at home. You shouldn't feel forced to go to work." He looked at Benjamin's face and almost smiled. "Uh, you should have your attorney look these papers over. If we're in agreement, all we need to do is get them notarized, and the checks will be deposited into your account monthly."

Jennifer stared at the papers. "I don't know what to say."

Bailey was starting to fuss and it was getting difficult to talk over him.

"Mom, do you want me to take him?" Jennifer said.

"Here, let me try to calm him down." Dennis realized too late what he'd said.

"Uh, all right." Rhonda put Bailey into Dennis's arms, instructing him on how to support the baby's head. He played along.

"Okay, Bailey, let's see if we can get you to stop hollering." Dennis rose from the table and walked with him around the living room, gently rubbing the back of the child's neck. Bailey became quiet, and Dennis enjoyed the feel of his son's warm body against his chest.

"Lawton," Mark said, "for a guy who doesn't want kids, you sure look like you're into this stuff."

Dennis swallowed the unexpected emotion. He handed a now-contented Bailey back to Mrs. Wilson.

Without making eye contact, he pretended to be sorting his copies of the papers. "Listen, I need to be going. I'll call tomorrow after you've had time to think all this over and run it by your attorney. Then we can get the papers signed and notarized, and I'll be on my way back to Denver."

Rhonda had just put Bailey in his infant seat when the doorbell rang.

Mark got up to answer it. Dennis glanced toward the front door, shocked to see the face of Flo Hamlin! Panic gripped his heart. He lowered his head and shuffled papers while Jed and Rhonda welcomed her to their home.

"The boys are in here," Rhonda said. She led Flo toward the matching infant seats set on the opposite end of the table from where Dennis was standing. He glanced up at just the wrong second, and his eyes locked with Flo's.

"Flo, please excuse us for a moment," Jed said. "Dennis was just leaving." Jed walked Dennis to the front door and held out his hand. "We appreciate everything, Dennis. By tomorrow afternoon, we'll have everything in order. Since we can't reach you, we'll wait for your call."

Flo spun around and gave Dennis a double take. "What did you say his name was?" A puzzled look spread across her face. "Why, he looks jus' like Ben Stoller—"

"Okay, then," Dennis said, his hand on the doorknob, "I'll call tomorrow afternoon. It was nice meeting you all."

He escaped through the front door and skipped down the steps. Everything else was a blur until he bumped his head as he flopped on the front seat of the rental car. Seconds later, he sped out of sight.

Jennifer deluged Flo with questions, and every answer pointed to what she didn't want to hear: Dennis Lawton and Ben Stoller were the same man.

"I can't believe it," Jennifer said. "My boys' first names are both tied to Ben Stoller, who turns out to be Dennis! It's so unfair."

"Jen, there's another way to look at this," Jed said. "Regardless of what name he used, his actions speak for themselves. So it was Dennis who risked his life for Flo and the boys. That doesn't change the act. Plus, he cared enough to make the video."

"Your father's right," Rhonda said. "I love the boys' first *and* middle names for all the reasons you chose them. That hasn't changed. I hope you won't change their names now."

"I won't. I love the names, too. I just feel so let down that Ben Stoller isn't who I thought he was."

"Maybe he *is*," Jed said. "Look how much he cared for the boys—and his actions the night Sawyer held them hostage. What a man does when he's facing death tells a lot about him, no matter what name he uses."

"Young lady," Flo said. "I'll be tellin' you somethin' about Ben— I mean Dennis. Somethin' inside him is fine, *real* fine. The way he was with them babies was nothin' he made up. I was with him day 'n night for a week. He's got a real good heart. I jus' wish I could know why he's runnin' so fast."

"Because he's a coward," Mark said.

Flo turned to Mark. "The boy was brave enough ta put hisself between us and that awful Sawyer fella. He ain't no coward. There's somethin' else botherin' him."

"Well," Mark said, "Lawton is either more generous than I gave him credit for, or that rich grandfather of his is holding a gun to his head. Jen, how come you didn't connect the name Bailey to Dennis's grandfather?"

"I don't know. Dennis always called him Grandpa. I never paid attention to his name. In fact, I've never met the man."

Rhonda put her arm around Jennifer. "You look tired, honey. Go lie down and let us take care of the boys. You need to clear your head."

"Do you love this guy?" Mark asked.

"Son, it's time to put a sock in it." Jed shot him a look.

"It's okay, Dad," Jennifer said. "I've been trying to figure out how I feel about Dennis. I know that I despise the spoiled, selfish playboy that I broke up with. But I could fall in love with the side of him that came through on the video, and the hero that saved the boys. But which is he?"

"I seen a lot o' good inside him," Flo said. "Maybe the boy's jus' strugglin' to find hisself."

"Maybe." Jennifer looked over at the boys asleep in their infant seats. "I just wish he'd hurry up. His presence in my life is disruptive, and I don't want the boys going through that. Dennis has to decide if he's in or out."

Dennis slowed down and set the cruise control, trying to imagine what the conversation was like at the Wilsons' after Flo told them everything she knew. All they had to do was connect the dots. He felt violated. Never once had he figured on Jennifer knowing it was he who had been there for the boys.

He felt like a wounded child that just wanted to run. He hit the steering wheel with the palm of his hand. What was wrong with him?

Dennis got tired of an annoying blue flyer someone must have put under his wiper when he stopped for gas. He pulled onto the shoulder and got out to remove it. He crumpled the paper and started to throw it away, then changed his mind, unfolded it, and started to read:

F.A.I.T.H.
FATHERS ACCEPTING INVOLVEMENT THROUGH HEALING
SUNDAY JULY 22, 7:00 P.M.
CHRISTIAN WAY CHAPEL, FIRST STREET AND MORRISON, ELLISON
NO ADMISSION CHARGE - COME AS YOU ARE

Fathers, if you're struggling with the pressures of taking responsibility for your children, we encourage you to attend this meeting and hear from other men who have overcome fears and pressure and have found not only peace and fulfillment, but also emotional freedom to enjoy their children.

Your problem is not uncommon! We can help. No questions asked.

THIRTY-ONE

Dennis paced in his motel room. It was six-forty-five. He wanted to run—but where? He reread the blue flyer. Could they really help him?

Dennis couldn't remember one time in his life when he had felt like any man's son. His feelings of inadequacy ran deep, and his fear of commitment ran even deeper. Dennis flopped on the bed. He picked up his cell phone and dialed. While the phone rang on the other end, he noticed it was seven o'clock straight up.

"This is Patrick Bailey's room."

"This is Dennis Lawton, Mr. Bailey's grandson. May I speak to him, please?"

"Certainly. I'm his nurse for this shift. Let me get the phone to him. Hold on." Dennis heard shuffling in the background.

"Hello."

"Grandpa, this is Dennis. You sound weak. Are you all right?"

"About the same. Can't complain. How are *you?*"

Dennis felt trapped in a long pause. "Grandpa, I'm not good at asking for advice, but—well—I'm…"

"What does your gut tell you, Dennis?"

"What do you mean?"

"What's your gut saying to you? All that churning has a purpose."

"I feel so *pulled,* Grandpa. I stopped by to see Jennifer and met her family and told them about the trust funds—and an offer of my own for child support that I haven't even talked to you about yet. Everything was going fine until Bailey got fussy and I offered to quiet him down. Jennifer's brother made some smart-aleck remark and I got embarrassed. Then Flo stopped by and recognized me, and now everyone is going to know that I was Ben Stoller. I left as quickly as I could. They're going to run the papers by their attorney, so I've got to go back tomorrow afternoon. Grandpa, what am I going to do? I'm freaking out."

"What is it you're scared of, that they've discovered Ben Stoller—or that *you* have?"

"Grandpa, I could never live up to that image. I did what I had to do. I told you, I was playing a part."

"I remember what you told me."

"But you're not buying it?"

"Neither are you or you wouldn't be calling me."

"Grandpa, this is too hard. I can't explain it, but I'm panicked. I really don't think I can do this…" Dennis paused to gather his composure. "I'm mixed up. Sometimes I feel like the little boy getting ditched instead of the father doing it. It doesn't make a lot of sense."

"Well, you've been both. Maybe it's time you stopped being either."

Dennis heard the sound of his mother's voice in the background. His heart sank. "Grandpa, I know you can't talk. I hear Mother's voice. I've got to go. Thanks for listening. I'll think of something."

Dennis turned off his cell phone and sat on the side of the bed. It was 7:05. Every fear he had was magnified in the quiet. He got up and grabbed his keys.

Beverly Stein sat in her hospital room with her husband Frank. Her heart ached for how lost he seemed.

"Bev, I can't get over the change in you," he said. "My heart's breakin' over here, and you're not bothered at all." There was resentment in his voice.

"I'm bothered plenty, but I'm not afraid anymore. Since I can't decide the outcome, enough already. I'd rather just sit here with you."

"How can it not matter if you die?"

"Don't mistake not worrying for not caring. Peace isn't something I can explain, but I'm grateful to have it. This feels much better."

"Seems weird to me."

"We've been through this, Frank. I respect the fact that faith isn't where you are right now, but it's very much where I am. What? I should apologize for finding the truth? What are you staring at?"

"You look so happy, Bev. Tell me, how should I feel about that? I may lose you—and you're happy."

She sighed. "I'm not happy that you might lose me. I'm happy that I'm found. There's a big difference."

"There you go again with the God thing."

"Frank..." She choked on the word. "Please don't spoil tonight."

He took her in his arms and embraced her. "I'm sorry..." He let his emotion out in quiet sobs. "I love you like life itself."

She nodded and held him tightly, wondering if this would be the last time.

Dennis pulled into the parking lot at the Christian Way Chapel and noticed fifty or sixty cars there. He didn't know whether to be impressed or overwhelmed. He pulled the rental car into a parking place near the exit and walked toward the front steps of the old stone building.

He felt like a lost kid and realized these were the same feelings he had grown up with—a sense of being abandoned, vulnerable, and out of control. They were powerful and debilitating.

Someone inside was already speaking. Dennis paused, then opened the heavy wood door and was greeted by a young man about his age, dressed in a plaid golf shirt and a pair of shorts.

"Glad you could make it," the man said. "The speaker's just getting started."

Dennis offered the man a moist handshake, then sat by himself in the back of the sanctuary. His anxiety level was off the charts. Why was he reacting this way? It was just a meeting. He finally calmed down enough to listen to the speaker.

"I'm not sure I ever remember feeling normal. In fact, I always wished I were like the other kids whose families were intact. I used to ache when I would see other boys come to the ball games with their dads. I'd hear every one of their dads' voices cheering from the bleachers. My father never once came to watch me play. If I saw him at all, he was drifting in and out of our lives, just enough to make me feel abandoned all over again. He didn't care about us. I'm not even sure why he bothered to come back. All it ever did was make me hate myself more. I figured it must be my fault. But I grew up determined *never* to do that to my own kids.

"And you know what? The very thing I didn't want to do is what I did. Sound familiar? None of it made any sense to me until I started coming to the meetings here. But when I got married and had kids of my own, something inside me was so empty that I couldn't commit myself to them. No matter how much I tried, I always messed up. Finally I gave up and just lived with the guilt, hating myself, deciding I was a failure and no better than my own father. Unfortunately, I was right. The difference is I really wanted to be different.

"For every man here tonight, there's one thing necessary for change: You have to really *want* to be different. If you have the desire, I have the solution. God can fill your emptiness. He can heal the abandoned child inside you, so that you can be the man you want to be for your kids. It's hard work. I'm not going to lie to you. But it's not as hard as carrying all the baggage you're already hauling around. Some of you had physically abusive fathers, or strict ones that were hard on you but never showed affection. Maybe your father was critical or drank too much or just ignored you. But the answer to healing the wound is the same. The beginning and ending of the story is your heavenly Father. Many of you may not realize that you have always had a Father who loves you and who is there for you. Did you know the God of the universe loves *you?* Getting ahold of that concept alone is life-changing.

"But there will be some choices to make—some courageous decisions on your part that will make all the difference in your future, and in whether or not your own kids will have a dad. Being a biological father is a no-brainer. The real question is: Can you be a dad? Do you have what it takes to take on the responsibility to be there for your kids?"

Dennis listened to his every word.

"There are three things needed for this to happen: God, this group, and guts. First, you must acknowledge you can't do this alone, that you need the help of a higher power. In this place, we believe that power is God Almighty, working through His Son Jesus Christ by the power of His Holy Spirit.

"Second, you also need the support of others who will not only be a sounding board, but will hold you accountable. God *will* take you through this, and you'll have a strong support group here at FAITH. These guys have been invaluable in helping me turn my life around.

"Third, you need to trust God to give you the courage, the sheer *guts,* to get past that abandoned child in yourself and grow up into the dad your children need. I'm living proof it can happen, but there are a number of men who are going to get up tonight and give their testimonies. The first one…" The guy became emotional, and stopped talking to gather his composure. "The first is my son, Jason. For twenty-five years, I ran from accepting my responsibility for bringing this wonderful human being into the world. I missed a huge chunk of his life because of nothing more than fear. Please listen to what he has to say. For most of you, it's not too late to pick up the ball while your kids are still young."

Dennis listened intently as Jason spoke to the group, and realized he wasn't the only one saddled with these emotions. The pain of feeling unworthy to be loved came rushing to the surface. Dennis couldn't hold back the tears as he listened to the young man talk about the healing power of God that had sealed his relationship with two fathers—the One in heaven and the one on earth. Dennis noticed that many of the other men were as shaken as he was, and he felt free to be honest with himself for the first time in his life.

Jennifer lay on her bed, her hands behind her head, her mind racing. Who *was* Dennis Lawton? Every time he showed up, she felt torn. She had loved Ben Stoller, and Dennis had taken even that from her.

And yet, how could she resent him after his generous offer? The figures were staggering. She might be able to earn half that much if she got the management position at the health food store. She knew making ends meet would have been a struggle. But with the amount Dennis offered her every month, she could raise the boys herself and never have to worry about the finances.

And the trust funds…Jennifer felt the tears sting her eyes. She couldn't even comprehend the opportunities that kind of money would open up for the boys. *Lord, this is more than I would have ever asked for.*

Why would Dennis do this? What was in it for him? Jennifer had never known Dennis to do anything that didn't benefit him first. *Lord, I don't love him. You know that. Why are You opening this door?*

Dennis listened as each man on the stage, one by one, came forward and told how his life had been changed through faith in God and with the help of the men of FAITH. As the last man approached the microphone, Dennis blinked away the tears, and when his eyes could focus again, he was shocked to see Jed Wilson!

"It's a privilege to be up here tonight. My name is Jed. Eight months ago, I was a bitter, resentful husband and father who had forfeited twenty-eight years of happiness to hold on to some old resentment that was running my life.

"At eighteen years old, I decided to accept responsibility and marry my pregnant girlfriend. I had been in love with her, and our families expected me to do the right thing. The trouble is, I made the choice out of protest and guilt, not commitment, and I wasn't any more effective in my role as a dad than if I had been absent. Oh, my daughter, who's now a Christian and has forgiven me, will tell you that my being there was better than abandoning her; but my son who hasn't yet found Christ is hurting just as much as all of you. I failed as a father. I failed as a husband. All I really brought home was a paycheck. I took my real 'presence' to O'Brian's bar with my buddies.

"By ignoring my wife, I caused her to feel depressed and empty most of the time. With both of us out of commission, that left my kids without a whole lot of nurturing, which gave them low self-esteem and a sense of not being wanted. Some dad I was.

The sad part is, I was the catalyst.

"You see, the man can make or break a family. His role is powerful. His wife and his kids respond to him, whether he uses or misuses it. I misused it. By shutting them out, I created a home atmosphere where we were all empty."

Dennis knew Jennifer resented her father, but she had never elaborated on the reason. And this explained why Mark had such a chip on his shoulder. Dennis had always assumed that it was the kids without fathers who were hurting. It had never occurred to him that even kids who grow up with fathers sometimes face the same feelings of abandonment.

As Jed concluded, he looked at Dennis. "Every child deserves a father. It took me twenty-eight years to wise up, and many of you aren't much older than that right now. Let the men of FAITH help you discover how to get this basic part of your life right, and everything else will fall into place. You have so much to gain and absolutely nothing to lose—except the fear."

As Jed returned to his seat, Dennis got up as inconspicuously as possible and slipped out the back door.

Ellen Jones sat on the screened-in porch, listening to the laughter of children next door running through the sprinkler hose. She had wanted to go to church today, but she didn't—again.

How her heart ached to know the truth. But in order to gain a relationship with God, would she have to lose the one with her husband, the love of her life with whom she had shared the past twenty-seven years?

It seemed miraculous to her that Blake and Melissa had survived the loss of their child without bitterness. And that Pastor Thomas had been a rock through the entire ordeal. That kind of faith is what she wanted. But if it meant losing Guy's love, could she do it? Should she?

"There you are," Guy said. "I'm game for banana splits. Want to go to Monty's?"

Ellen looked at him and smiled. "Sure."

"You seem glum tonight, honey. What's wrong?"

"Not glum, contemplative."

He sat next to her and took her hand. "You're not pouting because of what I said yesterday, are you?"

Ellen sighed. "I don't think I'm pouting. I'm depressed."

"About what?"

She didn't answer.

"Ellen, say it. I promise not to get ugly."

"My heart is being torn in two and I don't know what to do about it. We've been best friends since college. I love you more than anyone on earth. Until now, we've always believed the same things. But I've seen too much not to wonder if there's more. It hurts me to think our relationship might change if I pursue a relationship with God."

"Then why risk it?"

"I keep asking myself that."

"What's the big theological draw—that the FBI couldn't explain who Sawyer was shooting at in the church?"

"Guy, don't insult my intelligence. I've watched how Christianity affects people. Look at Pastor Thomas—and Blake and Melissa. They aren't even bitter. And look at Jed and Rhonda and Jennifer—same thing. And think back a few months at how people in this town let go of their anger because of Taylor Logan's testimony. The Kennsingtons never were bitter! It was amazing. And I was there when Sean McConnell died. I saw the look on his face—it was glorious. How can I explain all that?"

"Ellen, I can show you plenty of Christians who aren't worth the time of day."

"But it's the ones who are that I keep coming back to. I want to know what it is they have. Can you understand that?"

"No." He let go of her hand.

Ellen felt the hot tears roll down her cheeks. "Guy, please…this is so important. I have to know the truth."

Dennis gathered his clothes and toiletries and returned the key to the motel manager, explaining that something had come up and he was checking out tonight. He paid for the room and left Ellison the same way he had come.

But he wasn't ready to go home to his grandfather, nor was he willing to face what awaited him in Baxter. With a million dollars in his account, Dennis headed for Atlanta, hoping to find peace the only way he knew how.

THIRTY-TWO

J ed Wilson took Monday off without pay to take the legal
papers to Guy Jones and get his advice. Jennifer signed the
papers and Jed brought her home. They had been ready for
Dennis since one o'clock, but he had not even called.

Jed glanced at the kitchen clock: 4:40. He hadn't mentioned
seeing Dennis at last night's meeting. He was encouraged that
Dennis had found his way there, but wasn't surprised when he disappeared. Jed remembered all too well what it was like to feel
caged.

Jennifer stood in the doorway and exhaled. "He changed his
mind. I should've known."

"Don't be too hard on him," Jed said. "He probably got cold feet
after Flo recognized him. It doesn't necessarily mean he's changed
his mind."

"Dad, why does he care if we know?" Jennifer sat at the table.
"I'm surprised he's not bragging about being the hero."

"Judging from the men I've counseled with, they're afraid that
once people think they're capable of accepting responsibility, they'll
expect it. These guys are afraid of commitment."

"Some hero," Jennifer mumbled.

"I think he's very much a hero," Rhonda said. "The man's not perfect, but let's be fair. He did a great job helping Flo with the boys. Not only did he risk his life to save them, but he also risked your father's wrath coming here. The man is certainly not a villain."

Dennis answered the door and paid the classy looking call girl, then sent her away without inviting her in. He closed the door and stepped down into the posh living room of the hotel suite. The bottle of champagne he ordered earlier was unopened in the silver bucket and resting in tepid water.

Dennis sat on the white couch and stared at the Atlanta skyline. Had he ever felt this lost? Anything he wanted he could pay for and have delivered to his door—except peace of mind.

Martha Sullivan's words wouldn't leave him alone...*Let me tell you something, buster: If you walk away, some part of those little boys will stay broken on the inside, and you're going to have to answer for it someday.*

Dennis felt an ache deeper than any he had ever known. How could he inflict on his two sons the stigma his father had saddled him with?

Jed picked up the ringing phone and walked out on the porch where Bailey's crying wouldn't inhibit his hearing.

"Hello."

"Mr. Wilson? This is Dennis Lawton."

"Hello, Dennis. We've been expecting you."

"I'm sorry I didn't call. Something came up."

Jed waited. *Come on, Dennis...admit it.*

"Look, nothing came up. I chickened out. Do you think we could talk—just the two of us? I know you saw me there last night, but I couldn't face you. I've had all day to think, and I'd like to talk to you as a man of FAITH. Is that possible? I mean, would you be able to stay objective?"

"I'm willing to try. When do you want to meet?"

"Well, I'm in Atlanta, but I could meet you anytime—tonight, tomorrow, you name it."

"I have to work tomorrow," Jed said. "But I could meet you tonight. How long do you think it'll take you to get to Ellison...an hour and a half, two hours?"

"Sounds about right. It's five-fifteen now and I'm already out of the traffic heading your way."

"Okay, meet me at the church at eight o'clock. We'll figure out what to do from that point."

"I'll be there. Thanks, Mr. Wilson. I'm sorry about today. I'm trying. I really am."

"I believe you, Dennis. All's forgiven, but don't stand me up twice. By the way, Jennifer and Rhonda don't know you were there last night. We don't talk about what happens at the meetings. I'm not going to tell them who I'm meeting tonight either. This is just between us, so relax."

"Thank you, sir. Is that Bailey crying?"

"Yeah, he's pitching a real fit. Any suggestions?"

"He likes being held against your chest. Walk with him that way and rub the back of his neck. He usually calms right down."

Jed smiled. "Thanks. I'll go try it out. See you at eight."

Jed walked back into the house and was met with the looks of two desperate women unable to get Bailey to stop crying.

"Who was on the phone, Dad?" Jennifer asked.

"A guy who was at the FAITH meeting last night. He wants to talk to me... Jen, let me see if I can do something with Bailey."

"He's all yours."

Jed took the baby from Jennifer and walked into the dining room.

"Are you meeting with him tonight?" Rhonda asked.

"Yeah, eight o'clock." Jed held Bailey to his chest and rubbed the back of his neck. The child stopped crying and Jed stifled his laughter.

"I don't believe this," Jennifer said. "We've been trying to get him calmed down for half an hour. You pick him up, and he's perfectly content."

"He digs his grandpa, don't you, Bailey?"

"Well, we can use you here, *Grandpa,*" Rhonda said. "Can't someone else pinch-hit for you?"

"Sorry, no " Jed said. "The guy specifically asked to speak with me. You ladies'll just have to learn how to handle Bailey. I don't see the problem."

Jennifer collapsed into a chair. "Very funny, Dad. What did you do? We tried everything. It's maddening."

"Now, I can't let that out. But feel free to call on me anytime I'm available. I work for free."

As he held Bailey, Jed felt connected to Dennis and wondered how God planned to use him.

Ellen put a plate of curry chicken in front of Guy, then carried hers to the other side of the table and sat down. "What kind of day did you have?"

"You're not going to believe this," he said. "Jennifer Wilson got a financial offer from the grandfather of the twins. And a dandy offer of child support from the father. The Wilsons asked me to review the papers. It's confidential, of course." He smiled and took a bite of chicken.

"Oh, come on, Guy. Anything you tell me stays right here. Out with it." She laughed. "Don't make me beg!"

Guy told her the details of the two trust funds and the child support agreement. "It doesn't look like Jennifer will have to work unless she wants to."

"I'm so happy for her. She wanted to be home," Ellen said. "What an answer to—"

"To what?"

"Nothing," she said.

Ellen felt his eyes probing her thoughts.

"You were going to say this was an answer to prayer."

"Why would I say that?"

"People can come into money unexpectedly, Ellen."

"I know."

"Lots of people pray, and their circumstances never change. This doesn't prove there's a God. It's just a coincidence."

Ellen took a bite of curry chicken and tried not to smile. *Some coincidence!*

Jed pulled into the church parking lot and recognized Dennis's car from the day before. He glanced up at the church steps and saw Dennis sitting there. Jed parked his truck and added one last prayer to the many he had prayed during the drive over. He got out and saw Dennis walking toward him, dressed in khaki shorts and navy polo shirt. Jed couldn't get over how much the boys looked like him.

"I'm glad you're here," Jed said, extending his hand.

"Good evening, Mr. Wilson."

"There's just one rule for this meeting: You have to call me *Jed.*"

"Well, sir, it's a little awkward, you know?"

"Dennis, tonight I'm Jed Wilson, a man of FAITH. I'm not Jennifer's father or anyone else you know. I'm here to listen, and to help if I can. No one in this group is higher up than anyone else. We're all dads taking it one day at a time. Eight months ago, I was right where you are. You want to go have coffee or something?"

"Could we talk in that park around the corner?" Dennis said. "I know it's hot, but I'd be more comfortable if we weren't in such a public place. It's hard to talk about this stuff."

"No problem. You want to walk over there?"

"Yeah."

Jed walked beside Dennis on the sidewalk, stepping over the grass growing in the cracks the way he used to when he was a kid. Somewhere between the church and the park, Jed sensed that Dennis was starting to relax a little. When they got to the park, they sat on a wood bench under a huge shade tree. Jed finally broke the ice.

"It took guts to come here tonight, Dennis."

"Yeah, it did."

"Why'd you come back?"

Dennis sighed. "I'm tired of running. It hurts more thinking about what I'm doing to the boys than how hard it might be to deal with it."

"I know exactly what you mean." Jed told Dennis more details about his past and how hard it had been to change until he hooked up with the men of FAITH. "I spent a lot of time with my friend Mike at O'Brian's bar. While I was there, I felt good. But when I went home, I had the same feeling of being trapped. I always blamed Jennifer and Rhonda for my unhappiness. But it was me—something internal I had to work out."

Dennis nodded. "Yeah, same here. I blamed Grandpa and my father. Neither wanted me, and I guess I felt validated by all the women who did. As long as I had something going, I didn't have to deal with it."

Jed listened to Dennis share his past, not shocked by anything the young man told him but surprised he was being so open.

A few minutes passed before either of them spoke.

"Someone made a cutting remark when I was a kid," Dennis said. "Never have been able to shake it." He swallowed hard. "A neighbor was mad at me for something. I don't remember what I did. Probably picked his flowers or something. But I heard him on the porch, his voice raised at my grandfather, 'No wonder the kid's father didn't hang around. He probably couldn't stand him either!' I don't know which hurt more: what he said or what Grandpa *didn't* say." Dennis wiped his eyes. "I don't ever want Bailey and Benjamin to feel that way."

Jed squeezed Dennis's shoulder. "So much of our identity is tied up in our fathers, isn't it? We get their name. We want their approval. We need their love. When that's missing, part of us is empty. That's what happened to Jennifer." Jed paused, surprised at the emotion that surfaced. "I never wanted her. Jennifer was a continual reminder that I made a big mistake and would pay for it the rest of my life. Rhonda adored her. I didn't want anything to do with either one of them. My stubborn refusal to accept her as my own really messed up our family—and almost ruined my marriage. When I look at how God's healed us…when I think of where I was eight months ago…it blows my mind."

"Do you love Jennifer now?"

Jed blinked to clear his eyes. "Yeah. It's almost scary. I can't believe how much I've missed."

Jed admitted to Dennis things he hadn't told anyone but Rhonda, oblivious of time until the bells of the Christian Way Chapel rang twelve times.

"We sure covered a lot of ground," Jed said.

"After what I told you, I'll understand if you don't want me talking to Jennifer when I visit the boys."

"Where'd you get an idea like that? My past wasn't lily-white either. We all make mistakes. Growing from them is what separates the winners from the losers. You're no loser, Dennis. And you have a lot more to offer the boys than you realize." Jed paused. "As far as Jennifer's concerned, she's twenty-nine years old. I'm not going to tell her how to run her life. But she's changed a lot in the past few months. Your beliefs are very different. Do you want to start seeing her again?"

"She'll never trust me again after the way I walked out. But we need to learn to communicate for the twins' sake. I'm not looking beyond that right now."

"I don't think Jennifer's ready to jump into a relationship either."

"I want a chance with the boys, Jed. I don't know how well I'm going to do, but I want to try."

"Good. I hope you'll keep coming to FAITH meetings. You'll need the support. We meet every Sunday night at seven o'clock."

"I'm thinking I might get a place in Baxter so I can see the boys on a regular basis."

"That's a big step."

"Yeah, I know. If I leave Denver, I'll have to start over. I've worked for my grandfather's insurance agency since I got out of college."

"Will that change your offer of child support?"

"No. I don't want Jen to struggle. I'm sitting okay financially, so I don't have to work right away. Who knows? Maybe I'll start my own insurance agency."

Jed felt his eyelids getting heavy. "I've got an hour's drive back to Baxter and an early day tomorrow. This old body needs to hit the road."

The men walked around the block and back to the church parking lot.

"Jed, thanks for listening…and for not judging me."

"Hey, I live in a glass house, remember? I hope I'll see you Sunday night."

"I'll be there. But I may see you before that. I won't be able to stay away from the boys till then. What'll I say to Jennifer?"

"Work this out however you need to, Dennis. When I drive away tonight, I assume the role of Jennifer's dad again. She won't know I met with you unless *you* tell her." Jed put his hand on Dennis's shoulder. "I'm not sure what God's doing in your life, but there's no doubt in my mind that He brought you to this point. Only one other time has He allowed me to feel His love for someone the way I feel it tonight. You have no idea how much God loves you and is involved in your life. I hope as time goes on, you'll want to know more about that. Ultimately, He's the way to make this work out."

"You think God cares about me, Jed—after all I've done?"

Jed smiled and looked Dennis right in the eyes. "Oh yeah. He's one Father who never skips out. He's been waiting for *you* to come home."

THIRTY-THREE

Dr. Sarah Rice sat at her desk early on Tuesday morning, anxious for a return to normalcy. She heard a man cough and looked up, surprised to see Dr. Lionel Montgomery standing in the doorway.

"I guess you're anxious to get home," she said.

His silver hair looked disheveled and his eyes heavy.

"What's wrong, Lionel?"

He walked in and sat in the chair next to her desk. He buried his face in his hands for a moment, and then looked at her. "Beverly Stein is running a fever. There's evidence of early hemorrhaging."

Sarah leaned back and sighed. "I thought it was over."

"She must've known she was getting sick last night," he said, "because she left a note."

"Really?"

"It's rather touching."

"Where is it?"

"With her belongings. We're moving her to isolation."

"Does Frank know?" she asked.

"Not yet."

Sarah got up from her desk. "I want to see Beverly before I call him."

Dennis pulled up in front of the Wilsons' house and turned off the motor. *I can do this.*

He walked up the front steps and stood on the porch, his heart racing. He rang the doorbell and heard Jennifer's voice and then footsteps. The door opened.

"What do *you* want?" she said, smoothing her hair and straightening her bathrobe. "Haven't you caused enough confusion?"

"I'm sure I have. Listen, I'm really sorry. I chickened out after running into Flo, but I'm back because it's where I want to be."

"What if it's not where *we* want you to be?"

"Look, Jen, I really want to do the right thing. Help me out here. It's not easy coming back after standing you up yesterday." He put on his most pleading look.

"All right. Come in." She opened the door and Dennis stepped inside.

"Sit in the living room. I'll be right back. I need to check on the boys."

Dennis sat on the couch, his palms sweaty, his mind made up.

Jennifer came back and sat across from him in an overstuffed chair. "Talk to me, Dennis. No games—just honest dialogue. What's going on?"

"An internal struggle I can't explain very well. You know about my childhood and how miserable I was because my dad split. The last thing I want to do is skip out on the boys. I don't know why I keep doing it. I didn't have any problem when I pretended to be Ben Stoller. But Dennis Lawton keeps running, and I'm not sure what from."

"What made you come back to the clinic in the first place?"

"It started with this uncanny encounter with your brother in the Atlanta airport."

"So I heard."

"I had forgotten to bring my cell phone and was standing in line to use a pay phone. I overheard this young guy talking. He sounded pretty alarmed that 'Jen had been admitted to Baxter Memorial Hospital.' By the things he was saying, I knew it had to be Mark."

"He said you confronted him."

"But he wouldn't tell me anything, so I went looking for a TV. That's when I saw the report on CNN that the Thomas's baby was born dead. I panicked. That doctor gave your name. A reporter said there were reports of hemorrhaging. I figured you were doomed. And since I had just been with you, I thought I might get the virus—and maybe even the boys would."

"People overreacted."

"Yeah, I know that now. But it was real at the time."

"Weren't you afraid you'd be a risk to someone else?"

"Jen, I honestly didn't think about it. My mind started racing with all sorts of regrets. I realized I'd never done one unselfish thing in my life; and if I died, that's how I'd be remembered."

"That's why you came back?"

"What'd I have to lose? I'd already held the boys, so if I was going to get sick, I'd at least go down with one good deed under my belt."

"But why did you lie about who you were?"

"I don't know. When Flo answered the door at the clinic, she jumped to the conclusion that I was a volunteer from some agency. And when she asked me my name, I said 'Ben Stoller.' It was too late to take it back. Martha Sullivan knew who I was. But I think she was hoping I was back to stay, so decided to play along."

"Flo said you were amazing with the boys. What am I missing?"

"As long I was acting, I didn't feel pressure to measure up to anyone's expectations. I could relax and be Mr. Nice Guy."

"That's an understatement. You almost *died* for them." Her eyes seemed to be studying the knot on his cheek. "I guess that makes you a hero no matter what name you used."

"I couldn't stand by and watch Sawyer kill them. Jen, we came so close…" Dennis felt the emotion ball up in his throat.

Jennifer's eyes filled with tears. "Why did you leave? I would've thought you'd want me to know what you'd done."

"Martha Sullivan told me what you were naming the boys and why. You needed to believe Ben Stoller was the hero."

"Sounds like a convenient excuse to avoid commitment."

"Maybe. But tell me you weren't disappointed to find out it was me. The truth *was* disappointing—just like Dennis Lawton."

Jennifer's eyes dropped down to her hands folded in her lap. "Has anything changed?"

"I'm trying hard, Jen. I really am."

"Meaning what?"

"I'd like to get a place in Baxter and start spending time with the boys."

"You mean, *live* here?"

He nodded. "I'd like to give it a try. If things work out, I might consider starting an insurance agency of my own. One thing I *don't* want to do is be away from those boys. You don't look too happy about the idea."

Jennifer blushed. "Uh—I honestly never thought about sharing the boys with you. Part of me is still disgusted with you for writing us off. I can't switch emotional gears just because you made a choice you can live with."

"Well, then maybe you'll understand how hard it was for me when you made a choice I didn't think I could live with."

"Touché." Jennifer sighed. "So, you might stay in Baxter permanently?"

"I've been running from commitment all my life. If there was ever anything that could make me face up to my responsibilities, it's those two little boys. I—I really—uh—"

"*Love* them?"

Dennis looked into her eyes. "I guess that's what I'm trying to say. I've never actually said that to anyone before."

"Maybe you've never felt it before."

"I almost did—with you. But I shut off. I need time to figure out why I do that. I want to be a good dad to these boys. I'm sure someday you'll marry. But they'll still need to know their father loves them."

"Dennis Lawton, you're a real mystery. Why do you keep looking at your watch? You've been doing that for ten minutes."

"I'm surprised Bailey isn't up yet."

A loud demanding cry resounded from the nursery.

"Well, *Mr. Mom,*" she said. "Let's get his bottle and you can show me how to calm him down. You and my dad seem to be the only ones who have the touch."

Dennis followed her and tried not to laugh.

Blake Thomas stood looking through the glass surrounding the isolation room, wondering if Beverly was aware of his presence. Dr. Rice came and stood next to him.

"I thought I'd find you here," she said.

"At least she's not afraid."

"What makes you say that?"

"She gave her heart to the Lord—yesterday. It was amazing. She read the book of Hebrews and it all came to life for her." He turned to Sarah, his heart full of joy. "It's miraculous to watch the Holy Spirit work."

"Did you tell her about Jesus?"

"Yes, but not in the traditional sense."

"What do you mean?"

"You know she's Jewish? In fact, her father was a rabbi. All I told her was how Jesus became the Passover Lamb—the one perfect and final sacrifice for our sins. The Holy Spirit took it from there. She was thumbing through the Bible the other night and became enthralled with the book of Hebrews." Blake blinked the moisture from his eyes. "All the pieces of the puzzle came together. She asked me to pray with her to receive Christ."

"Oh, Blake…that's wonderful," Dr. Rice said. "You must be thrilled to see something positive come out of this horrific ordeal."

Blake leaned his head on the glass and closed his eyes. He could still see Beverly's face on the golden strand.

On Tuesday afternoon, Blake stood outside the glass room and prayed for Beverly, then went back to her empty room and stood in the doorway, remembering their conversations and the special moments they had shared. He spotted a wad of paper on the floor and walked over and picked it up. He opened it and began to read:

Dear Frank,

The past thirty-six hours have been the most difficult *and* the most wonderful of my life—difficult because I had to trust Jesus with my life, and wonderful because I was *willing* to.

God spoke to me through a Christian missionary. Go figure! After all Blake has been through, he was concerned for me, a fallen-away Jew who had completely missed her Messiah.

The scariest thing isn't that I might die, but that I almost died without accepting Jesus Christ and His saving grace. I know that's not what you want to hear, but I need to say it. Get a Bible and read the book of Hebrews. I think God must have put it there just for the Jews! It makes perfect sense that Jesus was the Messiah. Not only that, He rose from the grave, Frank. He's alive!

My future—here or in heaven—is in God's hands. Regardless of what happens, remember I love you as much as any woman can love a man. Shalom.

Bev

Blake wiped the tears from his face. He smoothed out the letter, then folded it and put it in his pocket. He heard footsteps approaching the door.

"Blake...there you are," Dr. Rice said. "Where's Frank?"

"Uh, he's already come and gone."

"The discharge papers for you and Melissa are all ready to go."

THIRTY-FOUR

The following Monday afternoon, Dennis moved into a furnished rental house not far from the Hunter Clinic. The old place had character, and it looked to him as if the landlord had simply walked away one day, leaving everything behind. He stood in the living room and admired the dark oak fireplace and built-in bookcases filled with hardbound classics, mystery novels, old encyclopedias, and back issues of *National Geographic*.

The doorbell rang. Who would be trying to sell him something already? He walked to the front door and opened it.

"*Mother!*"

"A little surprised, are you?"

"Why are you here?"

"I thought I'd drop by to see your new place. I already met my grandsons. Why didn't you tell me?"

Dennis felt his face and ears burning.

"I met Rhonda and Jennifer, too," she said. "We spent the morning together. You know, Dennis, she really is a lovely girl. And those boys look just like you. They're adorable!"

"How did you find me?"

"I'd been sorting the insurance agency's mail for your grandfather to look through. You know how he likes to control everything. Well, the phone bill came last week, and I noticed the calls made with your calling card. I had no idea why you'd be in Atlanta, but the two calls from Baxter really piqued my curiosity, especially with all the TV coverage about the quarantine. So I hired a private eye. It didn't take long."

"You *what*? Mother, how could you?"

"You practically disappeared in spite of the fact your grandfather is in the hospital. What was I supposed to think? And last time I saw you, you acted very strange and had that nasty bruise on your face. I knew something was up, but Dad wouldn't tell me a thing. The two of you exasperate me, you know."

"I know, Mother. I'm sorry. I've been so absorbed in all this, I haven't thought about much else." Dennis saw the worry lines on his mother's face. How awkward it must have been for her to track him down. Suddenly mindful that she was the one person who had never rejected him, he felt contrite at having shut her out.

"May I come in?"

"Sure. I'm sorry." He held open the door and she stepped inside.

"Charming place," she said, her eyes taking everything in. "Furnished, I see. Oh, and lots of wood, I love that…"

"What else is on your agenda?"

"Ben Stoller. I understand the two of you have a great deal in common. The missing young man has been touted as quite the hero around the country."

"Who told you?"

"Dad did—finally. But not until I threatened to have him declared mentally incompetent." She chuckled. "But he knows the Bailey side of me is determined enough to find out anyway." She poked her head in and out of doorways, smiling with approval.

"How long are you staying?"

"Now, that depends…"

"On *what?*"

"My, my, Dennis. Are you that anxious to get rid of me?"

"How long, Mother?"

"Don't worry. I just wanted to see for myself that you were all right. And I wanted to see the twins." She looked up at him, her eyes intrusive. "Dennis, what are you going to do?"

"Hopefully, the right thing—at least as I see it. I'm going to spend some time getting comfortable with the boys and then probably move here so I can be closer to them on a permanent basis. I don't want to do to them what my father did to me."

"Good," she said, a touch of bitterness in her voice.

"You know, he probably didn't know how to be a dad. Maybe if he'd had the support I do, he would've hung around."

"I've never heard you talk this way. You sound almost forgiving."

"I'm working on it. I'm hearing a lot about God from a support group I hooked up with. I suppose if He's willing to forgive me for all the messes I've made, maybe I can eventually learn to do the same for the people who've hurt me."

There was a long pause, and his mother just stared at him.

"Don't looked so shocked, Mother…look, I need mental space to work through this, and—"

"Would you mind terribly if I stayed here for a few days? I promise not to be obnoxious. And if you're planning to keep the boys, I'd be more than glad to help out. I haven't forgotten how. Imagine me…the grandmother of *twins!*"

THIRTY-FIVE

Blake Thomas heard the phone ring and couldn't remember where he was. He lay there with his heart pounding, then looked over and saw Melissa lying next to him. After a minute, there was a gentle knock on the door.

"Blake? The phone's for you," his mother said.

"Thanks, Mom." He rubbed his eyes and reached for the receiver. "Hello?"

"Blake, it's Dr. Rice. I wanted you to be the first besides Frank Stein to know: Beverly's fever's broken. She actually smiled at me!"

Blake groped for Melissa's hand and squeezed it. "Beverly's awake," he whispered. "Dr. Rice, that's incredible news. Can I see her?"

"Well, she's weak and we wouldn't want her to…what am I saying? You know better than I what she needs right now. I'm sure she'd love to see you."

"Thanks. I can hardly wait." Blake hung up the phone. He rolled over and took Melissa in his arms and held her tightly. He felt the emotion tighten his throat. But there were no words for what he was feeling.

Ellen sat at her desk enjoying a cup of coffee and reading Tuesday's issue of the *Baxter Daily News*. Her phone rang and she picked it up, a smile on her face.

"I left your cleaning in the hall closet."

"Uh, this is Sarah Rice."

Ellen straightened in her chair. "I'm sorry, Sarah. Guy's the only one who calls this early. What's going on?"

"Beverly Stein's fever broke!"

"Please tell me it's over."

"Time will tell. But with no new cases and the incubation period past, I think we've made it through."

Ellen sat in silence and let the reality settle over her. "Can I print that?"

"Let me talk to Lionel and call you back. We want to be a little guarded about declaring anything absolute at this point, but I think we're out of the woods."

Blake nestled in the passenger seat, admiring the leafy shade trees that formed a green canopy over First Street. He looked up at the spurts of sunlight that shot through the cracks as the car moved beneath.

"What are you thinking?" Pastor Thomas said.

"Nothing in particular, Dad. Just feeling His presence."

Pastor Thomas pulled the car up to the front entrance of the hospital and stopped.

"Take your time, son. I'll wait in the main lobby."

Blake got out and walked in the door, aware of the stares as he headed down the hallway marked "B Corridor." When he arrived at the isolation room, he stopped and looked through the glass. Beverly and Frank were holding hands. Dr. Rice looked up and motioned him to come in.

Blake opened the door, feeling the way he used to on Christmas Eve.

Frank Stein got up and shook his hand. "Bev's been wantin' to talk to you. Go on. I'll leave you alone for a while."

Blake sat in a chair beside the bed, his chin quivering, his heart overflowing.

"What? I look that bad?" She smiled slightly.

Blake laughed and cried at the same time. "You're almost as beautiful as Melissa was." He took her hand and held it, feeling as though he were somehow touching the hand of his Creator.

"Guess He didn't have my room ready," she said.

Blake sat holding Beverly's hand. Their eyes spoke and their spirits connected, but words would have to wait until she was stronger. He was aware of Frank Stein staring at them from the other side of the glass.

After several minutes, Blake gave Beverly's hand a quick squeeze and stood up. "I'm going to let you get some rest. Melissa sends her love." He left and walked outside where Frank was standing.

"Mr. Stein, I—"

"Hey, stop with the *mister* already. It's Frank, okay?"

Blake nodded. "I'm so happy for you."

"You and Bev seem to have somethin'," Frank said.

"We've been through a lot together. But then you have, too."

"I shoulda been stronger. I wasn't there for her like I shoulda been."

"She loves you."

"Yeah. I'm one lucky man."

Blake turned and looked through the glass. "Oh, I almost forgot..." He reached in his pocket and took out the letter he had found in Beverly's room and handed it to Frank. "I think you dropped this." Blake pretended not to notice Frank's red face.

"Yeah, thanks…" Frank's voice was emotional. "You know, I didn't think I'd ever see her again. I guess that's the difference, Blake…you believed you would."

THIRTY-SIX

O n Wednesday morning, the early crowd had already gathered outside the door of Monty's Diner when Mark Steele opened it.

George Gentry slapped him on the back. "Mark, old buddy, we've got some serious celebrating to do!"

"If I never hear the word *virus* again," Hattie Gentry said, "it'll be too soon!"

"Or *quarantine!*" Reggie Mason added.

Mark smiled. "Come on in, all of you. Grab a newspaper. Forget the quarter. It's on me!"

They all took their places at the counter, and Rosie Harris poured the first round of coffee.

"Can you believe it's *finally* over," Rosie said. "Maybe life will get back to normal."

"Wouldn't count on it." Mort took a sip of coffee. "Nothin's ever gonna be like it was."

George nodded. "For once, I agree with him. After a community's gone through something this traumatic, it's changed forever."

Rosie patted George on the shoulder. "Well, let's hope we're changed for the better. Don't you wonder what it feels like to be Beverly Stein? Or Blake and Melissa Thomas?"

"Don't wanna know." Reggie traced the rim of his mug with his finger. "But you gotta wonder why stuff like this happens."

"There's a reason for everything," Jim Hawkins said. "We just don't know what it is most of the time."

"What possible good can come out of something this horrible?" Mark asked.

"Maybe people will be more grateful for each day they're alive," Hattie said, squeezing George's hand.

"Good thought." Rosie poured Hattie a refill. "After all this, most of our complaints look pretty small."

George elbowed Reggie, a grin on his face. "What say you, Mort, O great and wise rabble-rouser?"

Mort chewed his pancakes and seemed to be thinking.

Mark moved so he could see Mort's face. "Yeah, what do you think we should learn from this?"

Mort washed down his pancakes with coffee, a more-serious-than-usual look on his face. "Since ya never know when yer ticket's gittin' punched, guess it couldn't hurt ta talk nicer ta each other."

Mark looked at George and shrugged.

"Nah." Mort dismissed his words with a wave of his hand. "That'd spoil all the fun."

Ellen folded the newspaper on her desk and walked over to the window. Was it finally over? She glanced outside at the early-morning traffic that clogged the streets of her sleepy town. The media couldn't leave fast enough to suit her. Ellen knew she couldn't compete with live television, but after things settled down, she'd write a feature story about the people who had been the most affected—something personal and meaningful to the community.

Surely something positive could be pulled out of this. Her thoughts were interrupted by the sound of her phone ringing. She glanced at her watch and picked up the phone.

"Good morning, Guy."

"The headlines are great, Ellen."

"Thanks. I'll never complain about the news being boring again."

"Sure you will." He laughed. "But I'm glad it's over. I'm anxious to see what feature story you come up with."

"Me, too."

"You've thought about it, haven't you?"

"Uh, yes. Of course."

"And?"

There was a long pause.

"Oh, no," he said. "You're not going to turn this into a 'religious thing,' are you?"

"This isn't about religion, Guy."

"I'm glad we agree."

"But I do think it's worth mentioning that God's hand seemed evident to those who reached out to Him during this crisis."

"Ellen, lots of people *think* they see God's hand. It makes them feel good, but that doesn't make it so. He's a myth. Think twice before you go there...Ellen?... Now you're mad!"

"I'm not mad. I'm weary."

"From what?"

She sighed. "Guy, I'm not going to hide my feelings anymore. I believe there's a God. I've seen too much evidence to deny it."

"What *evidence?*"

"Look, Counselor, how about dropping the courtroom tone? This doesn't need to be adversarial."

"What evidence, Ellen? Show me one piece of evidence."

Jed Wilson drove slowly until he spotted the tan brick bungalow that matched the description Dennis had given him. When he saw the house number, he parked his truck along the curb and waited for Rhonda's car to pull up behind him. He got out and helped Rhonda and Jennifer get the babies out of the car.

"I need a minivan," Jennifer said. "What a hassle."

"You nervous?" Jed asked.

Jennifer glanced at the house. "A little. It's hard to trust Dennis's sudden sincerity."

"Time will tell." Jed turned to Rhonda. "You want me to carry Benjamin?"

"No, I've got him."

As they went up the walk, an attractive, classy looking lady stood in the doorway. "Need any help?"

"No, I think we've got it," Jed said. "We're earning our *transportation* merit badges." He smiled.

The woman held open the door. "I'm Catherine Lawton. You must be Jed."

Jed extended his hand and shook hers. "Nice to meet you. I heard you stopped by the other day."

"Let me see those beautiful babies." Catherine's face seemed to glow as her eyes went from Benjamin to Bailey. "Come in. Dennis is out in the kitchen getting their bottles put together."

"Wow, this is nice," Jennifer said. "I like it even better than his house in Denver."

"My son has good taste." Catherine raised her eyebrows. "Gets it from his grandfather. Let me show you around."

Jed half listened while the girls talked about the details of the house. He liked the masculine feel to the place, especially the bookcases in the living room.

"And here off the foyer," Catherine said, "is a small parlor that

Dennis plans to turn into an art studio where he can paint and sketch. Wait until you see the kitchen. It has an oak floor and a corner brick fireplace. Dennis?... The Wilsons are here."

Dennis turned around when they walked into the kitchen.

"I'm glad you could make it. What do you think?"

"It's perfect," Rhonda said. "And you've got plenty of room."

"Yeah, I thought I'd better get three bedrooms so Flo could come stay on the weekends when I have the boys."

"A fireplace in the kitchen," Rhonda said. "I could handle this."

Jed sensed the awkwardness between Jennifer and Dennis. "Why don't we let the kids get the bottles ready while we entertain the boys?"

"Good idea," Catherine said.

Jed and Rhonda followed her to the living room and sat down.

"May I hold one of the babies?" Catherine said. "I just can't seem to get enough of them."

"Aren't they adorable?" Rhonda smiled. "Are we as obnoxious as all those other grandparents we've joked about?"

"Probably," Catherine said. "But isn't it marvelous? I never dreamed in a million years I'd ever have grandchildren."

There was a long, uncomfortable pause.

"Uh, Dennis is a fine young man," Jed said. "We've grown fond of him, and he's great with the boys."

"But not with Jennifer?"

"Jen has a lot to work through," Rhonda said.

"I like her very much." Catherine stroked Benjamin's cheek. "Do you think there's any hope for them as a couple?"

Jed heard giggling and squealing coming from the kitchen. He looked up in time to see Dennis chasing Jennifer, using a plastic baby bottle filled with water as a squirt gun.

Jed chuckled and winked at Rhonda. "You never know, Catherine. Stranger things have happened."

Ellen sat under the ceiling fan on the screened-in porch, knitting a baby blanket. Through the trees she could see the sunset painted across the sky with streaks of fiery pink. She heard footsteps coming her direction.

"I thought I'd find you out here," Guy said.

"I need to keep going on this second blanket for Jennifer."

"You didn't say much at dinner," he said.

"No, I didn't."

"Is that how it's going to be now?"

"Now?"

"You've as much as professed to being a Christian."

"I believe in God. That's a whole new thing for me. But I haven't figured out what I believe about Jesus. One step at a time."

"Is it that important to you?"

"I can't pretend to be someone I'm not."

He sat next to her on the wicker couch and put his arm around her. "I don't want that either. I'm scared, Ellen. What'll happen if we never agree? Will it ruin what we have?"

"That's up to you. On one level, I'm happier than I've ever been."

"And this isn't just because the FBI couldn't explain who Sawyer was shooting at in the church?"

Ellen put her head on his shoulder. "No, there've been a number of things I can't explain. I'm looking at those I can. It started last fall when Sean McConnell died."

"So you said."

"Guy, after all I've seen and heard, it would be harder for me to believe in coincidences than in Someone sovereign. But the best evidence I can present is how a relationship with God has changed people I know."

"You said that before, too."

"Well, how closely did you examine the evidence, Counselor?"

"It's circumstantial at best. And subjective. Wouldn't stand up in a court of law."

"Yes, you're probably right. Faith isn't something you can bag and put into evidence." Ellen sat up straight and began knitting again. "But I'm a key witness. I saw what faith *does*. No one will convince me otherwise."

"All right...I can tell you're resolved."

Ellen turned her head and looked up at him. "Does that mean you'll stop manipulating me with guilt?"

"Will you promise not to get fanatical?"

"Honestly, Guy. Passionate, maybe. But fanatical?"

He chuckled. "Promise me you won't get weird. I guess that's my biggest fear."

"But I'm already weird."

"No weirder then."

"Deal."

There was a long stretch of silence.

Guy pulled her closer. "Well, *I'd* sure like to know who Sawyer was shooting at in the church."

Ellen smiled. It didn't matter anymore.

Dennis decided to take a walk through the neighborhood, hoping the night breeze would make the temperature bearable. He strolled down the sidewalk past the quaint houses and stepped off the curb to cross First Street when his cell phone rang. Who would call him on a Saturday night?

"Hello."

"Heard you abandoned ship."

"Grandpa! How are you?"

"Alive, thank you."

"I'm sorry I haven't called."

"Catherine just got back. She told me about your new place—and about the twins. She's all excited about being a grandmother."

"Yeah, I know. I was surprised at how quickly she took to the boys, especially since she was ticked at me. Grandpa, are you home now?"

"Yes, I intimidated the doctors into kicking me out."

Dennis smiled. "I'm not surprised."

"They've stuck me with an occupational therapist an hour a day. Won't be long before I can go back to work part time."

"That's great, Grandpa. I miss working at the agency, and…"

"And what?"

"I miss you."

"That's a first."

"Uh, yeah, well, I—"

"No need to fumble around, Dennis. We always grated on each other."

"Well, like you said, Grandpa, there's a first time for everything. Maybe we can change that."

"Think you can change an old man, do you?"

"Well, you set *me* up, and look what happened!"

"I'm proud of you, Dennis. But you're a better man than I am."

"When your doctor gives you the okay, why don't you come down and visit? See the boys? They're a real kick."

"You've got enough trouble."

"Actually, I don't. Things are going really well."

"You're seeing Jennifer?"

"No. Yes. Well, we're not officially dating. But we're communicating well and are on the same page where the boys are concerned."

"She was pleased about the trust funds?"

"Thrilled. But I also made her an offer of my own. She won't have to work unless she wants to."

"Good move. I knew you liked her."

"You've never even met her, Grandpa. How do you know what I feel?"

"Because it's Saturday night, and you answered the phone."

Dennis smiled and decided not to comment. "I can't wait for you to see the boys."

"What if they don't like me? I'm not all that likable."

"If you get too obnoxious, you and Bailey can hang out together."

His grandfather chuckled. "Misery loves company, eh?"

"So you'll come?"

"I'll talk to the doctor. See what he says."

THIRTY-SEVEN

O n Sunday morning, the bells of Cornerstone Bible Church rang out across the community. Dennis Lawton went to church for the first time and sat in the front pew with the Wilsons.

Pastor Thomas's sermon was a personal testimony to God's faithfulness throughout the uncertain days of the quarantine.

At the end of the praise and worship, Blake Thomas told the church family about the golden strand and about Beverly Stein. Then Jennifer revealed that it was Dennis who had saved the babies—and about all that had happened since. One by one, testimonies came forth from others who experienced something positive during the quarantine. Dennis was overwhelmed.

Afterwards, Rhonda Wilson invited a number of people to the house for brunch. Though Dennis didn't know how to relate to this company of churchgoers, he listened with interest to their conversation.

"It's incredible how it all fit together," Jennifer said. "The only reason Blake and Melissa returned to the states when they did was because she was pregnant. If they hadn't left South America, they would've died with the others in the village."

Blake nodded. "God had a plan. The death of our baby set a whole chain of events in motion. But it also caused Dennis to come back and get involved with his sons—and, ultimately, to save them."

Jennifer looked at Dennis. "But if he hadn't thought he'd been exposed to the virus, he might not have come back. I don't know which nurse let him in the nursery, but it turned out to be a blessing."

"That's another of those unexplainables," Ellen Jones said. "I don't know who Sawyer was shooting at in Saint Anthony's either, but the incident prompted some religious discussions with Guy. For the first time, I found the courage to come right out and say I believe in God. It's so freeing."

"This seems small compared to that," Jennifer said, "but I can't tell you how much I prayed for God to take care of me and the boys. Having a second baby arrive unexpectedly threw me into a real test of faith. How was I going to raise twins as a single mom and not struggle every day of my life? But God knew Dennis was going to come back, and that my financial needs would be met. It blows my mind that I actually get to stay home with them."

"I'm relieved at how things turned out," Dr. Alex Harmon said. "It was a tough call not telling you about the twins. But I felt impressed to let God handle it. Your dad wanted to punch me in the nose."

Jed laughed. "Sorry about that."

"The Lord was speaking to you," Jennifer said. "Had I known, I probably would've panicked and let someone adopt them. And I would never have had more children." She looked over at Dennis. "And how weird that the very person who didn't want any responsibility ended up being the one who saved their lives and decided to support them."

Jed smiled. "Sounds like a divine setup to me. But this goes a lot deeper. Dennis gave me permission to share something with you. All his life, he's resented his father for skipping out. What he discovered as Ben Stoller is what gave him the courage to deal with his past. We know how that's impacting Jennifer and the boys. But some emotional healing is also happening between Dennis and his grandfather."

"And then there's Beverly," Blake said. "It was no coincidence that she was overcome with smoke during the hospital attack and had to be quarantined. Or even that she was sleepwalking. God had her where He wanted her so she would find Him. She's already telling her Jewish friends about her Messiah and causing quite a stir. It's hard to say how far her light will shine."

"So many good things have come out of this," Rhonda said. "But I'm relieved it's over. I've never been so scared in my life!"

Ellen shook her head from side to side. "I find it astonishing that while all of you were in the midst of the anguish, your faith didn't fail."

Dennis felt Bailey starting to stir in his arms. He glanced at his watch. If someone had told him a month ago that he would be living in Baxter, committed to building a relationship with twin sons he risked his life to save, he would have laughed.

Was it God working in his life? Was there a Father in heaven who wanted a relationship with him? He couldn't deny these people had something he didn't—something he wanted.

He looked over at Jed who sat with his arm around Jennifer. *God, help me stick with this the way Jed did. Help me get my life straightened out.*

Blake heard one of the twins fuss and felt a pang of longing. What would it have felt like to be a father? He took Melissa's hand, watching as Dennis stood and slowly walked back and forth across the floor, one of the babies held snugly against his chest.

As Blake studied Dennis's face, his heart started to pound and he felt a prompting in his spirit. He remembered having seen this young man's face on the golden strand! He thought of Beverly and was suddenly energized, struck by a thought he had never once considered: that God was calling him to another mission field—right here in his hometown.

Blake relished the moment, wondering how many other faces he might one day recognize, if not here, then in heaven. And he took immeasurable comfort in knowing that, at the other end of the golden strand, one little girl had already entered into glory.

Multnomah Publishers

The publisher and author would love to hear your comments about this book. *Please contact us at:*
www.multnomah.net/baxterseries

AFTERWORD

Dear Reader,

Learning to trust God in difficult circumstances is one of the greatest challenges of the Christian life. The Bible assures us that in all things God works for the good of those who love Him, who have been called according to His purpose. But bad things *do* happen to good people—even Christians.

That's why I wrote this story. I wanted the golden strand to leave a lasting impression that will remind us that God has a plan, even for the difficult and confusing situations that are out of *our* control.

The Thomases, the Wilsons, Beverly Stein, and Dennis Lawton couldn't make sense of their circumstances while in the midst of blood, sweat, and tears. And though I believe it would be a rare gift for God to reveal His plan the way He did to Blake Thomas, I hope you enjoyed being privy to the events being threaded together. In real life, we don't always know the reason we go through things.

But as the author, I controlled the story. I was intimately acquainted with the characters in this book and had a specific plan for each. Through them I accomplished my purpose. Sometimes it was necessary to put obstacles in front of them or to move things out of their way in order to give them space to make the choices I wanted them to make.

Now stretch with me for a moment: If you add perfect love, isn't that essentially what our God is doing with us? He's in the process of "character development." He's the author and perfecter of our faith, and the only One who knows how we fit into a much greater story. I guess you could say He's a meddling Father because He isn't willing that we should fall short of all He has planned for us.

Worrying only gets in the way and is often our biggest obstacle to trusting Him. The two are constantly at odds, and yet we know that the battle isn't against flesh and blood. It's a spiritual battle. And we need to put our faith and trust in the One who has already promised "it is finished."

In all of our worrying and striving, let us not forget that the blood, sweat, and tears from Gethsemane to Calvary were also part of God's perfect plan—down to the last drop.

I'd love to hear your comments about this book. Write me at www.multnomah.net/baxterseries.

I invite you to come back to the Baxter Series in book four, *High Stakes,* where you'll find out what happens to Dennis and Jennifer and Ellen. It's another page-turner, so catch up on your sleep!

In Him,

Kathy Herman

The Baxter Series, Book One
Dead Men Tell No Tales. *Or Do They?*

When a bizarre houseboat explosion rocks the close-knit community of Baxter, firefighters and friends stand by powerless as the blazing hull of their neighbor's home sinks to the bottom of Heron Lake. Have all five McConnells perished in the flames? No one wants the truth more than Jed Wilson, Mike McConnell's best friend. When rescuers recover the remains of all but one family member, suspicion spreads like wildfire. Was it an accident—or murder? Jed finds himself in a race with the FBI to track down the only suspect, and is thrust into a dynamic, life-changing encounter with his own past. Baxter's mystery and Jed's dilemma are ones only God can solve in this suspenseful, surprising story of redemption amidst despair in small-town America.

ISBN 1-57673-956-2

The Baxter Series, Book Two
Unrelenting Anger Yields Bitter Fruit in Baxter

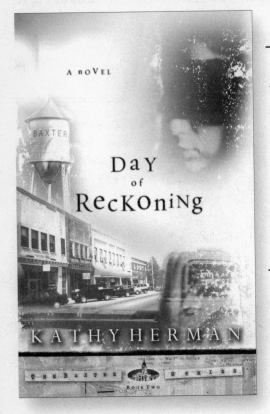

A NOVEL

DAY of ReCKOniNG

KATHY HERMAN

THE BAXTER SERIES
BOOK TWO

"Kathy Herman writes with a gritty realism and an emotional intensity that will keep the reader engrossed until the very last page."

—WAYNE JORDAN
The Word on Romance e-zine
(www.thewordonromance.com)

One man's hatred sets off a community crisis in a chilling page-turning read that is also startlingly inspirational. Textile magnate G. R. Logan lays off a thirty-year employee who dies weeks later, and the man's son means to make Logan pay. In her second novel in the dramatic Baxter series, Kathy Herman unleashes a kidnapper's unresolved anger and explores the honest depths of a believer's anger at God. Sinister messages threaten the lives of two teenage girls while the citizens of Baxter struggle to cope with the evil that plagues this once-peaceful town. How will they react when they learn who's responsible? Can anything break their cycle of bitterness?

ISBN 1-57673-896-5

On the Surviving Side of Gunfire

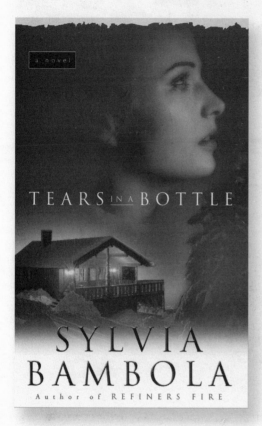

"*Tears in a Bottle* is a gripping story of betrayal, hurt, and triumph that accurately portrays the real truth behind the political correctness of 'a woman's right to choose.'"

—**Vicki Thorn**,
executive director, National Office of Post-Abortion Reconciliation and Healing

Becky Taylor, a young woman burdened by great expectations, is lying on a cold recovery table in an abortion clinic when she hears a man's voice, then gunshots. She holds her breath and lies perfectly still behind the curtain. When the gunman is finished, Becky is the only one left alive in the clinic. This act brings together two strangers who both seek answers to one of life's most wrenching questions: Are God's love and mercy big enough for every sin? The answer transforms multiple lives.

ISBN 1-57673-802-7

A FREE
"BEHIND THE SCENES"
LOOK AT YOUR
FAVORITE
FICTION AUTHORS!

www.letstalkfiction.com

Let's Talk Fiction is a free, four-color mini-magazine created to give readers a "behind the scenes" look at Multnomah Publishers' favorite fiction authors. **Let's Talk Fiction** allows our authors to share a bit about themselves, giving readers an inside peek into their latest releases. Published in the fall, spring, and summer seasons, **Let's Talk Fiction** is filled with interactive contests, author contact information, and fun! To receive your free copy, get on-line at www.letstalkfiction.com. We'd love to hear from you!

Multnomah® Publishers   *Keeping Your Trust...One Book at a Time*®